Ghostly Rites Anthology 2024

Plaisted Publishing House Presents

Ghostly Rites Crew

Acknowledgements

Mara Reitsma – Video Trailer and Teasers
Cathy-Lee Chopping – Proofreading, Editing & Admin

Mara Reitsma – Book Cover 2024

Alone with Ghosts

Isabelle Plaisted

Sitting alone in a home with no one around but me,
The ghosts are near, for them I hear
As they come for me

I sit alone, in a home forever waiting for thee,
The creaks and groans, and moans galore
As they come for me,
I know I'll die and here's the reason why,
I believed you would come for me

You betrayed my trust,
and so I must live alone eternally,
I thought you would come, and life would be fun

So the place I've come, now that I'm done
Is the place I'll never leave,
So here I'll stay, sitting in an empty home,
That's no longer a place for me,

The ghosts, they come and in the end I'm done,
Sitting here waiting for thee,
You left me here, in despair, for the ghosts to have their fun

Now I am gone, I find I belong
With the ghosts that have taken me

The Shadows of Todo O Nada

R. L. Burlech

In the heart of Mexico, where the sun kissed the earth with fiery passion and the wind whispered secrets through the canyons, there lay a cave forgotten by time. Hidden amidst the rugged terrain of the Sierra Madre Mountains, its entrance was veiled by mesquite bushes and guarded by the ghosts of ancient warriors.

Legends whispered of untold riches hidden within its depths, but none dared to venture too close, for the cave was said to be cursed by the spirit of a Comanche warrior, bound by duty to protect its treasures until the end of days.

Among the dusty plains and sunbaked mesas, there wandered a lone figure, a relic of a bygone era. Ole Pete, known to the Mexican farmers of the area as "El Gringo," was a weathered prospector with a heart as rugged as the land he roamed. For decades, he had traversed the wilds in search of fortune, his dreams fueled by the promise of gold and glory.

It was on a sweltering summer's day that El Gringo stumbled upon the cave, his eyes alight with a hunger that burned brighter than the midday sun. Ignoring the warnings whispered by the wind, he pressed onward, his footsteps echoing against the ancient stones as he ventured deeper into the darkness.

As he emerged into the cavern's chamber, his breath caught in his throat at the sight that greeted him—a treasure beyond imagination, glimmering in the dim light like a mirage in the desert sands. Gold coins spilled from ornate chests, jewels sparkled amidst piles of ancient artifacts, and the air was heavy with the scent of untold wealth.

But before El Gringo could take a single step towards his prize, a shadow materialized before him, its form flickering like a flame in the wind. It was the guardian of the cave, a spirit of the Comanche warrior whose restless soul was bound to protect its hoard for eternity.

In a voice as ancient as the mountains themselves, the spirit spoke but three words: "Todo o nada."

Ole Pete furrowed his brow, his mind racing to decipher the meaning of the spirit's cryptic message. But the words rang hollow in his ears, their meaning lost to him in a language he could not understand.

"What are you saying?" asked Ole Pete.

The spirit in that otherworldly voice answered, "Todo o nada."

"Git outta my way" said Ole Pete.

The ghostly visage answered, "Todo o nada."

Undeterred by the spirit's warning, El Gringo began to fill his sack with as much treasure as he could carry, the weight of his greed pressing down upon him like a burden too heavy to bear. Each coin, each jewel, was a testament to a lifetime of longing, a dream finally within his grasp.

But as he struggled beneath the weight of his desires, a sudden twang shattered the silence—a shaft of obsidian, tipped with feathers and stained with blood, pierced the air with deadly accuracy.

It hit its mark.

With a cry of anguish, El Gringo stumbled and fell, the treasure slipping from his grasp as darkness consumed him.

And as the last echoes of his pain faded into the abyss, the spirit stood silent vigil once more, its duty fulfilled, its treasure safe from the hands of those who would seek to claim it at any cost.

The spirit spoke one last time before fading into the shadows, "Todo o nada."

All or nothing.

I'll Be Waiting For You

Danny Buenaflor

"Hey. Sweetheart. Wake up. It's a beautiful morning!"

"Hmmm...so?"

"So...the sun is shining, the sky is clear, the breeze is cool. Good day for a walk. What do you say?"

"I'm tired, hon. Few more minutes?"

"Oh alright. I'll be waiting for you."

Aurora Petrova woke up with a start. "Oh hi, you're up! Sorry to startle you," said the small Chinese woman standing over her bunk, tying her dark hair into a low ponytail. She pointed to herself, saying "Chen Maylin. We met briefly before we left. You can call me May. The pod doors on our beds opened about half an hour ago. This must be your first time if you were still sleeping after stasis ended. So sorry, but Lorenzo made some breakfast for us. I'd get some while you can, before Commander Maksimov eats it all!"

"I'm not going to eat it all," said a brown-haired, middle—aged man with a Russian accent as he passed by in the tight corridor, "just most of it. And call me Stepan."

Aurora rubbed her eyes. "Thank you May. I'm up. I'll be there in a sec. Just need a moment." May smiled and nodded warmly before leaving. Aurora took in her surroundings. She felt like she'd been asleep for days (and indeed she had) and her environment felt familiar in the slightest way. She slowly recalled where she was as the dream that was her sleeping life slipped away into unreality. She'd never slept in stasis before, not like her parents before her, and the whole thing was very disorienting.

In front of her was what she remembered to be May's bunk. Lorenzo Sosa and Commander Stepan Maksimov's bunks were down the corridor on her left. After orienting herself for a moment, she noticed the photo pinned above her on her headboard. She remembered putting it there; a photo of a striking young man. He looked strong. Handsome. She stared at it for a good while, then kissed her forefinger and middle finger and placed them on the photo. "Good morning love," she said aloud, and she got up slowly, putting on some clothes. She stumbled into her shirt and pants, like a child trying on their parent's clothes, and made her way out from under the dark cloud hanging above her. She started heading down the corridor but stopped suddenly in her tracks.

A dark shape filled the other end of the dimly lit corridor. The shape of a man. "Commander Maksimov? Lorenzo?" she called out, but there was no answer. The dark figure remained still. Aurora stared intensely at it, trying to make out its features. She couldn't. A sharp chill ran up her spine as the dark figure suddenly moved, slowly and precisely, out of sight towards the common room and mess hall. Aurora swallowed as she carefully made her way down the corridor. She turned the corner, stumbling and disheveled, and searched the common room urgently for the dark figure.

"What's wrong, new girl?" said Lorenzo while serving May a portion of food, "you look spooked." He seemed charming to Aurora. He had tan skin, a Spanish accent, and long dark hair in a bun. His eyebrows were dark and dramatic and his short facial hair suited him quite well, she thought.

Aurora said "Oh, I...didn't any of you see that?" May and Stepan turned around, Stepan with a full plate of food.

"See what?" asked Stepan. Aurora looked at them confusedly.

"There was...something..." May walked over to her and helped her get settled. "Let's get you some food," May said to her, "a warm meal will set you right." Aurora tried her best to push it out of her mind. 'I'm just tired,' she thought to herself, 'that's it. Mother and father said sleeping in stasis has side effects, so I shouldn't worry about it.'

They all sat at a table under the cold LED lights, full plates before them. Stepan looked at Aurora, who ate quietly, and through a stuffed mouth, asked "so, why did NASA send an artist on this mission?" The others glanced up at the two of them, sensing a peculiar tone in his question and waiting to see what Aurora would say. "Well," she replied, "I suppose they think it's good publicity."

"What are they trying to publicize?" asked May.

"Propaganda, that's what," said Stepan.

Lorenzo gestured his fork in his direction, "everyone uses propaganda Stepan, not just NASA."

"They told me that my work would be inspiring to all," said Aurora, "to see our new home through the eyes of an artist. Supposed to make it a more attractive home to the survivors of the war, make it more human, but..."

"But what?" asked May.

Aurora looked down and said "I don't know. I don't feel like it makes much of a difference." Stepan said, "We do have cameras. Pictures are beautiful enough. They could have sent another scientist instead."

"Come on Commander," said Lorenzo, "Aurora here has her job, just like the rest of us. Leave her be, huh?"

Stepan put his hands in the air in defense. "I say nothing. Just, unnecessary is all. Apologies, Aurora. You are most welcome here, of course." A moment of silence, then Aurora spoke up. "I...actually agree with Comm— er, Stepan."

"Ah, you see? I haven't offended," he said.

May was quick to cut in however as she said "oh no, Aurora. Your mission is important. The world needs your vision!" said May.

"Honestly," Aurora said, "I haven't felt like I've had a purpose for a very long time."

May was insistent in her support. "Everything will turn out fine," May said to her, "you'll see. You were meant to be here. I know it." Aurora smiled at May's kindness. The morning meal was nearing its end when Stepan asked another question. "Aurora, your last name. Petrova. Forgive me for asking a personal question, but your family is Russian, no? How is it that you are working for NASA?"

"Well, my father was Russian and worked with Roscosmos, but my mother was American and worked for NASA. They met on a flight to Mars and, well they fell in love and my father immigrated to the United States before they had me. I guess NASA thought it would be good to have someone that can represent both the United States and Russia on this mission. Diplomacy and all that."

Stepan laughed a hearty laugh and lifted his cup. "Once a Russian, always a Russian, Ms. Petrova. It is clear to me now that you are a vital member of this team. The proverbial olive branch between our two countries. A toast. To the success of this mission." Aurora and the others raised their cups. "To the mission!" they all said, clinking their cups and drinking. Aurora half-smiled and sipped her orange juice, feeling better about her place on the ship, if not still a bit nervous.

Later that evening, Aurora sat with her knee up, quietly sketching away as she observed Lorenzo at work on the other side of the room. She wasn't used to capturing someone's likeness from behind, but she enjoyed the challenge. There was something about the subject's back being turned to the viewer that gave the sketch a sense of vulnerability, and perhaps a sense of focus, she thought. Focus. His eyes trained on the screens. What was he looking for, she wondered. Or perhaps he was hoping that there would be nothing to find, that nothing was wrong. She smirked as she realized she had been focusing just as hard. Much time had passed without her realizing, and before her lay a dramatically sketched Lorenzo, a snapshot of a moment in time. She was satisfied with her work and sure of its quality. The sketch showed his back, slightly hunched over in his chair as he studied the screens and buttons before him, the functions of which she knew not. The lines were clear, dark, and contrasted. His face could not be seen, but his emotions were clear. Focus. Purpose. Perhaps a sense of uncertainty. An unknowing of what the future held.

"How does it look? The drawing?" Aurora was caught off guard by Lorenzo's voice.

"I'm sorry?" she asked him.

"Was I a good subject?" he said to her. He turned his head with a charming smile. "I've been told by women before that I could've been a model. Ah, but science is my mistress. Of course, I'm still looking for a wife. That's different," he said.

"Oh. Right, yes, it turned out very well."

"May I see?" She got up and sat nearer to him and showed him her work. "It's amazing, Aurora. You really do have a great deal of talent."

"Thank you, Lorenzo."

"I recognize myself. Even from this angle. Impressive, really." He smiled at her again, and she smiled back, but her smile held something within it. A sadness. "Is something the matter?" asked Lorenzo.

"No. No, I'm fine. But thank you for asking." He took her hand and held it. "Aurora, I— "but he stopped. He turned her left hand over and saw that she had a ring on her left ring finger. "My apologies," he said, "I've been too forward. I did not realize you were a married woman." She smiled at him but withdrew her hand.

"It's quite alright," she said, "no harm done."

"Is he back on earth, your husband? He must miss you."

"You know, I really don't feel like talking about that right now, if that's alright."

"Of course! Of course. My apologies. It's none of my business." Lorenzo turned back to the screens, and a few seconds of silence followed. Suddenly, the lights in the room started to dim. They grew dimmer and dimmer, changing color temperatures from a bright white to a dim, flame-like amber color. Aurora looked up and back and forth, confused.

"Ah, it's just the day/night cycle," explained Lorenzo, "a new feature on these ships. It's supposed to help us with our circadian rhythm by tricking our bodies into thinking it's nighttime. We may be floating in space, but our bodies don't know that. It's a clever workaround. Of course, if you need the light, you can always turn it back on manually. I'm sure you'd need the light for your work." She didn't say it, but she actually liked the dim lights. They were peaceful and reminded her of her old home and the comfort therein. Everything in the ship was bathed in a warm glow. It made even the cold, utilitarian space around her seem welcoming. "I don't really mind it," she said.

A beeping sound interrupted her thoughts. "What's that beeping for?" she asked.

Lorenzo pointed to a screen on the lower right. "See this? This monitor alerts me once every hour. It tells me how many people are on the ship. Can never be too careful, right?" Aurora smiled politely in response. Footsteps grew louder as a Russian accent boomed from behind them. "Nightfall is here, friends. Are we all good here? Need anything?" They thanked him and said they were fine. "Good," said Stepan, "dinner at 1900." And he left.

After dinner, Lorenzo and May left to do some work in other parts of the ship before bed, leaving Stepan to wipe the dishes clean. Not wanting to leave without doing her part, Aurora grabbed some wipes and got to wiping. Stepan sat at the opposite end of the table from her, silent in the dim amber glow of the empty mess hall. Aurora tried to keep her eyes to herself, but noticed Stepan's expression, his face full of thought as he mindlessly wiped the same clean spot on a plate over and over. Realizing what he was doing, he put the plate down and grabbed another. Aurora returned her gaze to her own plate, but Stepan spoke to her anyway. "Ms. Petrova..."

"Oh, Aurora is fine."

"Apologies. Can I ask, I noticed during dinner that you were a bit distant. Not still feeling insecure about the mission, are you?"

"Not at all," she lied, "I know this mission is important. People need to feel inspired, comforted. A new home is a scary thought. New life forms, new diseases and pathogens, new weather. Even the days are longer. People need to be given something to look forward to, something familiar, something human. I see that now."

Stepan pouted his lips as he nodded slowly. "Even so," he said, "I get a feeling this is not the full story. As if something is holding you back. At dinner, your eyes..."

"What about them?"

"They were looking to the past, not the future, not even the present. Forgive me for prying. I am the commander, you see. It's partially my job to ensure that my crew is in their right mind. Stable. Happy. It's important for a successful mission, you see."

"So, this is just about the mission?"

Stepan laughed. "You misunderstand, Aurora! I do care. I'm not an unfeeling scientist. It's alright if you don't want to talk about it, but I can tell something is bothering you. I've flown many missions. I can recognize a troubled crew member right away. I hope we have not done anything to make you feel unwelcome."

"Not at all, sir. Everyone has been very pleasant. But...I suppose I do still feel a bit insecure about my part of the mission, after all. The three of you are such intelligent scientists and I'm just an artist trying to work through her depression and anxiety with pencils and paint. I get that NASA needs me to do this, I just don't feel...right. I haven't for a while. Not since before— "She stopped suddenly and looked at Stepan. He gave her a look, telling her to go on.

"Well," she continued, "anyway, ever since I woke up I've felt aimless. I have a mission, I have a goal, but I feel directionless anyway. And there's something around me. Something dark. I can feel it."

"Can you tell me more?"

Aurora thought for a second, then looked down, shaking her head, returning to wiping her plate. "Sorry, I shouldn't be going on like this. I'm fine, really. Just overthinking things. You don't need to be concerned about me. I'll do my part, I promise."

"Okay," said Stepan, not entirely satisfied, "well, I think you have the last plate. I'm going to retire for the night. If you need anything, Aurora, please do not hesitate to ask. Alright?" He smiled at her with his wide mouth then left her at the table, snorting from his large nose as he walked away.

The ship was so quiet. The white noise from small fans and pumps around the consoles and walls were the only sounds to be heard, but they barely registered as sounds to her. It was suddenly hitting her just how eerie the ship was at 'night,' even with the beautiful lighting. She continued wiping the plate clean, making sure it was as clean as possible. Get every stain, every spot, she thought to herself, then off to bed. Just a little bit more. It's a fine night for resting. But the atmosphere in the room disagreed.

Suddenly, a few strands of her hair jumped off of her shoulder. She gasped and stood up, swatting at her hair. She stood still, staring around the room in a panic. For some reason, she felt as if someone was watching her. Every corner of the room, every wall. She looked at each and felt something there, invisible, perceiving her, moving towards her. Then for a second, she nearly felt...comfort? Surely not, she thought. What is this? What is happening? Then the feeling changed. Whatever invisible presence she felt in there moved in on her suddenly. She panicked and sprinted towards the living quarters.

Not watching her step, she tripped and fell in the corridor of the living quarters. "Aurora?" asked May. She peered from around the corner in the room down the hall where the women's bunks were.

Aurora sat up slowly. "I'm fine. I just wasn't watching where I was going. Did I wake you?"

"No. I was just settling in. Okay, well, if you're sure you're alright..."

"Yes, I'm fine. Thank you."

"Okay. Goodnight then."

"Goodnight." Then May turned around and disappeared into the room. Aurora looked down at her hands as she turned over to stand up, slowly.

A sound. A tapping. Aurora quickly turned around back toward the women's bunks. "May?" asked Aurora. But no answer came. The hair on the back of her neck stood up. Not again, please, she thought to herself. "May? Are you there?" asked Aurora as she stood there.

Suddenly, from the women's bunk room, something peered around the corner once more. It wasn't May. Solid black, vaguely human-shaped, its features indiscernible except its eyes. A viscous, black goo dripped from its head but disappeared as it hit the ground. Two big circles with the brightest white scleras she'd ever seen and in their centers, two small black pupils. Its mouth (or where its mouth should be) was hidden behind the wall. Aurora looked on in terror at the thing in the room, trying to yell out for someone, but saying nothing. May, she thought. That thing is in there with May.

"Hee hee."

The dark figure giggled as it retreated into the room in a seemingly impossible horizontal motion. A burst of courage hit her as she ran to the women's bunk room. She turned the corner and there she was.

May lay sleeping in her bunk, her eyes covered with a sleep mask and ear plugs in her ears. Trouble sleeping most likely, Aurora thought. That explains why May didn't answer when she called out. She looked around. No dark figure. She peered around every corner, every possible hiding spot. Nothing.

She ran her fingers through her hair in a bewildered state of confusion. She posited that she may still be feeling the effects of stasis, although she knew this wasn't likely. She reluctantly settled into her bed. She lay there, fighting thoughts of darkness. The darkness of space. The darkness of the ship. The darkness of the future. The darkness of the figure in the room. The darkness of her past. And off to sleep she went.

Aurora woke up the next morning, still a little disoriented. She heard commotion, and although it was the sound of her crewmates waking up and getting ready for the day, she couldn't figure out what was going on. She fought to open her eyes, which seemed like they'd been glued shut. She tried to look around to see where she was and she remembered that she was aboard the ship heading to humanity's new home planet. She remembered she had a photo pinned above her on her headboard. She looked up at the photo of the young man and— wait, something's off, she thought.

She leaned in closer. Closer. The photo definitely seemed different. The young man in the photo seemed to be standing slightly more to the right than she remembered him standing. Then it happened. He winked.

Aurora jumped suddenly, sitting up and backing away from the photo.

"Good morning!" said May, sitting on the side of her bed, rubbing her eyes, "you alright? Bad dream?"

Aurora looked at her, then back to the photo. Back to normal. "You could say that," she said. She did her best to ignore what she just saw. But one thing was abundantly clear to her now. Something was haunting her. But what?

"Um, May, there's a crew conference, right? Before breakfast?"

"Yes, in about ten minutes."

"Okay, that's what I thought."

Then May asked her something, but she didn't quite catch it. May repeated herself. "I said, what was your bad dream about?"

"Oh. Actually, it was a...well, it wasn't a bad dream exactly."

"What do you mean?"

"I didn't want to say anything but...I think I'm seeing things. Terrifying things. Like...a ghost? Is that normal? For space travel, or..."

May thought for a second. "I don't think so. I couldn't rule it out, though. I've never heard of hallucinations being a side effect of sleeping in stasis or even just of being in space, but I suppose earth was so busy with war for so many years, we may have neglected study for some time. Do you want me to take a look at you later?"

Aurora shook her head. "Thank you, that's not necessary."

"If you're sure, okay."

"Please don't tell the others. I don't want them to worry."

"Okay, but if you see something else, you tell me. Understand?" Aurora nodded.

"Good morning, crew," said Stepan at the start of the crew conference, "yesterday was a good day to get settled in. Today the real work begins. The ship has been running on its own for quite some time. We have much work to do, da?" The crew all nodded. "Right," he continued, "Lorenzo, we need to complete diagnostics first thing, today."

"Sí. No problem."

"Aurora can assist you with that." She had never assisted in diagnostics checks before and feared that she may not know what she's doing. He continued. "And May, you're..."

"Preparing the sample kits for our arrival and fixing up med bay."

"Very good. Aurora, do you have anything for us this morning?"

Aurora stuttered in answering. "Uh, well—, n- no. Not really. I'm just going to try my best to help Lorenzo. And if I have time, I will be packing my art supplies for when we arrive later this week."

Stepan nodded and went on. "I hope you don't mind me volunteering you to help Lorenzo," he said to her, "diagnostics checks can take quite some time. You will have plenty of packing time after lunch. Good?"

"Good," she said, honestly glad that she at least had something constructive to do.

"I have a few conference calls this morning. We will have breakfast very soon this morning and lunch is at 1200. Today's morning conference is a bit short, so let us start the day strong. Lorenzo?"

"One stellar breakfast, coming up," he said. May reminded Aurora to come see her if her hallucinations persisted, and Aurora thanked her.

Later, at lunch, the crew had gathered in the mess hall and Lorenzo had tasked Aurora with finding some good music to play while they ate. Aurora had actually had a fairly pleasant morning. The diagnostics checks went well and anything that needed fixing was fixed by Aurora with guidance from Lorenzo. She was feeling particularly useful and she hadn't seen anything frightening. Whatever darkness that was surrounding her seemed to have gone away, at least for the morning. Aurora scrolled through the music options but stopped on one she liked. She pressed play and "It Never Entered My Mind" by Frank Sinatra started echoing throughout the halls of the ship.

"Ah! I love this song," said Lorenzo.

"I do not know this song, I think," said Stepan, "my country restricted much great music growing up."

"Surely you've heard of Frank Sinatra, Commander," said May.

Aurora chimed in as well as she sat down to eat with her crewmates. "People called him, 'The Voice,'" Aurora said.

"I have heard of him, yes. But not this song. Beautiful song," said Stepan. There was something about hearing a nearly two-century-old song echoing in a spaceship on its way to another galaxy that felt poignant, but beautiful in a sad way. It felt like a reminder of home, a home that most will never come back to. A piece of earth, alive on the ship, like a time capsule floating through space. The crewmates all seemed to be having similar thoughts. Their faces were focused, distant, much like Aurora's the day before.

May broke the silence, first with a smile, then, "this song reminds me of my boyfriend. He loves this old music. He told me that it keeps you grounded and connected to your past."

"I didn't know you had a boyfriend," said Aurora.

"Yes, we met at university. His name is Jun. I studied astrobiology and he studied music. You would really like him, Aurora. He has a very creative mind. We are engaged to be married and will be married in a year! We're hoping to get married on the new planet, once we're more established."

"An interstellar wedding!" exclaimed Lorenzo, "what a beautiful thing."

"We are very happy together. He has already secured a seat on one of the arks, so he'll be joining us very soon."

"That's wonderful, May," said Lorenzo, "congratulations. It's about time he proposed to you."

"It was actually me that proposed to him!"

Stepan laughed, "that sounds right for Jun. What about you, Lorenzo? I've never asked if you were married."

"Ah I was just telling Aurora the other day, science is my woman."

"Really?" asked May, laughing as she asked.

Lorenzo chuckled, but Aurora could tell from that chuckle that the truth must have been more painful. "No. Actually, the truth is I was married. Years ago. We married young," said Lorenzo. Aurora looked up from her food to see his face. There was pain there.

"Her name was Lila. I met her while I was studying in London," said Lorenzo, "she was— wow, she was gorgeous. Truly an amazing woman. Funny. Very intelligent. We dated briefly but got married fairly quickly. Her parents weren't very fond of me, but she loved me and wanted to marry me anyway. We uh...we were walking in town one day and she told me that she had something important to tell me. I asked what it was, but the air raid sirens went off. She looked at me with such fear. Her face, it's burned into my brain. I tried my best to find a nearby shelter but right before we entered one, a bomb went off in front of us. Everything went black and when I woke up, they told me that she didn't make it. Mi vida. I never found out what she had to tell me. She never told anyone else."

Lorenzo's usual charming smile was gone. His eyes were red, but he held back his tears.

"I'm so sorry, Lorenzo," said May. She had tears on her face, and Stepan was shocked, but Aurora was silent. She knew his pain.

"What do you think she was going to tell you?" Aurora asked. May and Stepan looked at her, as if they were unsure if that was an okay question to ask.

"I think I know. But I try not to think about it, considering what happened. In some ways I'm glad that I don't know. If I'm right, it would only hurt more..."

Aurora didn't know what to say, and so stayed silent. The echoing low sound of classic oldies still lingered in the background, mixing with the hum of machinery as the only audible sounds in the room. Lorenzo did his best to put his smile back on. "Well, I've had some years to process it since then. That was near the beginning of the war, so...it's in the past now. Um. What about you Stepan?"

Stepan smiled, "da. Married. Many, many years now. She's wonderful. Terrifying, very strong. Everything I like in a woman." Everyone chuckled at this. "Do you have any children?" asked May. Stepan hesitated slightly before answering.

"Yes. We had two children. My daughter Masha and my son, Alexi. My daughter, she lives with my wife. My son...he was called to fight at the start of the war. He didn't make it."

"Oh Stepan, I'm sorry. I didn't know," said May.

Stepan smiled. "It is okay. Like Lorenzo said, many years have passed since then. It has been a long war." Aurora could see that he was not okay. Aurora began to feel uncomfortable. Everyone was sharing their stories, and she knew hers would be next.

Stepan turned to her and asked "Aurora, what about you? I see a ring. How did you meet your spouse?" Lorenzo bumped him with his elbow and shook his head. Stepan realized his error and quickly apologized. "Hm? Oh, sorry." Aurora felt unsure. Should she tell them? Should she tell them what has been haunting her since before she accepted this mission, what has haunted her since she's awoken on this ship?

"I— I don't know if I can..."

"You don't have to tell us," Said May, "it's okay." She reached out and held her hand tight. Besides the quiet music in the background, a long silence punctured the atmosphere in the room, sharp like a needle but soft like a cloud of smoke at the same time. The darkness lingered near her. The same presence from before was surrounding her. How soon until the dark figure finds her once more, she thought. A deep breath in. A deep breath out.

"His name was Jonah. I loved my husband more than I've ever loved anyone." This was it. No turning back. It was time. Maybe in this room of strangers she would finally have the courage to face this. "I've known him since we were kids. I was always a troubled, angsty kid, but he knew how to calm me down. He always did. He completed me in a way I never thought possible. He would always tell me that he loved my quiet, brooding heart. He never asked me to change, but he inspired me to. He got me to pursue my art, even though my parents wanted me to follow them into science. He encouraged me to love freely, openly, and without condition. I mean it when I say he was my everything."

"He sounds like a very good man," said Stepan, "but if you don't want to talk about it now, you don't have to."

"No. No, it's alright. I think it's time I talked about it. I still haven't dealt with it and it's...it's killing me."

May said, "this war has taken someone from all of us, Aurora. We understand. I lost my father in the war." Aurora looked at all of their concerned faces. She couldn't understand how they were all able to relate to her and yet, she seemed to feel it all so much more than them. This is what she thought anyway.

"One day, he woke me up very early. Wanted to go for a walk, he said. I had had a very long night the night before. I was helping my cousin with some things and it went on a little late and just...I was so tired that morning. I only wanted to sleep for a few more minutes. But Jonah, he loved those walks and I should've just woken up then and gone with him. I don't know why I didn't just get up when he asked me. I told him I needed a few minutes. He said, 'oh alright. I'll be waiting for you.' But it wasn't a few minutes. He let me sleep for an extra two hours before he woke me up again. But when he woke me the second time, he was agitated, anxious.

"I asked him what it was. He told me he had to go, that he was being deployed on the east coast. That it was urgent and there was no time. I panicked. I was still out of it from waking up and didn't know what was going on. He held me and hugged me tight and told me he loved me. I told him I loved him too. He started walking to the front door, but I ran after him. I begged him not to go, knowing full well he couldn't stay. He turned to me one last time before getting in the car and kissed me. It was all happening so fast. By the time I had fully woken up he was gone."

"And then what happened?" asked Lorenzo. Aurora's voice broke as she went on, tears falling onto her plate.

"That was the last time I saw him. The last time I spoke to him. They say he's still considered missing in action, but I know. He's gone. I felt the moment he died in my heart." Aurora broke down and May went to comfort her. Lorenzo and Stepan bowed their heads in respect, unsure of what to say. "Every day, I feel this darkness around me," said Aurora through sobs, "I see things, things that taunt me. Sometimes I feel him close to me, but then the darkness takes over and all I'm left with is pain and loneliness. I don't know who I am without him."

"I'm so sorry, Aurora," said May, "you must know you're not alone. We know what you feel."

"May, I appreciate that but I don't know if you do. Every single day I think about what his last moments were like. The violence. The pain. I'll never know. I never even got to bury his body. How could you know what that's like?"

Aurora heard a light tapping sound coming from...somewhere.

"Trust me, solnyshko. We know," said Stepan. The three of them reached out to Aurora and touched her hands. "I just don't understand," she said, "why I feel it so strongly. This pain. It's so strong that I can practically feel it moving around me. Physically. Why can't I—"

A beeping interrupted her. They all turned their heads to a small console behind them. It looked similar to the one Lorenzo was working on the day before. "Lorenzo—" said Stepan. Lorenzo stood up and walked over to it, pausing the music at the same time; "I'm on it."

Aurora felt the hair on the back of her neck stand up.

"Guys," said Lorenzo, "it says that a fifth person has been detected on board."

This alarmed everyone. They all looked at each other in silence for a second. Aurora glanced over at the monitor on the console.

May said, "there aren't any ships here. How is that possible? Who could've boarded us?"

"Maybe we have a stowaway," said Stepan, "but I don't know why it wouldn't have appeared before. Lorenzo, where was it detected?"

Lorenzo leaned into the screen. "Living quarters. No, now the med bay. Now— Stepan, it's all over the place."

Stepan got up and entered work mode. "It's most likely a glitch but we need to be sure. Everyone take one of these." He walked to a locker and opened it. Inside were black stun batons. He grabbed four of them and distributed them among them. Aurora, still wiping tears from her face and feeling afraid, took one, confused.

"We need to check the entire ship, front to back. Aurora and I will go this way, Lorenzo and May, you go that way. Stay together. Okay?" May nodded and walked with Lorenzo towards the living quarters. "Come, it's alright. We just need to be sure," said Stepan to Aurora.

She was still confused and grieving but complied, "o-okay."

Stepan and Aurora made their way slowly through the tight corridors of the ship. She hadn't spent much time on this side of the ship yet and was especially concerned about getting lost. She made sure to stay close to Stepan.

"I'm sorry, solnyshko. About your husband," he said to her, "I wish we could have had a longer moment of silence for him. This timing, it is..."

"Thank you, Stepan. It's okay." They continued down the quiet corridor, listening for anything suspicious, but it was silent. Still.

"You remind me of my daughter, you know," said Stepan.

Aurora jumped slightly at his voice, booming still even in a hushed tone. "Really?"

"Really. You are very similar. You would get along." They went on in silence for a few more minutes, finding nothing. Aurora still felt uneasy. A presence was beginning to make itself felt near her.

"Lorenzo, check in," said Stepan over comms. "Nothing yet," was the response, and Stepan confirmed the same.

They came to a room that Aurora assumed to be the cargo bay. "This is the last room on this side," said Stepan, "let's check it quickly then we can go back."

Aurora nodded and turned on the flashlight on her phone, holding the stun baton firmly. "I'll check this corner," she said. Stepan nodded. Aurora approached a dark corner and pointed her light at it. A hard shadow was cast on the wall as she illuminated a stack of crates in front of her. She walked slowly around the crates and popped her light behind them. Nothing. Nothing at all.

Lorenzo's voice came through on her comms. "Guys, you're not going to believe this, but the monitor has detected a sixth person on board."

Then, she felt something. A light touch on her shoulder. A voice, right in her other ear.

"You know how to stop the pain, don't you?"

Aurora gasped and turned around. "Stepan?" she called, "did you say something? Stepan?" Not only did he not answer, but he was nowhere to be seen. She checked every corner of the cargo bay. "Stepan! Lorenzo, can you hear me? May?" No answer. Her breath quickened as she climbed her way quickly out of the cargo bay. She ran down the corridor in a panic, checking every room. "Stepan! Lorenzo! May!" No answer still. She stopped in the mess hall. The evening lights turned on, despite it not even being afternoon yet, creating a dim orange glow in the rooms. They didn't feel nearly as comforting now.

"This way, pet."

Aurora turned her head towards the living quarters corridor. She barely caught a glimpse of a dripping, dark figure disappearing past the entryway into the dark corridor. Reluctantly, she followed. Turning the corner, she stared down the corridor and shivered at the sight of a pitch black hallway going on and on indefinitely, lit only by her phone's light. She immediately tried to go back to the mess hall, but the way back was blocked somehow by a solid wall that wasn't there before. In full panic, she called out to the others, calling for any of them, all of them. "Stepan! Lorenzo! May? Hello?" Still no answer.

With nowhere to go, she carefully made her way down the dark hallway. The white noise of the machines, the whirring and clicking, felt louder than usual. Rather than the relaxing background sounds that they used to be, they now felt like specters, whispering insults and oppression at her. The whirring changed to the sound of steam hisses, the clicking to the sound of gears grinding. Aurora went on, tears flowing down her face as her environment changed around her in horrible ways. The clean and sterile architecture of the spaceship gave way to a dark tunnel made of rusted metal, rock walls and pipes.

"What is this?!" she said out loud, terrified. A pipe released a loud burst of steam in front of her. She screamed, ducking out of the way. She ran down the hallway, faster and faster, until she came to a descending stairway. She stopped herself just in time, almost falling down the stairs. She looked behind her. The dark hallway remained the same. Endless. Dark. She turned around and went down the stairs. Eventually she reached the bottom and in the almost pitch black room before her was a large conveyor belt, surrounded by boilers and other structures made of some dark metal. She peered over at the conveyor belt and on it was a steaming black goo. Disgusted, she backed away from it and went on through the room.

On the other side of the room, there was another hallway, but this one had a hint of light peeking out from under the door. She went to the door and opened it. Inside was a large, dark room with many doors, lit only by a single dim chandelier, covered in cobwebs. The wood floor beneath her creaked with age as she processed through. Looking around, she saw what looked like an old, Victorian room. Whatever color the furniture and walls were in there before, they were grey and dusty now. Perhaps they always had been.

She went to the left and grabbed a doorknob. She turned it and slowly pulled the door open. The door creaked quietly as she looked inside. She saw a dark stone temple, lit only by flames. It was quiet and people wearing linen loincloths and dresses lay about on low beds. Aurora recognized ancient Egyptian hieroglyphs on the walls in stellar, almost new condition. She saw bald men in linen clothes reciting something quietly over a man, sleeping on a bed. Over the man, on the other side, she saw something awful. A dark figure with a long frowning jaw stood hunched over him, black goo dripping out of its mouth and onto the sleeping man's face. She backed out of the doorway and went to another.

Opening another door, she saw a dark room in what looked to be a wealthy medieval style, lit by a fire in a fireplace. A woman lay on a grand four post bed and another woman (presumably a servant) was speaking to her. Aurora could barely hear her and what she could hear sounded vaguely like English but could have been another language entirely. From what she could gather, the servant woman said something about "filling the house with joy" and "having family over." Aurora felt somewhat safe in this calm, albeit dreary room and she was about to step through until she saw something move. From under the bed crawled a small, dark, impish creature, moving like a spider towards the woman on the bed. The creature left a trail of the same black goo. Aurora panicked, quickly shut the door, and tried another.

She began to lose hope. Surely this isn't real, she thought. Surely she would turn a corner and be back on the ship, heading towards the exoplanet. She opened a door and saw what looked to be an evening at a New York pier, but not the New York she knew. She saw men wearing bowler hats and women wearing long dresses. "It's the Carpathia, the Carpathia!" yelled a voice in the crowd. A large white ship was unloading people and lifeboats onto the pier. There was such a crowd and such a commotion. As people came off of the large boat, sobbing and embracing the people waiting on the pier, Aurora saw hundreds of dark figures erupting out of people's bodies, spreading black goo everywhere as they jumped from person to person, some of them licking and attempting to bite people. If the people could see these creatures, they didn't seem to be bothered by them. No one reacted to the creatures at all. Aurora felt a deep sadness, almost despair, as she looked at this sight. She could feel it draining her. She closed the door and tried one last one.

She opened a door and inside she saw, to her surprise, her old house back on earth. "I don't understand," she said out loud. She walked through the door and closed it behind her. She looked around. It looked nearly the same as when she'd left it, but all of her things were still there, not packed up in boxes. Suddenly, behind her, a door opened. It seemed to come from the front door. She went to it, not realizing that the doorway she'd stepped through to get here was nowhere to be seen.

In front of her she saw...herself. She was talking to someone. Aurora's heart sank as she realized what she was seeing. "I'm so sorry," said a male voice at the door. Aurora looked at her past self collapse onto her knees, sobbing. She cried seeing this, reliving the pain of the day she lost her husband. However, she stopped crying when she saw a familiar dark figure rising out of the base of her past self's neck. It crawled out of her as if climbing out of a manhole on a street.

"The day we first met," whispered a voice, "I've been with you for so long. You may be one of my favorites."

The dark figure turned its head to Aurora, its awful, big white eyes piercing into her. She stood, paralyzed in fear.

"Shh shh shh. I know, pet. I know. It's alright. I'm here now."

Aurora felt a pain in her heart. She cried out. The dark figure came closer.

"You know what can stop the pain. It's okay. None of this matters anyway. There's no end to your suffering here. You have no purpose without him. This will go on forever. Unless..."

The dark figure reached its hand out to her in a gentle, upturned position. She looked at its hand and then up at its horrifying eyes and featureless face. The round, bleached white scleras. The tiny, black marble pupils. Aurora cried as she slowly started to reach for its hand.

Then, a sound. In the distance. It was music. Frank Sinatra's voice.

Aurora turned to look for it. She turned away from the dark figure but she felt something grab her arm. It was the figure.

"Don't go. You need me."

Aurora ignored it and peeled its cold fingers off of her arm before following the sound of the music. She followed it to the back door of her house and after opening it saw not her backyard, but a beautiful cottage in the woods. The cottage was highlighted by a beautiful sunrise piercing through the trees. She turned back and saw the dark figure staring at her, its head tilted slightly. After a moment, it started to move towards her. Aurora shuddered, stepped through her back door and closed it before the dark figure could reach her.

She couldn't explain it, but she felt safe now. The sound of Frank Sinatra's voice was clear now and it seemed to be coming from inside the house. "It Never Entered My Mind" was playing. Curious, she followed it. Arriving at the front door of the cottage, she turned the doorknob and stepped inside. "Hello?" she called out. She looked to her left and saw a record player playing the music she heard.

"Aurora, in here!" called a familiar voice from the kitchen. Aurora's heart jumped. It was her husband.

"Jonah? Jonah!" She turned the corner of the kitchen and there he was, smiling at her in full dress uniform. She ran into his arms and kissed him deeply. He spun her around and looked into her eyes. She broke down, holding his face in her hands, kissing him over and over before hugging him longer than she'd hugged anyone in a long, long time. But then she stood back an inch. "Wait, are you really here? Is this real?" she asked.

"It's real, my love. I've tried so hard to reach you. I tried everything, but there was always something blocking me."

"I don't understand."

"That thing you left behind there. It always stops me. It was stronger than me, but you're here now."

Aurora backed away and shook her head. "No," she said, "no, this isn't real. I'm imagining things."

Jonah tried to reach out to her, but she backed up. "Please love," he said, "I promise this is real. How can I prove it to you?"

"You died and I'm seeing ghosts, visions. I can't trust my own mind."

"Aurora, look in my eyes. It's me. You're not in that awful place anymore. I've got you. You're safe."

Aurora went to him again, tearing up as she started to recognize her husband's true soul in this ghost. "It's really you?" she asked.

He nodded and smiled. "It's me, love. I tried to send you messages, but the only message I could manage to send you was winking at you through the photograph."

"That was you?! So you were the fifth person on the ship; or were you the sixth? Do you realize how much that scared me?"

Jonah laughed warmly, which warmed her heart. She laughed with him. "Sorry, my love. I thought it would be playful."

"I missed you. So much. Jonah, I...I can't live without you. I'm nothing without you. I'm a wreck. I need to come home to you."

"No. Don't talk like that."

"What can I do, Jonah? It hurts. So much. I don't understand how I'm supposed to go on without you."

"I know it's hard, love. But I'm always with you. Always. We will see each other again one day, but for now, I need you to be strong for me. You can do this; I know you can." Aurora balled her hands into fists and rested them on his chest.

"I can't," she said, "I can't do this. I just want to die."

Jonah looked behind her and saw the dark figure slowly opening the door on the other side of the yard. "Look Aurora," he said, brushing her hair behind her ear, "the more you think like that, the closer that thing gets."

"What?"

"God has other plans for you. You are not nothing. You are so much more. You are strong, you are important. Look at the path you're on now. You're leading people, other people who are going through the same thing as you, you are leading them to a better world. The living need you. Look at me, love. I'm okay. I'm alright." Aurora rested her head on his chest and closed her eyes. "I'm alright," he repeated, "you don't need to hold on to the pain anymore."

"I still don't know what I'm supposed to do without you though. It never occurred to me that I would have to wake up without you. Drinking orange juice without you...visiting my parents without you..."

"Do your best. That's all anyone can ask of you. And remember, I am always with you. I love you."

She kissed him again. "I love you too." Jonah and Aurora looked back at the door. The dark figure left, closing the door slowly.

"Is it gone now?"

"Not forever, I don't think. It can always come back. But hold on to hope. Lean on God. That'll keep it away."

"What are those things anyway? What was that place?"

"I'm not entirely sure what they are or what that place is, but I have a theory. I think you know what that theory is. Either way, it's not something they really talk about up here."

"And what is 'here'?"

"Actually, this is a cottage I was in the process of buying for you, back on earth. I was going to move us here."

Aurora looked around, amazed. "All of this?" she asked, "oh hon, it's beautiful. I wish we could've lived here together. They let you have this here?"

"They did. Don't worry, you'll get to come here one day. You'll see."

Aurora smiled and put her hand on his cheek. "I noticed you put on our song."

"Of course! I knew it would draw you here. You know, they let you listen to any song you want here. Even songs that don't exist yet. It's pretty amazing." They chuckled at this as they held each other's hands.

"What happens now?"

"Now you go back."

"Hold me?" He held her close and caressed her hair.

"I don't wanna go," she said, "please don't let me go."

"Never. I'll always be with you. Always."

"Please don't let me go."

"I'm right here. Right here. I'll be waiting for you."

"I think she's waking up," said Lorenzo, "there she is." Aurora opened her eyes sleepily.

"Aurora, how are you feeling?" asked Stepan. She sat up, dazed. "I'm alright."

"You gave me a fright, solnyshko. I turned around and you were on the ground."

May said, "Lorenzo and I didn't find anything on our side of the ship. It must have been a glitch."

Aurora smiled, "right, a glitch." They helped her up.

May took her arm. "Let's get you out of the cargo bay and into the med bay," she said to her.

Stepan gestured to Lorenzo and said to the women, "Lorenzo and I will run some diagnostics to see if we can figure out what happened."

In the med bay, while checking Aurora's vitals, May asked "what happened to you?"

"I don't remember fainting at all. I'm not entirely sure if it was real or not, but I remember hearing things. I saw a dark figure and it led me...somewhere awful."

"What does that mean?"

"I- I'm not entirely sure. I was walking down the living quarters corridor and it turned into this dark, lonely awful place full of coldness and despair. But at one point, I heard my husband."

"You heard your husband? While you were passed out?"

"It felt real, May. I think it might have been. He showed me the cottage he was going to buy us before he passed. It was beautiful."

May seemed skeptical but chose to believe her. "Well what did he say to you?"

"He told me he was alright. That he'd be waiting for me. I don't know why, May, but I think I actually feel some hope. For the first time since he passed."

"That's wonderful! Maybe you really did see him."

"I did. I know it. I feel it in my heart." They both smiled as May finished checking her vitals, giving her a clean bill of health. Life would be very different for Aurora from then on. Life would be better.

Three Months Later

Aurora stood behind her easel, palette nearby her on a foldable table. Before her was the eternal sunset sky she had been getting used to the past couple of weeks. It was dotted by several large nearby planets of varying size, sitting in the sky like many large moons. Being tidally locked, the part of the planet she had arrived on never saw nighttime. The small, red dwarf star that these planets orbited gave the sky a beautiful, dim crimson and peach hue. The rocks before her, covered in sand from sandstorms, gave way to gentle waves of water. Around her feet, the native flora grew generously, like a carpet, their black leaves stretching out to the cold, quiet sun.

"Good morning Aurora," said Stepan behind her, even though the planet never saw mornings, "some of the other crews wanted to call us before lunch, if you want to join us. They discovered some beautiful caves on their side of the planet."

"Oh, sure! I'll be there soon," said Aurora.

"Oh and I thought I'd tell you, my wife and daughter will be here in a few months. They're coming with May's fiancé. I'd love for you to meet them!"

"That's wonderful, Stepan. I look forward to it!" Stepan smiled and walked away, snorting from his large nose as he often did. From her right came Lorenzo and May.

"Hello, you two," Aurora said to them.

"Señora," said Lorenzo with a smirk.

May showed Aurora a basket of picked black plant material. "Look what we found. We think these may be edible. We haven't studied them yet. I'm going to look at them in the lab and if they're safe—"

"I'll be cooking them for lunch," said Lorenzo excitedly. Lorenzo went on, likely to wash his hands at their base.

"This is it, right? Your best piece?" asked May.

"Yes. I believe this will be the main painting that they'll use to promote this place. I will admit, as harsh and as different as this place can be, it is so peaceful and beautiful here. The warm, dramatic sky, the cool temperatures. The silence."

"Except for the storms!"

"Right, except for the storms." They laughed together. "I'm glad I came," Aurora continued, "Jonah was right. This is where I'm supposed to be right now."

"Do you ever see him?" asked May. Aurora shook her head but smiled wistfully. "Do you ever see that...thing?" May asked again.

In front of Aurora, in the water, she saw the head of a dark figure with bright white eyes and tiny black pupil's half rising out of the water.

It stared at her intensely before disappearing once more below the dark, gentle waves. "Sometimes."

"Are you sure you don't want to talk to someone about it? About the dark figure? And the black goo that you mentioned?"

Aurora took May's hand and held it, hugging it with her thumb.

"No need. I think everything is going to be just fine."

The End

Once Upon a Tidal Cove

Cathy-Lee Chopping

As they sat and watched their children play in the sand, Sarah and Margot smiled gently at each other. It had been an incredibly long time between visits, and Margot thought her sister looked very well after last winters 'flu had made her incredibly sick for months. The children giggled as the water lapped gently around their legs, the twins sitting either side of Archie in the hole their mothers had dug for them. The late afternoon sun glittered on the surface of the ocean, and Sarah stretched in its warmth. "Thank you for inviting me." She said, just loud enough for Margot to catch her words over the blonde trio's mirth at the seaweed swirling in their sand bath.

Margot reached over and took her sisters hand, smiling sadly. "It was the least I could do, I've missed you guys all very much." Sarah grasped it tightly, emotions from the years they hadn't seen each other unable to pass her lips. "It's – been hard." She choked out, unable to meet Margots gaze. "My girls..." Her marriage had disintegrated around ten years ago, her life had almost been over from the pain, and she still had nightmares about that time of her life. Her loss had been excruciating.

Smiling at the identical twins sitting in front of them, now splashing each other and Archie with the sea water, Margot remarked, "They look a little bigger today." Looking over at them, Sarah was suddenly splashed with the cool water after one exuberant splash by Archie. She laughed lightly, "I think it's this place."

Margot had booked the holiday after a horror decade for their family. They had lost several loved ones to car accidents, cancer and other illnesses. The running morbid 'joke' was that they were cursed, and Margot almost thought it true when they lost another person the year before to a freak accident at his workplace. "We all needed this." She waved at their parents walking up the beach towards them. "All of us."

The women watched as their mother and father walked slowly up the beach, arm in arm. Her mother gazed up at her husband of forty years like it was the first time seeing him. Sarah snorted, "It is almost gross, how smitten they still are after this long." They snickered as their parents reached them, their mother, Annabel looking down at them with slight surprise as if she hadn't seen them at all on her walk along the beach. "Oh hello you two! How has your day been?"

Sarah gestured to the three freckled toddlers, now intently pouring warm sand on her legs, patting it down and slowly burying her feet. "It's been hectic and...just absolutely amazing." She smiled up at her mother, who stepped forward and hugged her daughter. "Good – I just can't get over how amazing this place is." Sarah squeezed her back gently, "Me too. I've really missed..." She watched her girls filling the bucket with more sand. "Everyone."

Annabel stepped back and took her husband's hand. "We're going to have a meal in the restaurant, and then we might go for another walk to watch the sunset." She looked up at him, eyes full of love. "It's been a very long time since we have caught a sunset together." Sarah and Margot smiled as Paul and Annabel walked off together, oblivious to everything else but each other. "It's so nice to see her so happy." Sarah remarked. Margot nodded, a lump forming in her throat. Words that remained unspoken swirled around them, and they turned their attention to the three children, now working on burying Margots legs. They laughed and suddenly scooped Archie, Matilda and Sophie up, running down to the waters edge and splashing each other. Footprints washed away in the surf as the children's laugher rang out across the otherwise empty beach, and Sarah felt like all was as it should have been.

It was the last night of their stay, and Margot couldn't sleep. She slipped out of bed and checked on her son Archie, snoring lightly in his bed. She smoothed his hair over his forehead, marvelling on how big he was getting. She tucked him in, her eyes memorising the dusting of freckles across his nose, and the sweet curve of his mouth as he smiled in his dreams. Leaving his room, she walked across the hall to Sarah's door. It was slightly ajar, and she peeked in to see Sarah and her girls sprawled across their bed in the moonlight. The twins were soundly sleeping, holding hands, which tugged at Margots heartstrings. Another memory to lock away.

"Are you alright?" Sarah asked softly, making Margot jump. She hadn't realised that Sarah was awake. "Yeah, I'm okay, just about to make a hot drink. Would you like one?" Sarah nodded, sitting up slowly as to not disturb the girls. Matilda let out a light snore, and Sarah smiled down at her, gently pushing the curls off her tiny forehead, like Margot had just done to Archie minutes before. The girls excited voices from dinner that night rang in her ears, timeless echos as she focused on their faces. She wouldn't ever forget this moment. Her heart ached and she felt bereft as she left the room.

They sat together at the breakfast bar several minutes later, watching the ocean outside their villa glitter in the full moon. It was a perfect night, a slight breeze ruffling their hair as they sipped their tea together in silence.

"This place really is amazing." Margot echoed her sister's words from earlier, her eyes searching her sisters face. Nodding, Sarah wiped away a stray tear. "I cannot thank you enough for everything." Margot smiled again, "I had to bring you, there was nothing else for it. This was something we all needed, and I'm so sorry that life has been so cruel to you." Sarah wiped at her face, now streaming. "It has been unforgettable, and exactly what I needed. I didn't want to go to sleep in case it were all a dream. I've missed them so much." Having committed the pamphlet to memory, Margot recited it, "For time with those you have loved most, at the time when you were happiest."

Smiling through her tears, Sarah nodded. "Yes, I thought that this place was a scam at first, a gimmick that was just going to rip us off, but here we are." Margot patted her hand as she continued, "This was absolutely the time when I was happiest. Thank you so much for this trip, I wish I could repay this." She finished her drink. "Thank you for the tea."

Margot shook her head. "It was my pleasure. Now, you need to go and hug and squeeze those beautiful girls of yours until you go back to sleep. Don't waste another second with them." Sarah agreed, "I don't really want to go home tomorrow. This time with everyone has been priceless." She hesitated, "I'm going to struggle to leave." Margot hugged her sister, "Try and sleep, it will be an emotional day tomorrow."

The morning came too quickly. Margot had given up on sleep after several more hours of tossing and turning, and had just laid on Archies bed with him as he slept soundly. As he started to stir, she slipped back into her room and had a hot shower, not ready for the goodbyes to come as they would head back to reality. She could hear the twins bouncing around the loungeroom boisterously as she came out, towel drying her hair, and found Sarah wrangling them for breakfast, laughing at their energy as they pounced on each other from the couch.

She found her mother and father sitting at the kitchen table, Annabel holding onto Paul's hand for dear life as he turned the pages of the newspaper with his free hand. Coffee sat untouched between them, and Margot could sense an overwhelming feeling of sadness emanating from them. No one likes goodbyes. Leaving them to their silence, she turned to the girls rolling on the floor, laughing and squealing as Sarah dressed them, kissing them all over and hugging them hard until they squirmed away. She met Margots eyes, unspoken words once again hanging over them. Her gaze pleaded for more time. Margot smiled sadly. It was nearly time to go.

"Wow – is that how small we used to be?" A young man's voice cut through the laughter, and as he spoke, everyone in the room seemed to stop and hold their breath. The illusion was finally shattered as Margot turned slowly, and watched as a sleepy Archie walked into the room. His long, lanky legs and pre-teen body was a stark contrast to the chubby toddler he had been yesterday, and the twins squealed and wrapped their arms around his legs as he stumbled to the couch to hug them in a cuddle puddle. Margot caught Sarahs eye, shaking her head helplessly as a lump in her throat prevented all speech.

"Yes." Sarah said softly as she sat by a twelve-year old Archie, wrapping the girls up into a huge hug between them. The two-year olds were giggling and bouncing in their seats. Matilda ruffled Archies hair, and Sophie planted a big raspberry on his arm. He squeezed them tightly, the beginnings of a teenage crackle running through his voice. "I think I remember how happy we were. We were always laughing like this. I remember..." Tears spilled over as Sarah stood, allowing Archie to give his final goodbye hugs to the twins. "You really all were so happy together. They loved you, Archie." She could feel her mother's eyes on her as both her and their father stood as well. "We need to go now."

Margot swept the girls up into her arms, kissing their chubby faces all over, smelling their hair which still had the faint scent of newborn baby clinging to it. She whispered words of love and wishes for them to be able to come back home with them. Sophie and Matilda patted her face back, cooing and returning her kisses. Archie got up to hug his grandparents, squeezing his Grandad extra long and hard. "I don't want to go." He murmured, moving to his mother's arms as the twins again wiggled away to go to Sarah. Margot nodded too, taking his hand in hers. "Me neither, but we have to let them say goodbye." Archie smiled sadly and followed her out the door into the sunshine.

Several minutes later, they sat in silence on the porch swing, taking in the beautiful morning there on Tidal Cove. Margot heard the door swing closed behind her, and turned to see her sister, almost doubled up in pain. She was up in a moment, hugging her tightly. Sarah whispered, "I almost couldn't leave them." Margot nodded, unable to speak. Behind them, the door opened again, and Annabel walked out; alone. The sisters pulled her into their hug, and they stood there for what seemed to be a very long time.

"Mum." Archie's voice cut through their collective grief, and they looked up to see their car arrive. He stood and took their bags down to the car, and as their driver loaded them in, Archie leaned against the back door. Margot watched her son, almost a teenager now, quietly looking back at the house where they had spent an amazing week together as a whole family again, for the first time in over eight years.

Margot took Sarahs hand and began leading her gently down to the car. They heard a knock behind them, and they turned together, to see their father standing at the window, holding Matilda and Sophie, forever toddlers. The twins waved cheerful goodbyes, not quite understanding what was going on. Their father's sad eyes never left Annabel, and she stood stock still, staring back at him.

As Margot helped her down the stairs, Sarah winced with both emotional and physical pain. Since the car accident ten years ago, she had never been the same. She closed her eyes as the screech of tyres, the shatter of broken glass and the smell of gasoline filled her senses. The flashback brought a roaring sound to her ears as the car once again twisted and crumpled around her and her family. She heard her screams echo in her ears as she watched fire fighters gently remove two tiny, broken bodies from the wreckage of her car; still felt the ache of the bruises from the paramedics hands holding her down to preserve her spinal column, and the everlasting bruises on her heart that would never heal. She gripped the banister with her other hand to steady herself, as Margot watched her struggle with her internal thoughts with concern as she tightened her hold on her hand.

The very babies that were her entire world had been torn from her in an instant by a drunk driver. The rest of that year had gone by in a blur; a whirl of fragmented memories, pain relief, rehabilitation and heartbreak. The police visiting her in hospital, near comatose as she cried inconsolably for the children that she would never again hold, kiss and lay in their cribs. Every time Sarah awoke, she remembered again, the pain as fresh as that first night without her girls.

Margot held her as the flashback continued, a bane of her existence and the price she would always pay for driving home so late on a Friday night. A memorial service that ended with two tiny coffins lowered into the ground, Sarah's heart-wrenching sobs as she tried to stop the groundskeepers from filling in the holes, screaming that her girls were afraid of the dark. The averted gazes filled with pity of the other mourners as they either looked away or moved to her side to gently pull her out of the way.

Sarah shook her head as the vision cleared, looking up at her sister with shame and sorrow. She visited their graves every day, and every day her heart hurt more knowing what they were missing out on. She watched Archie grow into a young man with pride, and with sadness, always wondering what her girls would have been like as young women. Margot turned with her as she waved back at her babies in the window, smiling and crying at the same time. This week, her heart had healed a little, knowing that she had been able to squeeze them tightly again anytime she had wanted to. They had been warm, real, and alive. It had been ten long years without her Sophie and Matilda. She finally reached the car, and with exhaustion she leaned lightly against Archie, who put his long arm around her to comfort her. "It's okay, Auntie. We can always come back."

"Mum." Margot walked back up onto the deck and touched her mother's arm. "It's time to go." Annabel jumped, jolted from her reverie. She looked at her daughter like she hadn't realised that she was there. "Margot." She looked at Sarah, leaning on the car. "Sarah." Her face fell, and forgetting her own pain, Sarah was back by her mother's side in a moment. Margot and Sarah each holding one of her hands. "Mum, we have to go." Margot repeated.

Annabel smiled at them sadly. "I can't go home." She turned her gaze back to her husband, who smiled sadly back at her. Margot frowned. "What? What do you mean?" Annabel embraced them both for a long time; Sarah first, and then Margot. "I'm really sorry, I should have told you earlier."

Realisation dawning on her first, Margot looked at her mother in shock. "What happened?" Annabel pulled away, stepping back towards the door. "It was just before we left. I was doing the dishes, and then... I fell..." She brushed her hand across her forehead as she struggled with her thoughts. "I can't remember anything else, but I know I was coming here, and the next thing I knew, I was here with your dad. And you were both here too. And the children." Sarah let out a low moan. "Mum, no."

Running back up the stairs, Archie flung himself into his Nanas arms. "Please tell me you are coming home with us?" Annabel squeezed him tightly, and then stepped back again, even closer to the door of the beach house. "I'm sorry my love, I can't." Sarah and Margot clung to her hands, feeling an overwhelming sense of loss and grief. "No, we can fix this, we can get back in time..." Sarah trailed off, looking between her mother and Margot helplessly. Annabel smiled sadly, "It really is too late, I'm here now."

The door behind her opened, and Paul stepped out. His face was full of sadness. "It is time now, Annabel, you need to say goodbye." Sarah burst into tears as she hugged her mother yet again. Margot enveloped them both tightly as Archie moved to hug his Grandad.

Tapping from the window had them all turn to see Matilda and Sophie blowing great big raspberries on the glass, dissolving into uncontrollable laughter together. They all chuckled through their tears, as Paul took one of Sarah and Margot's hands in each of his. "I will look after your Mum until you can come back to visit us." Archie moved away to the window, waving and blowing kisses to the twins as his eyes filled with private tears listening to their goodbyes.

Paul continued, "Sarah, I will always look after your girls, I always have, but you must promise to look after yourself. Please." She nodded silently, tears streaming down her face. He turned to Margot, smiling at her proudly. "Archie is a wonderful lad, and I can't wait to see how he grows up. You're a great mum, and a strong, wonderful woman." He looked back at Sarah, "You both are. I am so proud of you both, and you will be okay. We are all going to be here waiting for you when it is your time." Enveloping them both in a giant hug, he then kissed them both on the foreheads as he used to every day before his work accident the year before. "You need to take Archie, and go home now."

As Margot and Sarah cried and hugged their mother one last time, Paul turned and embraced Archie tightly once again. Pride beamed from Paul's face as he spoke in soft tones to his grandson, and asked of him a favour. Archies face was set and determined as he nodded his assent through his tears at his grandads request, accepting the kiss on his forehead as they pulled away reluctantly from one another. Paul then moved to stand by Annabel, placing an arm around her waist as he guided her gently back into the house. The trio left standing on the porch watched as the twins screamed with glee as their Nana joined them at the window, a sorrowful look on her face, hand never leaving her husbands.

As they drove away from the house, the sisters sobbed quietly together in the backseat. Archie stared out the window towards the ocean as their car travelled towards the bridge and the portal home. Margot reached out to her son and placed her hand gently on his shoulder. "Are you okay buddy?" Archie turned and took her hand in his, and nodded, the developing apple in his throat bobbing up and down against his emotions. "Did Grandad ask you something at the end there?" She asked. Again, Archie nodded, squeezing her hand. Margot continued, "If you don't want to tell us, that's alright. I'm so sorry, that we didn't know about Nana... We can come back again another time to see them again."

Archie shook his head, clearing his throat as he fought for the right words. Sarah looked up as he began to speak. "Grandad asked me a favour, and I told him that I would try my best." He looked at them both before staring out the back window at the quickly receding blue beach house on Tidal Cove. "What was it?" Sarah whispered, clinging to Margots other hand. Archie looked at her and smiled through his tears. "He asked me to live my best life, and to look after you both." He looked back at his mother.

"I told him I would."

The End

Always Love You

Adria Northman

Part I

"What do you mean, you're not coming?" She all but whispered into the phone as she stood just outside the airport, alone and soaking wet from the rain.

"I'm not going with you." He replied, sounding rather distant and distracted.

"I don't understand. I thought…" She had started to say, but when the soft feminine laughter that usually warmed her heart, echoed through the phone, it wasn't butterflies she felt fluttering about inside. It was more like knives.

"I'm staying home to take care of our girl." He meant his girl, because their tri-lationship was more of a him and her, than a him and them these days.

"Fine. Whatever. I'll go alone." She was not missing her sister's wedding, even if she had to show up alone.

"Dammit, Darla. Don't be like this. You know Miranda's been sick, and she needs someone here to… " The only thing Miranda needed was some ice cream, a soft blanket, and a good movie. She was pregnant, not crippled.

"Dillon, just take care of Miranda, okay." She didn't wait for him to reply, hitting the end button and slipping her phone into her pocket.

Her phone rang. She ignored it.

It ran again.

Then the ringtone changed.

"Great." She shook her head, for now they were both calling.

With a long, drawn out sigh, she continued to ignore the phone, picked up her carry-on bag, and made her way back inside the airport. After checking in, again, she hit up the bathroom and quickly changed out of her wet sweater and leggings. Eyeing herself in the mirror, she wasn't surprised to find that she looked like a drowned rat. She couldn't meet her parents like this. Hell, she couldn't meet anyone like this.

Nonetheless, she did her best to make herself look presentable. She wiped all the streaks from her cheeks, dabbed at the mess of mascara that was supposed to be waterproof, and tied back the loose strands of her long, chocolate-brown hair. It was as good as she was going to get without her make-up bag, which was somewhere between security and the belly of the plane. So, hoping that she could just grab a blanket and nap on the flight, she hurried from the bathroom and found a seat near the large bay windows that looked out over the runway.

It was here, that twenty-three-year-old, Darla Anne Benson, had started contemplating her choices as of late. In fact, she was about to call the last four years of her life into question and run them through the ringer.

What. The. Hell. Was. She. Doing?

Dillon. Miranda. That thing they all had going on.

Dillon Mitchell was the twenty-five-year-old heir to the family goods, not that his father, or grandfather for that matter, were going anywhere soon. Still, he had the beach-blonde hair that fell to his shoulders and those ice-blue eyes, the sinful voice and charismatic charm that had somehow captivated her enough for her to agree to what came next.

Miranda Tessario had been Darla's best friend since grade four. They'd lived on the same street, went to the same school, had the same teachers, same friends, same frenemies. They'd shared everything while growing up, from clothes and toys, to makeup and jewellery and shoes, and when they were old enough, they even shared their cars, and their boyfriends...

Now, Darla was a good-looking woman, with waist length, chocolate-colored hair that she kept pulled back for work, and eyes that '...shimmered like honey in the sunlight...' he'd once told her. She wasn't skinny like the models on the billboards plastered all over the city, but she felt pretty confident strutting along the beaches in a barely-there bikini while holding Dillon's hand. She had the hips, the round butt, the ample melons as it were, and she had a wicked personality; at least, she thought so, but Darla was no Miranda.

For starters, Darla thought she was far too pale. Sure, she tanned, if only to keep up to the all-natural sun-kissed goddess that was her best friend. There was also the matter of her height. She wasn't tall and lean and full of energy at the drop of a hat. She wasn't as playful or as confident, often keeping her thoughts to herself when in truth, she wanted to scream.

Miranda, on the other hand, had everything a man was looking for in the world of exotic and erotic, barely having to lift a finger to achieve the drop dead gorgeous look she was always rocking. Long, black hair, thick thighs and pretty brown eyes, a skinny little waist and a butt that Dillon was absolutely obsessed with. Okay, so maybe Darla had been a little obsessed with it as well, which is why they'd ended up in the situation they were in now.

It was one big love-triangle. Darla loved Miranda, probably more than she loved Dillon though she'd never admit it out loud, and Miranda, well... 'I'm in this to be with you.' Dillon, on the other hand, had claimed to love them both, but Darla knew the truth, ever more so now that Miranda was pregnant.

"Excuse the interruption, passengers, but due to bad weather, flight five-seven-two out of Edmonds to Cassus had been delayed. For more information, please visit..."

Wait, what?

Quickly pulling out her phone and ignoring yet another call from Miranda, she pulled up the flight itinerary and almost lost her lunch. That was her flight, and the update blinking at the bottom said that it wouldn't be leaving until one in the morning. It was only seven, and she really didn't want to wait around for another six hours. Chances were very high that Miranda would be upset enough to demand that Dillon bring her to the airport, so she could talk to Darla; and it wasn't really Miranda's fault that Dillon was the way he was, but Darla really didn't want to see anyone right now.

Checking the time again, she shook her head. Man, she could drive and be pulling into the city of Cassus before the plane even left the runway. She could drive straight to her parent's house and surprise them. Except, she could hear the conversation now…

'Hi, Mom. Hey, Dad. I'm here for Amy's wedding, and I'll be staying a few weeks. Hope that's okay.'

'Oh my, is everything okay with you and the others?' Her mother would ask.

'Where is that meat-head boyfriend of yours? Miranda keeping him in line?' Her father would inquire with a frown, though he adored Miranda, he didn't think very highly of Dillon. He'd end with an *'I just want you to be happy.'* and they'd all go inside and have breakfast, and chat about her sister's upcoming wedding.

Yeah, she could totally drive, and then she'd have her truck and wouldn't have to rent a car. That would save her a few hundred dollars and she could come and go as she pleased, not having to bother anyone. It was beginning to sound like a great idea.

Her phone rang again, and she shoved it back into her pocket, rose to her feet, and proceeded towards the flight desk. After confirming that her luggage would indeed arrive at the Cassus Airport tomorrow afternoon for her to pick it up, she swung her carry-on over her shoulder and made for the parking lot. It was still raining, but that no longer hindered her mood. She was going on a road trip, and as long as she didn't run into Dillon or Miranda on the way to her truck, her mood was sure to improve.

Part II

The mini-mart had had everything she needed, including a small cooler she had packed with ice to keep her snacks and cans of iced coffee and sodas cold for her trip. Having loaded everything into the truck, she filled the gas tank and hit the road, heading east on the highway. It had been a good two hours before she reached the turn-off she needed, and then she was heading north towards Emory Falls, followed by Bexsville, where she'd stop and grab some more snacks, stretch her legs a little.

The highway was long and boring, but with her windows down, music cranked, and another can of iced coffee in hand, she was in a phenomenal mood as the wind blew through her hair. It had stopped raining a half hour ago and the skies above were clear, the stars shining bright. Nothing but them and her headlights to illuminate the big white signs as she passed them. Finally, she found the one she'd been searching for.

Bexsville 100

Turning off the highway, she began the trek down the winding road that followed the base of Hawk Mountain and remembered all the camping trips and beach parties that had taken place at Hawk's Point. It would be amazing to visit the old stomping grounds, but then, it wouldn't be the same without Miranda.

"Shit!" She hissed as her eyes started to water. "Happy thoughts. Think, happy thoughts." She scolded herself, and cranked the music even louder.

A remix of one her favorite songs came on, and she sang along as best she could, shouting her heart out into the open night sky. "Do a little dance..." She blurted out, weaving back and forth in her seat, which in turn made the car weave back and forth along the darkened road. It was all fun and games until the song switched over and *'I Will Always Love You'* came on; and try as she might, she just couldn't hold back the tears, though nor could she muster the strength to reach out and switch the station.

As the song played on, the tears fell faster, until Darla had to pull the damn car over and use her sleeves to wipe the traitorous droplets away. This was their song. Her's, Dillon's and Miranda's, but the truth hit hard once again, and she cringed. Dillon didn't love her. Not like he loved Miranda.

"Mother-trucking-damn-it-all-to-hell.... FUCK!" Darla rarely swore, but tonight, tonight was different.

'... always... love... youuuuuuuuuuuuuuuuuuuu......' She could hear Miranda's voice in her head, and pictured her dancing about the living room.

She wondered what the two of them were doing at the moment. Her phone had stopped ringing, or maybe it had died, she wasn't sure, and she wasn't about to check. She needed time. Needed space.

Oh, wow...

With her emotions overwhelming her, she felt her head spin, the need to vomit, rising fast. She barely had time to pull the truck over, whip off her seat and throw open the door before the snacks she'd devoured at the start of her journey, proceeded to make a surprise comeback. Emptying her stomach on the side of the road, she hoped like hell that no one drove by. She was in no condition to deal with people at the moment, for chances were high that she'd break right down and confess her whole life story to a complete stranger, who may very well end up kidnapping her.

At that, she pulled the door closed and locked it. If she had to puke some more, she'd use one of those chip bags she'd emptied. The thought alone was enough to make her stomach churn and a shudder ran through her, like the blood in her veins had been replaced with ice.

Great, now she had the chills. What was next, a raging fever and mild hallucinations? Or was it the other way around?

Man, if she had food poisoning...

Her mental rant was cut short as she caught sight of the strange figure, weaving along on the opposite side of said road. At first, she couldn't tell what it was. A large, dark mass that weaved about. Was it a bear? A wolf? Both were common around Hawk Mountain, but as the figure drew closer to the light thrown by her headlights, she noted that it walked on two legs. It was a person, and with the one step forward and two steps, arms flailing on either side, they were either walking an imaginary tight rope, or really, really drunk.

Sliding down in her seat, she felt the whole world spin, her heart began to race in her chest, and her skin grew clammy. "Just keep walking." She whispered, peeking out the window to find the figure now directly across the road from her. "Just keep walking."

As the seconds past, Darla held her breath and watched the shadow stumble off into the night. When it disappeared from view, she let that breath go and sank even further into her seat. In and out with slow breaths, she tried to calm herself. She was still smelling the roses and blowing out the candles when something slapped against her driver-side window and her heart skipped a few beats before sputtering to a stop. She slowly opened one eye, and then the other, and spying a set of massive, filthy palms, she jumped in her seat and instantly went for the door locks. With a clunk, they engaged, and she bolted into the passenger like being two feet further away would up her chances of survival somehow.

"Fuck. Hello? Fuck, fuck, fuck. Hello?" At least, that's what she thought he was saying, but between the rain beating down, the music playing, and the fact that her heart was now beating so damn hard it felt, and sounded like a freaking freight train rolling through her chest, she wasn't sure. Still, the guy kept tap-tap-tapping on the glass and the deep, muffled voice was speaking to her.

What did he want? What was he saying?

Then the hand wiped the rain away, and a face slid up against the glass. The guy was soaking wet and had short, dark, curly hair that dripped rain down his cheeks. He wore a baseball cap that had a hawk holding a football on the front, and the deep grey eyes hidden beneath the brim were so familiar, but the moustache and beard were throwing her off. There was something about him that left her both relaxed, and extremely on edge. She knew this face, or perhaps, a younger version of it.

The rain had petered off and again he was speaking to her, but the words were jumbled mumbles amidst the ringing in her ears. "...la? .... me.... arla."

"Go away." She shouted back. "Just leave me alone. I have nothing for you."

"Is... la!" He continued, and by the look on his face, he was really sorry about something.

"GO AWAY!" She shouted, reaching forward to silence the radio.

"Dar..... please. Darla. I'm Sorry." Wait, that was her name. Had she heard that right? How did he know her name? "Darla, come on, it's cold out here." Now that, she heard clear as day, and it left her with a feeling of deja-vu.

She'd heard it before. That voice. That very line, but it had been years ago. "Russel?" She whispered as she sat forward and rubbed at her eyes.

"Darla, please. Let me in."

In the blink of an eye it was like she was a teenager again, living in Cassus, going to high-school with her best friend, partying with all their friends, dating whoever they wanted, even the captain on a rival school's football team. Oh, she'd done this before, and this was the part where he was still drunk and apologizing for doing something stupid; except this wasn't high-school, and she sure as hell wasn't his girlfriend any more. She hadn't even seen the guy since they'd broken up five years ago.

Nah, this couldn't be right. That couldn't be him. And yet...

"I'm sorry I drank too much. Please, don't go." Okay, that sounded way too much like Russel to not be Russel, and she shimmied back across the front seat and slowly rolled the window down an inch. "Oh, thank God. Look, I know you're mad, but you can yell at me on the way home, okay?"

"What?" She choked out, unable to fully comprehend what she was hearing.

How could he be here? Right here. Right now. Like he just had to take a drunken walk down memory lane, on the very night she'd be passing through.

"Please. I just need to get out of the rain, D." Ah, and there was the nickname.

"Russ?" She muttered, staring at the beard, trying to picture him without it.

"Darla, please." The guy sagged against her truck. "I swear, I had no idea what we were drinking. I can't... I can't find my truck."

"What?" Darla recoiled. "Russel, what are you doing out here?" She kept the window to a crack, but found her hand sliding towards the door locks. "Where is your truck?"

"I... Uh..." He was slurring his words pretty bad, and the stench of alcohol hit in her in waves each time he spoke.

"Where were you?"

"I was just..." He slipped a little, knocking his chin on the roof of her truck, and laughed. "Ha, I was hanging out with the guys."

She tried to picture his two best buds in her mind. What were their names again? They were like the gruesome-twosome, always creeping in a stealing Russ to go do stupid shit. Casey? Carllen? Crap, it had been so long ago, and those two had been so, overly annoying.

"Yup. Me, Cam, uh, Luke and a few others. We were... uh..." The guy took off his hat and scratched his head, and nearly fell over in the process. "Whoa. Fuck."

Same old Russel. No manners. No morals. "Where is your truck?"

Russel shrugged, which again, almost caused him to fall over. "I think..." Clearly, he couldn't think, and Darla sighed, rolling down the window down some more. "Do you need a ride home?"

"Uh..." He removed his hat again and rubbed at his eyes before hanging his head. "Yeah. Probably best."

Darla nodded to the passenger side and unlocked the doors, then watched as her ex-high-school-sweetheart slid across the front of her truck with the grace of a drunken hyena, swung the door open with the strength of a gorilla, and poured himself into the seat beside her.

"Wow." Darla let out with a laugh as she helped him with his seatbelt, trying to ignore the stench of deep-woods musk mixed with campfire and some kind of home-brewed fire-water that permeated from his pores.

Rolling his head to the side, he smiled and closed his eyes. "Did you miss me?"

Was he serious? "Sure." She replied, rolling her eyes, and pulled the truck back onto the road.

It was a forty-minute drive to Bexsville from Hawk Mountain, and she hoped her little detour wouldn't take much longer than that. She had places to be. People to see. A life to get on with.

Despite being unable to hold his head up, let alone keep his eyes open, Russel was grinning like a madman. "I love this old truck."

"She's been good to me." Darla patted the steering wheel. "More so than others." She added with a sigh and instantly regretted it.

That brought a frown to the guy's face, but he kept quiet as he reached forward and turned the music back on, and then he just stared out the window.

Part III

The storm had come on suddenly, and despite having excellent tires on her truck, Darla was having trouble keeping the truck in line. The rain was hitting hard, the wind was howling and flashes of lightning making Hawk Mountain look like something out of a horror movie. In the distance, Darla could make out the lights of an oncoming vehicle, but her wind-shield wipers were doing a piss-poor job of keeping things visible.

Russel had fallen asleep in the passenger seat, which wasn't unusual, for the guy could fall asleep anywhere. Good thing too, because her stomach had been churning again, and she didn't have the energy to entertain anyone at the moment. She needed to find a bathroom, and quick. Wasn't there a gas station along this route?

And just like that, the bright neon sign of the local petrol station flashed up ahead. "Perfect timing." She muttered as the burn started in her stomach and slowly rose up to her throat. "Oh man."

Maybe she shouldn't have wolfed down that sandwich so fast, or gorged on those potato chips? Or was it the chocolate bars? The beef jerky? She'd been so hungry lately, and tired. She couldn't remember the last time she'd gotten a good night's sleep, what with Miranda being pregnant and Dillon spending all his time with her, she'd been left with everything else.

Another wave of nausea rolled inside her belly as she parked the truck, jumped out, and raced inside. Snatching the keys from the clerk, she made it into the bathroom stall with little time to spare, and once again, emptied her stomach.

With her head spinning, she sat down on the toilet to catch her breath and wipe the nasty taste from her mouth, thinking she could totally go for some ginger-ale right now. Then she remembered the four cases of the stuff that Dillon had brought home for Miranda the day before Darla had left for the airport. It was probably still sitting in the hall. She'd thought it was because he'd be coming to her sister's wedding, and he didn't want Miranda to leave the house for want for anything while they were away; but that had not been the case. Not even close, and a sudden rush of anguish hit her, bringing her to tears.

"It's fucking ginger-ale, for crying out loud." She cried, and hung her head in her hands. "This is so messed up." She whispered.

Darla loved Miranda, but right now, she really despised the woman, and through no fault of Miranda's own. She'd been loving, attentive, passionate, and Darla had to face the fact that the woman was her best friend, the rock that had kept her grounded most days. So why was Darla feeling this way? Like Miranda was slipping away? No. More like, Dillon was stealing her away?

After a good cry, she dried her eyes and left the toilet stall, feeling more than a little foolish. She washed her hands, splashed some water on her face, then dried off, and had a good hard look in the mirror. She had to get a hold of herself. She had chosen this lifestyle. She had chosen Miranda, and Dillon.

"Don't be an asshole." She grumbled, and noted that not letting the asshole out had left her with wrinkles, frown lines and bags under her eyes. "Uh, I look like crap."

After returning the keys and purchasing a bottle of ginger-ale, hoping it would help, she headed back for the truck. The rain was still coming down pretty hard, thunder rolling through the skies followed by bright flashes of lightning. She'd missed the thunderstorms out here and she took a moment to breathe in the fresh air before getting back in the truck.

Swinging the door open, she climbed inside. "You still sleeping?" She inquired as she shut the door and turned towards him. He was. "Right. Let's get you home." She laughed.

Russel and his mom lived near the old lumber mill, at the far end of Nelson Rd, right before it met up with the highway again on the other side; but unlike the rest of the roads running through Bexsville, Nelson was comprised of mostly gravel, having been built atop a dyke that ran through the farmers fields to accommodate the logging trucks. So naturally, it was filled with hundreds of ruts and potholes, and the ditches on either side were something else, some four feet below and filled with water. Risky, at the best of times, but if she dropped Russel off and continued down Nelson, it would cut almost two hours off her trip and get her to her parent's house even earlier.

It was a rough, bumpy ride and with all the rain, Darla was white-knuckling the steering wheel. The fields between the houses were massive, and often filled with cattle, but on a night like tonight, even they were tucked away inside a barn safe and warm. In their absence, water had formed massive black puddles that resembled giants patches of oil that filled both field and road, and the rain kept coming, creating little streams that ran off into the ditches to either side.

"This is bad, Russ…" She spoke up, but when she turned to face him, he was gone. "What? Where… Russel?" She recoiled in shock. "Russel?" She shouted, searching the seat, the floorboards, the closed window. "Where…" She mouthed, just as one of the tires hit a deep rut, jerking the truck to the left.

Darla tried to make the necessary corrections, which was hard to do when her brain was trying to figure out where the hell Russel had gone, only to have said tire give way just as she tugged on the wheel and the whole truck began to spin out of control. In slow motion, she watched as the view in the window switched from road to field, field to road, and so forth. Rocks went flying, some pinging off the hood of the truck, others slamming into the windshield, and then there was a cracking sound as the glass finally shattered, giving way to whatever had hit it. Glass went flying into the interior of the truck, forcing Darla to let go of the wheel and shield herself from the onslaught.

Moments later the whole truck flipped onto its side, and then the roof, slamming Darla into the steering wheel and window, before continuing to ass-over-tea-kettle it down what could only have been the ditch.

Thank the lucky stars that she'd remembered to put on her seatbelt, for she'd have been tossed around like a rag-doll, perhaps even thrown from a broken window to land in crumpled heap of mangled limbs. Instead, she felt the pull of the belt as her entire body lifted up and out of the seat, and she was slammed, one last time, face-first into the steering wheel. She could hear the crack as her nose gave way, feel the warmth of the blood running down her face as her eyes filled with tears.

She knew she had to get out of the truck, but she was bleeding from a pretty nasty head wound, every muscle in her body ached, her left leg was bent at an unnatural angle, the straps of her seatbelt were digging into her chest and stomach, and her vision was fading in and out. Barely able to keep her eyes open, she could see just enough to tell that she was indeed, dangling upside-down from the seatbelt like bait on a hook.

What was worse, the seat beside her was still empty. She hadn't imagined that part. Panic set in, flooding her broken body with adrenaline, and her head started to pound. He'd been there when she got back from the bathroom, she was sure of it.

"Rus...sel?" She managed to get out, but that seatbelt was making it harder and harder to breathe. She had to get herself free. "Russel?" She shouted, then recoiled, for the sound of her own voice made her head ache even worse. "Oh God..." She whimpered, as fresh blood dripped down her face and dribbled across her lips.

She had to concentrate. She couldn't give in to the aches and pains, she had to... Where was her phone? She needed her phone. If she could only... What was beeping? Was that her phone? Her alarm? What was that noise?

"Darla?" She heard her name being called, but she couldn't tell which direction it was coming from. "Darla?" It was getting louder.

"Russel?" She muttered, licking her lips, but all she tasted was the metallic tang of fresh blood. "Where... you go?"

"I got you."

"I... hurt. All... over."

Part IV

She came to, slowly, her body filled with aches and pains. She had no idea where she was, or why she couldn't move, her arms and legs refusing every command given to them. Her eyelids felt as if heavy boulders sat upon them, for which she lacked the strength to move, and her throat was rough like sandpaper as she inhaled each scorching breath.

What the hell had happened to her?

Why was she in so much pain?

"Oh, God..." She opened her mouth to speak, but what came out sounded more like the croak of a frog and a pang of pain lit off in her throat.

"Darla? Sweetheart, can you hear me?" Wait, was that...

"M... Mom?" She let out another croak, forcing the word past the lump in her throat, caring not as to the how, only that the woman was here. "Mom?"

"Oh, honey. Hush now." Came the cracked reply, and then someone was holding her hand, stroking her arm and kissing her cheek. "It's okay. You're going to be, okay."

"W... what... happened?" Darla struggled to sit up, but the pain shot through her like a bolt of lightning, and she felt dizzy and sick to her stomach, letting out another groan.

"No. No. You just lay there, I'll get the doctor." Her mother let go of her hand.

"Mom?" Darla barked, panic welling inside of her. "Mom?"

"Hey, I'm here. You're okay."

"Mom?" She whimpered. "I can't... why can't I see?"

"It's okay, the doctor's coming?"

Sadly, her mother's words did nothing to ease the anxiousness that was building in her chest, and like a fist it squeezed at her throat, as if trying to choke back her words. "Why can't I see?" She shouted again, caring not that it made the pain worse. "Why can't I see anything? Why can't I move?"

"Easy, Darla." It was the voice of a man.

"Why can't I see?" She cried out. "What happened to me? Why can't I move?"

"We can remove the bandages that cover your eyes." The doctor's gruff voice spoke words meant to bring relief, if only temporary.

"Please. I want, no. I need, to see."

"Alright, but let's do this, slowly. Don't rush things here." The doctor said as he moved about, his voice all but echoing off the walls.

It hurt like hell, but when the weight had finally been lifted, the air felt cool against her lids. They tingled a little, but they seemed to stuck. "Why, why can't I open them?" She tried to lift her hand, to wipe away whatever it was that still covered her eyes, but her hand wouldn't budge.

"Just relax, Darla." Her mother's voice hovered to one side, and she caught the change in lighting right before she felt something cool pass over her face.

Was it a cloth? Were they... Oh please, let her be able to see. Please let this work. She couldn't go through life without her sight.

"There. Now try again." The doctor spoke.

The light blinded her with the first crack of her lids, the pain lancing through her temples like a knife through butter, and she shut them again quickly. "Owww." She moaned, but attempted again. The light wasn't as bright, but her vision was blurred. After a few blinks, she looked around as best she could and began to see the dark blue walls and the stainless steel counters, the glass-front cupboard with all the little boxes and packages of medical equipment inside. There were monitors, wires, and tall poles with bags hanging from the tops, and beyond them, a bay of windows from which a handful of doctors and nurses were watching her.

This wasn't your usual hospital room, in fact, she'd never seen one so decked out before and an overwhelming urge to run washed over her. She wasn't supposed to be here. "Mom?" She yelped in alarm, wanting so badly to see the woman's face, to know that she was real, and she was here. "Mom?" She shouted, louder this time.

"I'm right here, Baby." And that face, that beautiful face was hovering over her, those honey-colored eyes, just like her own, staring back at her. "I'm right here." Her mother smiled, stroking Darla's cheek with her thumb.

"Where am I?" Darla whispered. "What... happened to me?"

"It's okay, Darla. You're in the hospital."

"No, it's not okay. I can't..." She blinked her eyes again and again, trying desperate to hold back the tears. "I can't move. Why can't I move? Am I..."

"You've been through a lot, Sweetheart. Your body needs time to heal is all." Her mother tried to smile, but there was something hidden in her eyes.

"I can't even lift my arm."

"You will. I promise. You are doing so much better than before."

"Before?" Darla murmured and her mother looked away, but Darla could still see the worry that plagued her.

"Darla, what's the last thing you remember?" The doctor's face came into view, a darker face covered in greying beard, and a pair of thick glasses trimmed in black.

Wow, okay. What did she remember? "Uh..." Come on, what did she remember. "I... uh..."

"It's okay. Just take it slow. Sometimes it takes a while for our memories to catch up after an ordeal such as your own." The doctor squeezed her hand. "Can you feel that?"

"Uh, I think so."

"Good." The man smiled as if she'd made some huge achievement, but she still couldn't lift that hand, or wiggle her toes.

"What happened to me? Why am I here?"

"There was an accident, Sweetheart." Her mother's voice was filled with anguish, and her eyes had clouded over in sadness. "You rolled your truck..."

It took a few seconds, but everything came back to her in waves. The call from Dillon. The cancelled flight. The decision to drive, and getting sick, and picking up her friend. Her breakdown in the bathroom. The hard rain, screeching tires, smashed glass and an insane sense that she was rolling. They'd gone off the road, they'd...

"Russel?" She shouted, and like her motion had returned with her memories, she shot up in the bed, and instantly regretted it.

Pain ricochetted through her body and she actually wished she could go back to the unable-to-move-state she'd been stuck in before. Every nerve in her body had come alive, and man were they pissed at what she'd done to herself.

"Where's... Russel?" She gritted out through the onslaught of what felt like stabbing knives and relentless nausea attacked her insides. "Is he okay?" Oh, wow. This was, not good. The pain radiated from head to toe, even laying down hurt. "Okay." She hissed. "I'm... okay." But the room was far too silent, save for the subtle beeps of what she assumed were her monitors. "Where is he? Where is Russel?"

"She means Dillon, her boyfriend." Her mother smiled, taking her hands and squeezing them tight. "He's been calling day and night." The fact that he'd been calling, and wasn't actually here...

"No, Mom. Not..." Darla tried to shake her head, but that was a bad idea, for the pressure grew and the alarms on those monitors started to freak out. "Shit." She lay still and closed her eyes, waiting for the spins to subside. "Where is Russel? He was with..."

"Mrs. Benson?" A third voice entered the room, and Darla's heart made the monitors shrill as it skipped a few beats.

"Miranda? You made it." Darla's mother squeezed her hands again. "Come in. Come in. Look, Darla. Look's who's here." The relief at her arrival seemed not only to calm Darla, but also her mother, the woman's smile more genuine, the weight on her shoulders lifted slightly.

It took less than a few seconds for Miranda's tear-streaked face to come into view, and then the vision was blurred by even more tears. "You're alive." She managed to choke out.

"I am." Darla replied and tried to smile, but even that hurt.

"I am so sorry..." Miranda started in. "We should have been with you. If I hadn't stayed home, he never would have... and you would have gotten on that plane instead of..." The tears were streaming down her face. "You shouldn't have been out there alone."

"I wasn't alone."

"What?" Miranda gasped and looked to the floor. "Who... who were you with?" The hurt in her eyes was real, though she tried really hard to conceal it. "You can tell me."

"I wasn't cheating on you. Or Dillon." Darla sighed and closed her eyes. "I ran into Russel, or rather, he ran into my window."

"Wait. Who?" Miranda inquired, taking one of Darla's hands from her mother, so she could hold it; and her hands shook like crazy.

"Russel. Hawk Mountain High. Football player. Drank too much. I'm not surprised you don't remember him." Darla chuckled. "He hated that you and I were friends."

"Oh, I remember him. And the feeling was mutual." Miranda replied with a roll of her eyes, but then her mouth dropped open and her eyes opened real wide.

"What?" Darla cranked her head to one side, ignoring the pain.

"Where did you say you found him?"

"Who is this boy?" Darla's mother cut in.

"He's a guy Darla used to date in high school. Real charmer." Miranda answered, then turned back to Darla. "Where did you see him?"

"Uh, he was stumbling down the road. He was beyond drunk and mumbling about needing a ride."

"And you gave him one."

"Yeah, I did. It was raining, and he was a good forty minutes from home. So I drove him home." She stopped short. "Or, at least, I tried to." She added. "Where is he? Is he okay?"

"Darla." Miranda started, but then let out a long, drawn out sigh.

"Where's Russel?" Darla was trying to sit up again and she didn't care about the stupid monitors and their annoying alarms. "What happened to him?"

"What's going on, Miranda?" Mrs. Benson was just as curious it seemed, eyeing the young woman up and down.

"Where did you say the accident happened?"

"Uh, Bexsville I believe." Darla's mother replied with a shake of her head. "They said it was an old dirt road. Um, Nelson something."

"Russel lives on Nelson Rd." Darla groaned. "I figured, I could drop him off and just follow the road through the old lumber mill, come out the other side and meet up with the highway. It would have cut two hours off my travel time, but the storm..."

"That road is sketchy at the best of times." Miranda frowned.

"Well aware of that." Darla groaned. "The guy was passed out in my passenger seat, what was I supposed to do, bring him with me to meet my parents?"

"Darla..."

"Don't Darla me. There is nothing reasonable about any of this. I was helping a friend get home, and we crashed. Now, can someone tell me where he is, or how he's doing?"

"Russel is dead, Darla. Has been dead, for three years."

Part V

One week later...

Her mother had gone for the night with a promise to return with her father in the morning, and Miranda had disappeared downstairs to find something worthy of being called food, for them to snack on. She had been amazing, staying by Darla's side through every minute of her recovery, even had a cot brought in, so she didn't have to leave at night. She was Darla's emotional support person, the one who could defend her from the petty nurses, and rock the matching silk pyjamas and fluffy slippers, belting out show-tunes as she wheeled her down to the halls to every physio appointment. She'd also spent many of the past few nights assuring Darla that she wasn't crazy.

It had been three weeks since the accident, and a week and a half since Darla had woken up in that hospital bed, for the second time, as she'd been told. The first time hadn't gone so well. She'd come to with superhuman strength and a will to escape, ripping out the tube that was lodged in her throat, tearing wires from her chest and forehead, and nearly strangling herself with the own I. V lines that got wrapped around her neck; which explained why her throat had hurt as much as it did, and why they'd had to sedate and restrain her.

'They said it happens to a lot of people. Like their bodies have rebooted and they don't remember where they are, or what they're capable of. They just, don't understand what's going on and lose it.' Miranda had done her best to her explain it, but sadly, she was no doctor.

Darla laughed out loud and leaned back in the bed, staring out the window. She had learned a lot about this place, and the accident which had landed her here; but some things just didn't make sense.

Like Russel.

Her sight shifted from the window to the drawer beside her bed, and she went for the folded piece of newspaper inside. Her mother had brought it in for her after doing some digging, and Darla couldn't believe what she'd read.

The article was dated October the sixteenth, two-thousand and fifteen.

It is with great sadness that we announce the passing of our son, Russel Malcolm Anders, aged twenty-three.

As she sat in her hospital bed, no longer connected to the pesky monitors and tubes, she read the obituary for the umpteenth time, still trying to wrap her head around it all. She was getting better, so why did she keep seeing him in her head? Like he was there? Clearly, he hadn't been. Couldn't have been. The guy had died. Three years ago, and creepy enough, in almost the exact same spot where she had crashed her truck. She had made it further than he had, but the road had claimed both vehicles.

Dammit. She had picked him up that night.

She was so certain of it. Every part of her very being rejected any notion that stated otherwise. For crying out loud, she could see still see him sitting there in the passenger seat of her truck when she closed her eyes. She could hear him slurring his words, and oh how he wreaked of alcohol. Even now, she wrinkled her nose.

How could any of it have happened?

Had she gone on a road-trip with a ghost?

Or, as the doctors claimed, had she been so stressed out and suffering from a mad bout of food poisoning, that she'd been hallucinating?

"Hey, look what I found?" Miranda's sudden appearance in the doorway was a surprise and made Darla jump, which in turn struck a nerve in her broken leg, and another in the shoulder that had been severely dislocated from its socket. "Okay, that was not supposed to hurt." She frowned and dropped the bags she held at her sides.

"I'm good. I promise." Darla threw on a smile as she repositioned herself on the bed.

"Liar." Miranda came forward and set the bags on the rolling table, and wheeled it over.

"Ha! What gave it away? Was it the grunt? Or the grumble?"

"Your face. You're an awful liar." Miranda shrugged, and then looked at her with her head cocked to one side, as if something about Darla left her puzzled. "Sorry." She shook her head and started into the first bag.

"For what? Being honest?" Darla scoffed and waved her hand. "Please, out with it." But when Miranda handed her a small package, she shook her head. "Not the snacks. What's bugging you?" Other than the fact that it had been almost two weeks and Dillon was running out of excuses on why he couldn't be here yet.

"I'm scared." Miranda replied, staring at the thing in her hand.

"You bought it." Darla teased, nodding to the brightly wrapped whatever.

"No. I'm scared about you."

"What! Why?" Darla blurted out so fast, she nearly choked on her own tongue. "What's going on?" She sat forward as far as she could and reached for Miranda's hand. "Is this about me not wanting to go home, because of Dillon? I didn't mean I never wanted to go home, just, not yet."

"No. It's about you and the fact that you really do suck at being a liar." Miranda looked to the floor, and then back to Darla.

"Okay, what did I lie about?" Darla took the small package and sat back, focusing on the high-precision task of unwrapping the paper while she waited with a rock in her stomach for Miranda's answer.

"That's just it. You didn't lie. Not once. You really…"

Oh look, it was a little bun shaped like a panda. How cute…

"You talk about Russel as if he was actually there."

"Because… he was. I told you I'd been feeling sick." Darla left out the part about the song and getting all emotional over the whole Dillon incident, on purpose. "Maybe I was seeing things that weren't there. My father always said I had a wild imagination."

"I believe you." Miranda sat down across from her. "If you say he was there, then he was there."

"And what, his ghost travels the long dark roads between Hawk's Point and home?"

"A home he never reached." Miranda looked so serious, then she shrugged as she pulled her own Panda bun out of the wrapper and bit off an arm. "If you think about it, he saved you. You said yourself that he pulled you out of the truck, and the paramedics did find you under a tree…"

"Maybe I climbed out by myself?"

"In your condition? I highly doubt it."

"Okay, that is beyond creepy." Darla took a bite of a leg and revelled in the warm chocolate taste.

"You're the one who picked up a hitch-hiking ghost."

She was interrupted by the most annoying ringtone in the world. It was the same one Darla had set for Dillon, and surprisingly enough, just like Darla, Miranda was ignoring it.

"Anyhow, like I said, if you say you saw Russel, I believe you."

"You shouldn't. I'm crazy."

"Well I'm pregnant, and people call pregnant women crazy all the time, so we're a perfect match. But I hear, crazy people have all the fun. They get to do what they want, and eat what they want." At that she sat forward and burped. "Okay, maybe I was wrong about the eating part."

"What's wrong?" Darla grew worried.

"I don't think this kid likes those pandas." She added, bringing her hand to cover her mouth, and burped again. "Wow."

When her phone rang again and Miranda just stared at the thing, Darla found the courage to finally ask what the hell was going on. Clearly, something was wrong in paradise. "You going to answer that?"

"Why, so he can tell me again why he's not flying out tomorrow? Maybe it's because his mom is sick now, or no, it's his co-worker's going away party that he just got told about. Quite frankly, his car could be on fire with him in it, and I wouldn't care."

Darla laughed so hard she snorted. "But you love that car."

"I do, but I'm not so sure I can say the same about the driver anymore." Miranda simply shrugged again, and wrapped her hands around her swollen belly. "Unlike you, he lies very well. Took me a while to catch on, and now..." She rubbed at her belly again. "... there are strings attached."

"And you will be a wonderful mother."

"Do you want to watch the game? It'll take your mind off things." Miranda choked out.

"What?" Darla let out.

"That's what he said. When I told him your mother had called, and that you had been in an accident, I wanted to get on a plane and fly out that very minute. He, wanted to watch the game and take my mind off things. Those things, every last one of them revolved around getting to you and making sure you were okay, and he wanted to watch the fucking game..."

That was a hard hit to take, but then, Darla had already come to the conclusion that she was third wheel in their relationship; she'd just never considered that Miranda would leave as well. Because that's what she was doing, right? Contemplating the inevitable? God, Darla hoped so.

"... for you, not him. I mean, sure, he was fun. All men are fun, for a while, but you seemed so attached to this one, and then I got... well, I got pregnant... he is... Dammit... messed up." Miranda was lost in a whirlwind of a rant.

"Wait, wait, wait. Slow down."

"Oh, God, Darla. Dillon is not the baby's father." Miranda's hands came up to cover her mouth. "And he knows. I found out the night after you left. I was going to tell you too, but you wouldn't answer the phone, and I freaked out."

"Who, is the father?"

"You remember that party we went to, Dillon disappeared with those girls and we had a little fun of our own?"

Darla gasped, for that night had been wild, and the first of many that left her questioning Dillon's true feelings. "We did. But you did your own disappearing act that night if I recall."

"I did. I had a free pass, as did you. Not my fault that you didn't use it with anyone other than me." Miranda let out with a smirk. "Anyhow, before you ask, he was wearing a mask, so NO, I don't know who he was. Nor will I be attempting to find him."

"And Dillon?"

"He's mad, of course, but what can he do? I showed him the results of the paternity test. He's not the father."

"Like I said before, you will be an amazing mother, Miranda, but I..."

"Not without you I won't. Don't you see, without you there, I don't have anything to go back to. Me and this little bundle, we're good to go, wherever... you go."

"Wh.. wher...ever I go?" Darla stuttered, she hadn't pictured herself going far.

"Yeah, just don't go off driving any more ghosts around, or getting into any accidents, and we should be fine." She teased, but that was how

Miranda was, always making light of a grim, or in this case, mind-boggling situation. "This can be our baby."

"Even though I'm crazy?" Darla just had to check.

"Even though we're both crazy." Miranda kissed her forehead. "Now, eat and get some sleep. Doc said you may be able to move to a big-girl bed tomorrow. No more chaperones." She grinned as she sat back and pulled out two take-away bowls of Pho.

"You, are an angel." Darla's mouth watered, and she was glad her appetite had finally returned.

"Nah, but I bet Russel was." And didn't that leave Darla in a state of awe.

Not a ghost, but an angel.

Sure, if he hadn't gotten in her truck, she never would have had a reason to go down that road, she'd never have crashed into that ditch, but perhaps, if not that ditch, another?

And he wouldn't have been there to pull her out of the wreck.

And without the accident, Miranda wouldn't be here, and they wouldn't be discussing their future over Pho noodle and panda buns, or chatting with the night-nurse before crawling into bed.

Russel had not only saved her life, but he'd secured her future as well.

"I think you're right." Darla let out a short while later as she lay next to Miranda. "Russel was definitely an angel."

The End

In the Middle of the Night

Donna Clancy

When all is quiet
In the middle of the night
The voices begin
Not another human being in sight.
Black wisps appear
Taking menacing forms
Floating closer and closer
Old hags with horns.
You're coming with us
I hear in my head
My heart beats faster
I'm filled with dread.
The closet door opens
It is the Devil himself
The glow of red fire
Reveals Hell itself.
A boney hand
Reaches out for me
I'm not ready to go
But I must pay my fee.
I've been rich beyond dreams
I have lived a good life
And now I will leave

None will ever find me, not even my wife.
I will pay with my soul
Come take me away
But leave my family safe,
With my last words I'll pray.
I hesitate at the door
Drop my wedding ring to the floor
My last act alive
Me and my soul will exist no more.

Undead Things

Chrissy Moon

Hi Mom,

As I told you over the phone, I'm sending you this flash drive so that you (or one of your colleagues) can physically take it to Dr. Sorey onsite. Even better would be if someone can print it out and put the papers in her hand, because I imagine she's knee-deep in artefacts right now.

Thanks again for recommending my translation services to her. This project was, well, really one in a million. It was absolutely fascinating, and the last part was a special kind of challenge.

This was an amazing experience. It really helped that Dr. Sorey and her people took hundreds of photos of the restored pages. Especially those last ones!

Talk to you soon.

Love you lots,
Isa

Document found in an antique metal coffin with two skeletons. Coffin was stuffed vertically in a big well.
   The following is translated from Old French (Burgundian).

It is strange, writing a letter to no one. Yet I do that now.

Do not be fooled; I did not think of this on my own. My tutor gave me the idea without realizing it. He does not write facts; he writes his own feelings, as if keeping records. Well, *his* feelings are all religious because he is a priest.

But I do not want to write about my religious thoughts. I want to write about what I think, and about things that are happening to me. I cannot tell anyone, and I am about to burst.

These events began with a wedding.

My father, aunt, and I traveled to the home of someone in town for their wedding, to help them celebrate. I did not know that John would be there. He is the man whom my mother had wanted me to marry. There are two things that I remember about her: that she had beautiful green eyes and that she wanted me to marry John, because we were close in age and he came from what my Aunt Agnes called 'a good family.'

I miss my mother, but I do not want to marry John. I want to marry someone I love. I want magic and laughter and nightly kisses to die for. So when I saw John at the wedding, I did not talk to him much. But I was not rude! I simply did not 'engage him' the whole night, which was what Aunt Agnes wanted me to do. For example, I would smile briefly at him and then go on to do other things.

Now, I did not believe it was rude, but my father and Aunt Agnes felt differently. As soon as our feet stepped out of our carriage and onto our estate, my aunt's yelling filled the air. "Katerina! I do not know what is wrong with you, but you treated John horribly. That is NOT what I told you to do. You did not act as a lady should!" She stomped her feet to make her point; my father sighed heavily and began walking past us, probably to go to his bedchamber.

"We must apologize to John's mother next week. She is, after all, going to be family," my father said over his shoulder. He shook his head at me, as if I were a worry for him.

"I am *not* going to marry John!" I cried, stomping my feet as well. "You will NOT force me!"

Aunt Agnes gave me a *look* and hurried past me to catch up to my father. "Reginald," she began, and then they spoke among themselves in low tones. When they saw me watching them, they walked away, still talking.

I then ran to my own bedchamber and closed the door. And then I remembered Father Richard and his written record of religious experiences. Well, maybe I was not having a religious experience, but I *did* need God to help me deal with my stubborn family, because I will never marry John, no matter what!

So I found some fancy paper that Father Richard had given me after I told him that I wanted to practice writing words. The truth is I already know how to write words, but I wanted more paper so I could write this long letter to myself. I think when I tire from writing for the day, I will put it underneath a loose piece of wood in the floor in my room. You see, the piece is loose and so it is a good hiding place. I keep a lot of things in that spot – a piece of coal, a black and brown spotted egg – whatever catches my eye. It is a place of secrets, and I adore secrets.

They make life worth living. Do you agree?

Oh, damn. I hear someone coming. Goodbye for now.

It is the next morning. Oh, I know! Maybe instead of writing to no one, I will write a letter to myself. Hello, Myself!

Yesterday, I was correct when I wrote that someone was coming. That someone was Alanna. She is my new nurse. She is here more often because Father Richard is travelling far somewhere, and my father and aunt need someone to 'watch' me. I like Alanna because she is nice, but often I tell her I do not need anything and she can go back to the room she uses when she is here. I do not know if I can trust her with my secrets just yet.

This morning everyone is busy, and where they went I do not know. I do not care. They do not want me to go see the *trouvere* passing through this night. More than anything I want to hear his poetry. I am determined to go. I am old enough to be a bride, so they cannot tell me what to do. They cannot stop me!

I will tell you what happened tonight. My hands are still shaky, so I hope you can read my writing.

I snuck out of my room so I could find where the *trouvere* performs. I was just very tricky and put pillows underneath my blanket to look like my body, and when it sounded quiet in the hallway, I left.

I knew I was in the courtyard of my home when I smelled the grass spread over the leavings from the animals. It was familiar, so even though the sky was dark, I knew where I was, and I had the moonlight to guide my way.

But going outside of the walls is harder than I expected. I really thought in order to get to the nearby town, I should head southwest through the small forest behind my home. I did that, unafraid as the moon was shining very brightly for me. But in the forest, the ground had a hole that I did not see – I tripped and fell, and somehow this hole turned into a slope and I, screaming, shot down a more vertical hole thereafter, falling and then landing awkwardly on a big pile of hay that was spread out over a smooth, stone floor somewhere.

Perhaps if someone else fell into this strange place, they would get excited with the adventure of it all. But that is not what I felt. Something felt very wrong down here in this space so close to my home.

I looked up, discouraged. Unless I suddenly became a bird, it would be impossible for me to leave the way I came. I would have to find a different way.

The ground felt very cold beneath my cloth slippers. The place was clean, as if someone had been sweeping the floor periodically, and there were even lit sconces on the wall. This scared me – falling so far down in the woods, landing in an empty place that was well-lit.

Nothing good could happen here.

I began to feel more and more as if I should not be there. Hurriedly, I took a sconce from the wall and walked down the only possible direction, my heart pounding, my lips moving in whispered prayer.

The end of the journey took me to a peculiar-looking space. It was built like a big circle with a hole in its center.

I took a timid step towards the hole. It looked like a well in the ground, but it didn't have a rope, bucket, or anything else someone could use to draw water with.

Why would someone have a well that you cannot draw water from?

And how could I not know after all this time, there had been a well hidden near my house?

I took another unsure step towards the well so I could see what lay inside. Surely there was something in there – water, at least. I wanted to see what was inside. I had to see.

I would like to explain something to you, to myself when I read my own letter, or if there is someone else out there who likes to read a letter not addressed to you. This secret room near my home was very still. There were no windows or trees down here, no wind blowing, no animals resting in the corners.

This is why, when something did move, I was very startled.

A white flash of something shone in my eyes, and when I looked at it, I realized it was a woman. I gasped when I saw her. I did not breathe, and my heart beat very fast.

As I watched, the woman – who did not even seem to notice me – walked past me to the well, looking down. And then she turned around like she saw someone behind her, her mouth moving for a few minutes as if talking, only I did not hear a word. And then, she looked in a different direction, her mouth opening again but this time much broader than before, as if screaming. She dropped quickly to the floor as if struck on the head, and then she disappeared.

I collapsed on the floor, shaking and crying. I did not know how to process what I just saw. You see, I knew who that ghost was. I had seen paintings of her all my life.

That ghost was my mother.

Hello, Myself.

It is one whole day later. Wait until I tell you my adventure! I still don't understand it all.

I could not wait until nighttime; I wanted to go as early as I could, so I could investigate everything. But I could not do it right away. First, our cook made me eat – I never really liked breakfast, so she brought me some pieces of fruit on my favorite plate. It is a tin plate that is curved and is shaped like the moon when it's a thin, curved strip in the sky. I knew she would not leave until I finished my food, so I nibbled on it absentmindedly while playing with the pink ruffle on my curtains.

And then, as soon as I was alone, I left to find the well again. Oh, do not worry; I did not have to walk into the forest again. Last night after seeing the ghost, I found a door not far from the well. I opened it, and found a stairway leading upwards, and when I got to the top, I was in one of the courtyards of my house! I was coming from a door that did not look like a door from the outside, but rather looked like part of the wall and decorations.

I was happy when I found this closer path to that mysterious place. You see, I am not scared of the ghost now, even though it did frighten me at first. But how can I be scared of my own mother? I missed her. I wanted to see her again.

I must tell you something interesting now. There was something else I saw briefly, because at the time I was scared and just wanted to go home so I did not look at it very closely.

I saw something in the well. Something which didn't belong there.

It was silver, or metal that was the color of silver. I don't know, but it was like no coffin I had ever seen before. First of all, it was shaped weird. In the middle of it was a cross.

Why, oh why, is there a coffin inside a well?

I know, it sounds like I am some crazy type of talking bird who does not know what she is saying, but I swear it is true. And there is one more thing I have to tell you.

When I got back to my bedchamber and went to sleep, I had more adventures. I had a dream that was not a dream. I know it. I feel it.

I know what is inside that coffin. My mother is not in there – I know where her body is buried – it is a man in the well. I know because he came to me in my dreams and we spoke. He is alive, but not exactly living. A handsome man but one who looks strange, as if he had been drowned or killed. One would think, seeing the way he was shoved down the well, that he was some horrible sort of person who deserved this endless prison.

And it is true, I am haunted by him – by his eyes, in the best way possible. He is a beautiful person, especially in his heart which feels pure, though perhaps it has been broken many times. He says he is a combination of many creatures because his family condemned him to Hell. Yes, he actually says the word Hell, and now I say it too. I am not afraid.

He said his given name was Béraud, but his family called him Damion before they tricked him into the silver coffin and threw him down the secret well many years ago.

I asked Damion about my mother's ghost. He says he sees her often.

"Does she see you?" I asked him.

He shook his head. "No, never. She is stuck in a world of her own. She sees no one except for those who killed her. Wake up now, Katerina.

Your mother wanders the well-room now. Come follow her to learn what you can."

I did as he requested and woke up. Now I knew the proper way to get to the Well-room, all I had to do was sneak over to the outer courtyard and take the hidden stairway down to the well, where I would surely see my mother again.

Also, I wanted to find a way to open the coffin so Damion could live again in the real world with me.

When I got there, it was as he had said: my mother was there. I watched as she looked in the well, just like last time.

Then she looked behind her and spoke words I could now hear. She again talked to someone I could not see or hear, but because she said his name, I knew who she was talking to this time.

She looked frightened – frightened and in tears. *"I just had to see it for myself. Your family is playing God, Reginald." She sobbed as she spoke. "I want to take you away from this horror. You speak of strange creatures you and your father conjure. These creatures come from Hell! Reginald, your family USES them to keep control over people and money! And using these creatures to attack others? Please say you love me more than you love power. Please, let's run away and forget about all this."*

She screamed two words before she seemed to get hit on her head and fall to the ground, and I went back upstairs to my bedchamber, my mind racing, my heart reluctant to accept it, my soul wondering how I was going to survive this insanity.

She had screamed, *"No, Agnes!"*

Hello, Myself. I made a mistake.

I told Aunt Agnes what I saw, and asked her about the man in the coffin. But I did not say I talked to him in my dreams, because I know it sounds stupid.

At first, she would not even face me. She kept her back to me as she fixed her own supper, saying, "Nay, it is not a man in the well but a monster, and he is very dangerous! You will not believe me when I say he drinks people's blood until they die!"

"We killed him," my father joined in from the other side of the kitchen. "Our family is special. We are gods in our own right. We control who dies and who does not die. This man in the coffin you speak of was truly evil – so evil he did not even die when a blood-sucker killed him. Nor did he die when an undead person bit his throat. Only an evil man can defy death like this."

I listened to them both, scared and doubtful. My father thinks *he* is a god? If only Father Richard overheard him, he would have some strong words to say.

I doubted my family, and I struggled to figure out who I should believe. It is hard going against the people you have known all your life, but sometimes you have to stop and ask yourself what you *really* think, what *really* makes sense.

And these were the facts: Aunt Agnes could be very mean to me. Some days when I had no nurse or tutor around, she would starve me and bolt my door closed. Some days, she would beat me. Beyond this, there was a bigger history of horrible things she did to me, and I do not wish to list them now. The point is, inside my heart, I knew who was lying, and I knew who was telling the truth.

Hello, Myself.

Things are getting bad. Things are getting very, very bad.

But first, Damion.

Damion came to me in my dreams again, and oh, how much fun we had. We did not dance by the stars because he is not very graceful, but instead we talked and talked. Never before has talking to anybody been so easy. I did not have to try or search for something new to say to impress him. We just spoke to each other as if we had been talking together our whole lives. We told jokes and sang songs and discovered we liked some of the same things.

While we were talking, I told him, "I wish there was something I could give you, something you can take back to your coffin to keep you company."

He shook his head. "That would not work. I cannot take items from dreams, only thoughts. What would you give me, Katerina, if you could?"

"Jewelry!" I exclaimed. "A ring, perhaps, to remind you of me, something to cheer you up until I figure out how to release you from your coffin."

"Now, Katerina, it is much too dangerous. Please do not do anything like that. Also, I already have something even more precious than jewelry."

"What is that?" I wondered.

"I have you. You are better than any gold or silver. You are my gold, and thus you have already given me more than anyone ever has."

I laughed with delight and threw my arms around his neck. Even if it was only in a dream, the feel of his neck was a wonderful experience.

He made me happy – so happy I woke up giggling, opening my eyes to find Aunt Agnes standing there with an ugly knowing frown on her face.

"I heard you!" she accused. "You said his name. You said *Damion.* You said many things you could not possibly have known unless he really was talking with you in your sleep."

"I do not know what you mean," I replied.

She smirked at me now. "I know him better than you do, you idiot, and I happen to know he is a Dreamwalker. Do not take me for a fool, Katerina! He is my uncle, and what you are doing with him is disgusting."

"He married into this family, which killed him," I said quietly. I did not know how to defy her just yet, but I wanted to. I really wanted to. "We do nothing but talk, even if it is only in my dreams. And he is your uncle, but he looks young."

"That is the curse, one of his many curses, one of many ways in which he should be dead! You understand nothing, and you are playing with fire. Do you know what it means? He is dangerous."

"YOU are dangerous," I retorted immediately.

She slapped my mouth so hard tears squeezed out of my eyes. I cried out and stumbled back; I should be used to this treatment by now.

She screamed and screamed and screamed. "You do not know what we have done for this family! Do you think keeping this money and this home is as easy as taking a walk and smelling flowers? No! Sacrifices must be made. Control must be taken when others do not give it. That is the way of the world, Katerina, and you must learn this now or else suffer the same fate as this Beloved Damion of yours."

She closed my bedchamber door so hard that it hurt my ears. And then, to my horror, I heard a key in the lock.

She had locked me in for the night.

I supposed I could have simply gone back to sleep so I could converse with Damion again, but I was so upset – she had slapped my face and threatened my life. Sadly, this was not the first time she had done either one.

I was still crying when the door was unlocked and someone came in. I braced myself, thinking Aunt Agnes was back for more, but to my surprise, it was Alanna.

She was very concerned for me – she had been in her room down the hall and had heard screaming. She had also heard when my aunt struck me. She asked what happened, and I made the decision then to trust her. I told her everything, looking deep into her kind eyes as I did so.

After I was done, she whispered to me, telling me some of her own secrets. She had heard my family talking just now, which was easy because my aunt was still shouting due to her being so angry with me. This was the conversation:

Agnes: We have to do something to keep her away from there. She is sure to open the coffin and let him loose. If that happens, it is over for all of us! Damion will punish us – he might find the King and tell him *everything*!
Reginald: Argh! You told me you had her *handled*!
Agnes: I *did*, but there were some things I did not think would happen.
Reginald: Pathetic excuse, my dear sister. Now, I am going into town tonight. *Handle this*, or I will handle *you*.
Agnes: She will be dead before sunrise, Reginald.

I could not be quiet any longer – I sobbed loud and hard. My father was never the most loving man, but I did not think even he would condemn me as if I meant nothing to him. As I cried and wiped my eyes, I thought about how quickly my life changed for the worse. The only thing that was good about it was Damion.

My family did these horrible things so that we could have money forever? I felt sick to my stomach. This is not how life should be.

They had killed my mother to protect the family secret.

Alanna helped me dry my tears and said she would go into town to get some help. It made me nervous, and I began crying harder. Her eyes got big with even more concern and she said, "Ah then, what? What, my dear? Everything will be okay. I will go quickly and return with help."

I told her I did not feel good about it. I had a bad feeling. I begged, in a voice so desperate it did not even sound like my own, that I should go with her. She finally agreed, and I was so relieved I cried yet more. But first she had to make sure my family was not wandering around the estate, because she did not want to be seen sneaking out. She told me to get my things, and she will be back, but I have a dreadful feeling now, because I have had time to write all this, and still she has not returned.

Oh my God! My hands are shaking. I'm terrified. I just came back from seeing... from seeing...

My stomach hurts and I am vomiting everywhere.
They killed her. They killed Alanna, my lovely nurse who only tried to help me. They took her face… and…

Oh, I feel sick. They put her face over a vegetable and put a candle inside. They put it on the floor next to the well. Is this a warning for me? Will they also do this to me?

I don't know why, but I feel like I MUST write this down. I also do not feel I will be alive much longer, because Aunt Agnes has no reason to spare me. Perhaps if I write as long as I can, using any liquid I have to make a mark on this paper, keeping these papers inside my clothes, then this evil family – a family I denounce and am no longer a part of – will be found out. That is my final hope.

The man in the well who harms no one but sits in my presence in my dreams – he was far gentler than these people who claimed to be my family. This man in the well, the man everyone referred to as a monster, the man who was part blood-sucker and part dead was the most loving out of anyone.

I ran back to my bedchamber quickly, and I have been here for some time. I think Aunt Agnes is trying to make me as afraid as possible before she kills me too, but I am only getting stronger. I will not permit this. Even though I might die, my willpower will survive. It is my mind, my spirit will remember.

My family and especially my aunt have never truly loved me. I was always told what to do for the sake of our *'image.'* I was never seen as a person by *that* family – I was only a part of a machine, part of mechanical clock and nothing else. During my life, I would keep getting angry at these people because of how they treated me, and then I would switch back to accepting their cruelty.

My love for them has been killed and revived so many times, but now there is nothing left. There is no resurrection here. They are not my family. Family does *not* make you feel ashamed for existing.

They are the monsters.

My hands are shaking so much. I am going to try to release Damion from his coffin. I am going to kill *his family* if they try and stop me.

(Translator's note: This next part was hard to read – the words were very thick and possibly written in blood. Dr. Sorey, thank you for taking hundreds of photos in multiple angles and lighting.)

She got me. Hit on head. Bleeding. Cannot see. I have many pages. Put in coffin with him. He is alive, chained, cannot move. But he talks and I write his words. I write until I die.

The pain of watching you being betrayed by your family, the same family I married into – it destroys me, in ways no dark creature ever could.

I always knew there was a reason why I kept myself alive when I should have died. And now, My Gold, I have met the reason, and her name is Katerina. And now that you die, I also will die. I will follow you to any place – Heaven, Hell, or Earth. I will always find you, I will always protect you, and I will never leave your side.

I love you. We are forever.

The End

The Belfry

Mary R Woldering

Yesterday, upon the stair,
I met a girl who wasn't there
She wasn't there again today
I wish, I wish she'd go away...

It all came back as I read the article on my screen. I'm sure you've been there, too. You're having your lazy Saturday morning coffee but the bagel in your hand ends up cream cheese side down in your lap because you just saw a reminder from your past. It was something that had happened in my childhood of many moves as a "Navy brat". This memory, I thought, had faded over time only to resurface when my daughter was born thirteen years ago. I named her Susan and planned to call her Sue after a friend from a very tumultuous seventh grade. My Mom gave me a noise about it because it was something she thought I had put behind me. I had thought so too.

My Sue is now twelve going on thirty and married to her phone with the latest Tok. She's a good student and great big sister to her younger brother and sister Todd and Tammy who weren't named for any previous friends. She's a junior high cheerleader, an acrobat and will be a great young woman in a very few years. She's the world to me and my own Mom. We're both widows now; and we share a house but we've become more like sisters.

"Mom," I called out to the woman making the pancakes for the rambunctious crew's morning feast. "Remember this place? There's an article here about some renovations on the old Holy Sepulcher in DC. Looks like they're finally putting that steeple on it."

Her answer was a half-disinterested "I remember," followed by "And I remember how much you hated that school, too. Good thing your Dad wasn't stationed there too long." Then she said: "Pancakes everyone!"

All through breakfast, I managed to keep my family from noticing my concern, but the memories, terror, and shame along with the feeling that I had lost my mind came back. As soon as I ate my food and packed the dishwasher I knew the screen would be waiting for me before I settled to my work as a realtor. The kids were off to their tablets and Sue was texting a friend. Mom got on to her crafting in preparation for our local Christmas in the Sun craft fair.

The article stated that the church was one of the older ones in the DC area but for its entire 150-year existence it seemed unfinished. A steeple and bell tower were never successfully perched on top of the gothic entry with its tall tower magnificent rose window. Long ago a spire had been planned, but every time the builders tried to erect one, bad things happened: Workers fell, lightning struck, bells came loose and fell. The project had been abandoned almost a hundred years ago as hopeless.

This morning, as I made calls and set up appointments for walk-throughs or current listings, I saw the random article. It triggered something darker than awe at the stunning architecture and interior of a beautiful American Gothic church. I stared at the picture of the way the tower had looked when I went to church and school there and at the architects' plan for the new tower. Then I thought about Sue from seventh grade in Holy Sepulcher Elementary School thirty-five years ago and the tower without a spire that everyone in school said was haunted.

We had just moved to DC. It was an odd time of year but as a navy brat, I had grown used to dropping in and out of classrooms and being expected to hit the ground running. Most of the kids were polite enough, but not too chummy having already picked out long-standing cliques for the year. That was fine with me. My favorite thing was reading, not playing yard games or listening to gossip about kids I didn't know. My second day in the new seventh grade class, I noticed a girl with light blonde hair sitting in the desk next to me. It had been empty yesterday. She wore a navy-blue sweater/jacket with what looked like a monogrammed badge on the front. It wasn't very fashionable and made her plain shirtwaist dress look cheap. The badge said: "All Saints Children's Home."

'*All Saints Children's Home? An orphanage?* Is she an orphan?' I thought. We were in the back of the classroom, so I felt comfortable in making a whispered contact low enough so that Sister Catherine in the front wouldn't hear me.

"My name's Marsha Smart. What's yours?"

"Sue. Sue Lorrenz. You're new here?"

"Uh Huh. My Dad's in the Navy. Lawrence?" I asked and she shook her head then peeled open the lapel on the sweater blazer to show me S-U-S-A-N L-O-R-R-E-N-Z. and I repeated. "Lorrenz. Your name is on your sweater?"

"Have to. All Saints Rules." She answered, still whispering "I'm not there anymore. Shh. Sister's coming." And she became silent because the stern look at me or any of us could freeze us in our tracks for fear of being yanked up out of our chair and exposed to the other students as disrespectful.

At recess we talked a lot about nothing, just the two of us stayed off to one side by the swing set. I don't remember too much except sometimes the other kids gave us strange looks. She told me she wasn't a real orphan. Her Dad had died, but her mother was poor and so she went to live at the home during the week. There were some mean girls living there so her mother took her home again but she wore the sweater anyway.

I talked about the Navy and the way we had to move a lot.

"Is she watching us?" Sue asked because more than once she saw Sister Catherine staring in my direction when she made her rounds on the playground. She always had a puzzled look on her face.

"Maybe." I remembered saying.

Not long after that, Sister Catherine asked me to try the Children's choir because they needed more good voices for the Christmas Concert. Sue looked excited too, so we agreed to do it together. We laughed and had fun at recess playing tag and then we'd sing. "Gloria in Excelsis Deo" really loud at practice until Sister scolded that we were supposed to get our voices to blend with the other children's voices *not* make it a screaming match. I just didn't think any of them could sing as well as Sue and me.

That's about all I remembered until *'it'* happened.

We were getting ready for the concert in just a few days. Sister Catherine had gone downstairs to check the sound while Sister Frances played the big pipe organ. Sue and I sang gently then and we "blended". Unbeknownst to them, Jeanne who was in our grade was talking about the fact the belfry was haunted. We weren't supposed to talk about ghosts in a church or anywhere in school because the only ghosts were devils. The story was about a storage room, but my classmates agreed it was something terrible.

"Oh cool – wonder what's in there." I murmured, instantly garnering some positive attention for bravery. Sister leveled *that* stare and clapped her hands, calling our classmates to collect the books and folders. The bigger boys were assigned to help her and Sister Frances carry things down the winding steps to the vestibule. Sue and I fell in line at the end as everyone marched behind them.

There were three doors in the anteroom outside the choir loft. One door went to the loft. A second sealed off the anteroom. The third door, almost always shrouded in darkness led up into the forbidden storage which would have led to the unfinished belfry. That day I noticed the doorway to the Belfry, was ajar.

Grabbing Sue's dark sweater, I whispered:

"Hey that door is open. Want to see what's up there?"

She shook her head "no". I didn't understand. Sue had always been happy-go-lucky on the playground. I had thought she would love the naughtiness of sneaking off for a moment or two to have a look at what was in the creepy old room.

"Aw. Come on, Sue." I urged "We won't be long."

"OK" she shrugged but really didn't seem happy about it. "They could be waiting for us though."

Without a further thought, I grabbed her arm and we crept into the slightly open door that led to the upper room of mystery.

It stank of dust like anyone's nasty attic. Spiderwebs streaked across our faces and made us spit as we pushed on up the steps; determined. It guessed birds had come in and died up there from the loose feathers we stirred. There were low ceilinged rafters, empty picture frames, bent candelabra, incense thingies and statues in stages of broken or chipped with eyes that --- I squeaked in fright, then laughed at myself, adding "Oh cool."

Something *was* moving around behind them – two or three somethings. I noticed the beady eyes and the whiskers. *Rats. Big ones.*

Sue was backing up too.

"We'd better get out of here!" I almost shouted, turning around and heading back down the rickety stair. "It's just broken junk up there anyway."

When we both blasted through the door, however, I saw that the door to the loft was closed. I had just missed Sister Catherine who had locked it and had probably gone to put the box of books in the lower storage closet.

"Sister –" I called out, not caring that if Sister Catherine came back I would be punished in class and my parents informed which meant more punishment later. There were no sounds other than Sue who had started to cry. That upset me. She hadn't wanted to go up there and I had insisted. Now she was scared and probably wouldn't want to be my friend anymore. "I'll just go bang on the closet door." I suggested, "I know we're going to be in trouble, but I don't like Sister. She gives me these creepy looks anyway."

Sue was looking really scared now. She stood over to one side with her head down while I went to the storage closet door and tugged on it, then beat on it. "Sister –" I called "It's Marsha and Sue! We're still up here.

I stumbled inside the lightly closed storage room and fell against the bookcase. Sister wasn't in there. Leaping out, I closed that door behind me and listened to the satisfying click. Maybe not too late! I had thought. "C'mon, Sue! We can catch her."

In the distance I thought I heard the nun mumbling: "Goodness Mercy! Who opened the door to the old attic. Glad I fixed that."

I heard the door that opened to the vestibule being pulled solidly shut and keys locking it as she muttered aloud. "I bet it's that Smart girl. If that's who did this, I think I'll be calling some parents."

"Hey!" I shouted. "Sister Catherine! Don't leave! We're still in here! Help!" I shouted but silence answered except for Sue crying a little louder and coming to beat on the door with me.

Just to check, I ran back up and tugged at the choir loft door. *Locked*. I went to the door that had led up to the storage room below the roof and thought I heard something scurry and make a schlumping noise before I beat on the door. It sounded larger than a rat but no less scary. Now I was worried.

"Did you hear that, Marsha?" I heard Sue's faint voice call. "It's them. They're going to get me. Help!" and her voice rose in a crescendo. "Get me out of here."

I didn't know what to do, because, for some crazy reason I wasn't that scared. It was near Christmas. I knew someone would be cleaning or doing some decorating in the church. I was sure someone would hear us.

Sue sat on the step at the door to the vestibule, unconsolable. What she was saying did give me pause.

"They?" I asked "Who? There's nothing here but a rat and maybe a seagull stuck up in there. Besides, if we can't open that door maybe they can't either."

The way she was crying upset me. I knew Mom would be waiting for me to come home from school. I usually tagged along with Sue and a gaggle of other kids that lived near enough to walk home, but I was always alone by the time I arrived. I really sure where Sue lived, but she never asked me to come over. I knew my baby brothers were keeping Mom busy so I shouldn't bring her to my house either. Now we were stuck. If we *weren't* lucky it might be late at night or even in the morning before someone came back to the church and heard us. I knew we just needed to keep trying.

Thump! Thump! Thump!

Sue was sitting on the bottom step kicking at the heavy door hard enough to make pale marks in the darkened oak finish.

"Help Us! Help!" She shouted over and over again.

I stared at the little moon shaped marks from taps on her heels. Taps. Cleats. I remembered wondering about taps then. My Mom had told me that kids sometimes had those on their shoes when she was little to keep the heels from scuffing down. On Sue's skinny legs, they were doing an awesomely damaging number on that door.

"Sue!" I cautioned "Stop! Your marking that door up. It's old and real expensive! The Church'll make your Mom pay for it."

She didn't stop; her feet making an almost drumlike rhythm on the door, marking and chipping while she sobbed.

Something in me just switched off. As I thought back I remembered something seemed so unreal about that afternoon. Sue was there screaming and crying, but I wasn't. In a strange way it seemed almost perversely funny. I just wanted her to stop kicking the door. The church was a historical gothic style and everything about it was just magnificent. It seemed so wrong that little tapped shoes were busily scarring the lower panel of the door beyond repair.

"Sue, you've got to stop with the door!"

"I don't care. I don't want them to get me!" more kicking.

"There's nothing up there but an old empty dirty attic. And I'm here. They'd have to go through me." I realized something had changed. She looked disheveled and teary as she kicked a few more time, then as if there had been a miracle, she stopped.

"Will you protect me from them? You're bigger than I am."

"Who?" I asked. "There's no one here but you and me, Sue." I pouted, glad she was calming down just a little bit but worried she would start another round after she caught her breath – kind of like my baby brothers. True. I was taller and she looked frail. I guess moving a lot counted for making me stronger on the inside.

"They chase me – all the time." She mumbled softly

"Who? Bad men?" I wondered, because on the way home from school we had always been safe and she had always been in that desk when I arrived.

Sue shook her head.

"Girls. From the Home." She cried softly "They put paste in my hair and cut my new dress."

"Girls? Well they aren't in the attic, that's for sure."

She didn't say anything back, as if she knew her worry was over nothing, but then added. "No one does anything about it. They just let them do it."

The ambient light in the stairwell grew dim. I knew it was getting dark outside. I leaned back against the wall and prayed silently that someone would find us before much longer. Sue made a few more sniveling sobs and kicked the door a few more times. I was hungry and getting drowsy and hoped my prayers would be answered. I think Sue scooted over to me and lay her head on my shoulder before we both slept.

I shook my head in hopes of ridding it of a bad memory. Staring across the room at my daughter, I wondered about the effect that goofy event had on the rest of my life. Chose an Architectural Art degree. Failed to find that sort of employment. Became a realtor. Got married. Had three kids. Ben was cut down by gunfire in a robbery. Wrong place, wrong time. Did it start there? Stupid me, getting nosy and getting locked in the stairwell. If it had only been that simple. It wasn't.

"Merciful heavens!" a woman's voice called. I woke to the sound of jingling keys on a ring. The door was flung open and I was looking at one infuriated Sister Catherine and a man I assumed was a janitor. Worse than that, my Dad, still in uniform, was standing behind them with an expression on his face I never wanted to see again.

"Miss Marsha Smart!" the nun called out. "What on Earth are you doing in here? Do you know people have been looking for you for hours? Your family was worried sick!"

'She actually seems worried'. I thought I had seen a different crease in her frown. None of that mattered. Despite his obvious anger and my knowledge that I was likely going to be banned from television or anything else other than the basics of the Holiday and maybe even not allowed to open my presents until after the New Year I leapt into his arms, excitedly.

"Dad!"

"Glad you're safe, Marsh." But then he turned to the nun and apologized with an "I'll take care of this from here, Sister." then tugged me quickly toward the big double door in the front of the church. I knew we weren't going for sodas. I was in big trouble, but at that moment, none of that mattered. I didn't see my friend. I looked quickly around the vestibule as my Dad towed me to the stone steps.

"But where's Sue? I asked, feeling a strange surge of panic that had nothing to do with the punishment my parents or anyone from the school had in mind for me.

"Sue?" Sister Catherine repeated, an odd look crossing her face.

I tried to pull away from my Dad's grasp to look up the now opened stairwell but he wasn't going to let go of me easily.

"Sue Lorrenz from school, Sister, my friend." I answered, feeling really puzzled. "She was with me and got stuck in the stairs with me. She was crying a lot, even though I told her someone would find us." I began to feel really small from the looks Sister, my Dad, and the janitor were giving me. "We were just trying to see what was up in that storage room just under the place where they were supposed to build that bell tower a long time ago. It wasn't locked."

"Young lady. You know it's a sin to tell a lie." Sister warned. "I saw that door was open and locked it myself before I left. No one was up there." She turned to the janitor.

"Weather sometimes pops it open." The janitor darted up the steps to jiggle the door then called down. "Locked up tight now, and that's a mercy. There's bats up in there and maybe rats. Don't need them coming out during Mass."

"But Sue?" I complained because it was just not believable that she had somehow slipped out past everyone and that no one noticed.

"Child." Sister Catherine stared me in the eyes. I think she had hoped I was shorter then so she could look down at me. Both hands were on my shoulders. "You were by yourself when we opened the door. There wasn't another little girl." She looked at my Dad who then seemed much more worried.

"Mom?"

I heard my daughter calling. "Are you okay? You've been staring at the computer ever since you sat down after breakfast."

I startled. The article about the bell tower was still displayed.

"I'm fine, I'm fine, Suze. I was just remembering something." I nodded. I didn't think I had ever told her the story of how Sue and I had gotten trapped in the stairwell after my daring exploration of the closed off upper room – which ended in a bad place. Sue hadn't been real. It started that night with Sister Catherine looking odd and flustered, claiming there was no Sue with me and, in fact, she had really never seen me playing with anyone in my short time at Holy Sepulchre School. She'd evidently talked to my parents about how I had been seen playing by myself and talking to non-existent persons. She had been worried.

There never was a Sue. It was a sin to tell a lie.

At school the next day right before Christmas break, I sat at my desk wondering if Sue would come to school so I could point her out to the dumb nun. She didn't. The desk next to me was empty, but before I could ask Sister Catherine about it a girl with neat red side braids took Sue's seat.

Before I could say anything to the new girl, Sister Catherine announced:

"Class. As you can see, Henrietta Gresham is back today. Her doctor says she has to rest at recess for a little while longer but because of everybody's prayers and good wishes she is getting better and stronger every day. Welcome back, Henrietta!"

The class clapped. I clapped twice to avoid looking rude. My jaw dropped. It seemed wrong – like a violation. I sat staring as the class said a happy and quick prayer of Thanksgiving. I didn't want to pray. I wanted to know what had happened to Sue.

"Was that the church where it happened?" my daughter asked in a whisper.

"What happened?" I decided to play dumb.

"That girl – In the old Belfry. The one you named me for. Sue and Laurice on account of it sounding like Lorrenz – sort of."

I looked into her face and rubbed my own more than tired eyes, not sure what to say after that opening. My parents had been mortified that

I had made up such a tale about a girl that wasn't there. I even repeated that dumb poem kids say to get the thoughts out of my head about Sue, but swapping the gender so it would fit.

Yesterday, upon the stair,
I met a girl who wasn't there
She wasn't there again today
I wish, I wish she'd go away...

I had promised myself that I would do my best to strike it from my thoughts, yet here was my friend's namesake taking a seat beside me at my desk.

"She was this girl I made up when I was a little bit younger than you, Babe." I started. You know how I told you Gramps was in the Navy?"

She nodded obediently, putting down her phone as a signal that what I had to say was going to be much more interesting.

"Well there were a few years in a batch where it seemed like he was getting shipped and transferred every two seconds. I know it wasn't really that often, but I was always the new kid at school, and girls were kind of mean to me because that was the way kids were in those days. You were either one of the gang or running from the gang."

My Sue shrugged.

"Kinda still is." She said. "I don't let people push me around. But then I've never been the new kid. We've lived in Oahu forever."

Oahu. Yep. We didn't stay in DC long after that. Dad was lucky and got transferred to Hawaii for his last years of active duty and there we settled. It was good weather, cleaner air and much for a young girl to do. After a while I didn't think about Sue, but what my daughter had said about mean girls bullying new girls wakened another memory.

'Will you protect me from them? They chase me – those girls - all the time.'

Some protection I had been. I never saw Sue again either. Pretty soon it was easy for my parents and whatever counselors and therapists they took me to – to convince me she had just been part of my pre-teen imagination, because I had been a lonely new kid with no friends at school.

"Well I stayed by myself and after the Sue thing. When they heard what happened and about Sue, no one would play with me and the nun who was my teacher just acted super upset and creepy, yelling and standing over me over the slightest thing, making me stand in the hall with all my books "because liars don't belong in her class". – even getting Grams to take me to a doctor."

I didn't tell my daughter how I wanted to hate her for the way she treated me but couldn't.

"I didn't let it alone, Sue." I continued the story to my daughter "I wanted to figure out if there *had* been a real Sue they somehow didn't want me to know about. A week into the new year I asked Sister Catherine about All Saints Children's Home. I was polite, but she snapped at me about listening to gossip and told me it was shut down and torn down and that now unfortunate children were placed in foster care."

"So what happened then?" Sue asked, staring at the page I had been reading and remarking "Place looks creepy. I would have been scared to death, If I had been locked in there."

Scared to death. I remembered more. She had been scared. I had thought she was a little crazy she was acting so scared, kicking the door with those tap shoes.

I felt my daughter leaning in over my shoulder just as I was about to get up and walk around before settling to make some calls to potential clients and times they might be available for showings. Then:

"Oh wow. Hey Mom, look here."

"Sue –" I complained. "I have to get to work now; make some calls.

"No." she protested, sticking her phone in front of me. "That article about the church you were reading was old. I looked it up on my phone while you were telling me what happened." She looked me in the eye with that going on thirty glance that let me know something was up. "It was from over a year ago. Look here. This is newer. And it's a News Story."

I refocused my eyes and saw the picture of a woman – a reporter – broadcasting something. The headline was a banner from a DC television station. It read: "Does a historic church tower hide the scene of a crime? Skeletal remains to be removed today."

All the blood left my face.

"What?" was all I could manage.

Sue clicked the little speaker icon and amped up the sound for me.

'—In an odd turn of events the renovation and construction on the seemingly cursed spire and tower at the Church of the Holy Sepulcher has been stopped once again. Saturday, while the upper storage room was being cleared, a void was discovered. At the bottom of what looked as if it had been a small elevator were human bones. The medical examiner and local authorities are in the process of attempting to identify –'

"Sue!" I shrieked and couldn't close my mouth after the scream.

"Mom?" Sue's face was equally pale now. "You don't think –"

My own mother, quilting hoop still in hand, rushed in to see what the commotion was and skidded to a stop by my desk where I had busily brought up the current article on my large screen.

"She was real!" I snapped, remembering the scolding, the pleading the visits to a psychiatrist when I couldn't be dissuaded.

"Marsha. You certainly don't think –" she started after a quick scan of the headlines and then self-corrected. "They could belong to some other unfortunate person – Maybe a homeless person or something."

I felt the tears wanting to start as the pain and the gaslighting from teacher, and parents replayed. I didn't notice that the video of the story was still going until my daughter nudged me.

"Oh cool." She said "Watch. They're taking the bones out now."

As I watched I saw the skull, with wizened and mummified skin patched over the exposed white bone. I noticed the blond hair, but the clincher was the tattered navy-blue sweater that looked like a bad blazer.

"They'll find her name on the collar." I rubbed a tear out of the corner of my eye. It'll say Susan Lorrenz and it'll be from the All Saint's Children's Home." my voice lowered into a mumble. "You know – that orphanage I tried to find out about.

The long bones were pulled up and the shoes with metal taps located. I remembered the way she had kicked at the big door, but found me calming enough that she stopped being afraid and fell asleep in my arms.

'There never was a Sue. It was a sin to tell a lie.' That's what Sister Catherine said.

"No." It was my own Mom's turn to show shock. "The nun said you made that up because you didn't have any friends." She paused in deeper thought.

"Mom's psychic. I bet you saw her ghost. Oooo..." My Sue teased and appeared to start a text to friends but I glared at her.

I didn't think it was funny.

"Not out of this house – no messages until we know the whole story." I spoke in the "I'm serious" through my teeth tone.

The reporter ended the segment stating that more would be posted as the details were discovered. For now, the steeple would not be put up – once again – at least until the mystery was unraveled.

That Saturday was scrapped. I struggled through the current listings and setting up appointments, dressed and went out, but Sue was texting me about the fact that now there was some investigation on the news and that missing children's files were being searched. I didn't want to know any more.

I wanted to be mad at Mom and even my Dad who had been gone almost as long as my own husband. I wanted to be mad at them for not believing me and for insisting Sue was made up. Was she? I knew I never saw her again. After all those years imagining her seemed the likely answer.

Or -- maybe my own Sue was right and she was a ghost but the next question was why did I see her? Was she trying to tell me something – like how she died or maybe even if someone killed her and stuffed her in an old dumbwaiter shaft,– There were just too many questions and unless something of her essence showed up after all these years and told me about it, I'd never have an answer.

I dreamt about Sue that night. At least, I thought it was a dream, until I knew it wasn't. Once again, we were in the stairwell and she was crying.

'They always chase me, those girls.'

"I'll protect you from them, Sue." I whispered and the fact that I was talking in my sleep woke me. *I looked at my watch and it said 3:33 Angel number. New Age nonsense. Unity, Moving forward. I need to sleep.*

I didn't protect her, though. If she was, after all, real, she was a ghost. She was already dead when I saw her in school and on the playground. I remembered that no one else could see her. No one believed I was seeing something real either. She was already dead and in the shaft but for some reason she picked me and needed to tell me something.

When I came home last night at three
The girl was waiting there for me

At first, I thought it was moonlight reflecting off a place on my bedroom wall but then I saw the form of a girl in a vague outline. Sue. She wasn't solid like a real person. She was translucent and looked lost as if she wasn't sure I was her old friend. It didn't make sense because I had memories of her being real – of being able to grab her by the arm, push her, and ultimately the way her head felt on my arm when we fell asleep.

"Sue." I called out quietly enough that my voice didn't carry beyond my room to my Mom's, Sue's or the boys room. "It's me Marsha."

The image moved slightly as if she heard me.

"Remember? From the belfry stairs?"

Marsha. You got out? Grown up? She seemed to be saying. *I was asleep. The bad girls.*

I remembered studying about spirits with friends when I was in high school and memories of Sue were a little fresher. That was when I decided she was a ghost. I had avidly watched "Ghost Whisperer" as a young adult and new mother. The mantra was: If you see a spirit or one appears, remain calm and ask it why it is there and what it wants. See if you can help it *'cross over.'*

"Sue, those girls weren't in our class. They weren't in the belfry. No one was chasing us" I wracked my half-asleep brain trying to remember names of any of the girls in that class until I remembered other things that made Sue look like a long dead past tense. Taps on shoes when kids didn't wear those now. Sneakers or soft leather dress shoes were allowed even at private schools because teachers didn't like the tap-taps down the hall. The blazer said All Saints Children's Home which had been torn down by the time I went to school. It meant she must have been dead for quite some time, but thought she was asleep.

They were there, Marsha. She insisted and added: They were just grown up like you are now.

I felt a creepy feeling starting up my spine.

"Names. What were their names?"

Katie Marie and Flora from All Saints. They were mean. I saw them smoking and stealing things. I was going to tell.

"Oh my God." I tried to hide that revelation. *Sister Catherine and Sister Florence.* Had to be the connection. My heart was pounding double time then. *They killed you?*

They chased me into the street at night. No one saw. Sister Evangeline, the Mother Superior's car.

I noticed the image of Sue was starting to wink out. *Don't forget me, Marsha.*

It was just like that silly poem the kids at that school sang at me.

I sat bolt upright in a quiet and empty room, then reached for my phone to look up All Saints Children's Home and found a reference to a charity house in DC by that name that was run by some nuns. There was a black and white newspaper photo shown in the article of Sister Evangeline and a group of girls all wearing the navy-blue blazer over plain pastel looking dresses. No Sue in that group, though.

Sister Evangeline she said. The woman ran over her and must have killed her right away. It was an accident. Maybe what happened afterward was the real crime. She blamed the girls and for chasing her into the street and made them help her hide the body - or did she?

And then they both became nuns? Was that religious zeal or guilt? And the dumbwaiter shaft where they directed choir and went up and down stairs a zillion times?

I thought about Edgar Allan Poe's *'Telltale Heart'* and knew if I had been either one of those girls, being a nun to atone for bullying Sue into a street in the middle of the night wouldn't be enough penance to allow me to ever set foot in that choir loft again. They didn't know Sue was there.

It was razed in 1947 and the old school I attended was built there. That too was gone now in favor of a modern building with all the bells and technological STEM whistles. The Mother Superior was obviously dead now and Sister Catherine and Sister Florence would be in their nineties if they were even alive. I just didn't know how I could help Sue without causing a lot of trouble halfway around the world – not to mention upending the balance of sanity in my own family.

Just find the truth. Katie Marie will tell you. Hurry to hear her. She needs to tell someone.

And then there was nothing – not even the hint of a shade.

So what was I to do? I hadn't been Catholic in years. It wasn't anything in particular. We just drifted. I missed choir and singing Gloria In Excelsis Deo loud through the nave and the feeling that I would be heard by angel choirs the most. I also missed the architectural wonders of the older churches created by decadent rich men in my opinion who were, as the song said "Buying the Stairway to Heaven." It led me to get a degree in Architectural Art. I laughed once again at the way I had been more upset with Sue kicking dents in that solid one hundred fifty-year old oak door with her taps instead of our plight.

In a week there was another article stating that all attempts at locating the *'Sue Lorrenz of the belfry'* relatives had come up empty. Her remains were with the coroner's office. A collection to provide her a nice grave in a local cemetery had fizzled. *'In time, if there was no action they would be cremated with a group of other nameless dead and buried.'*
Katie Marie will tell you. she had said.
And then I knew what I had to do.

I wasn't sure if the old nun knew who we were that afternoon. It must have a shock to see three generations of women descending on her room in the Sisters of The Precious Blood Retirement home. She had been seated facing a sunny window and praying her rosary – maybe the same old black one she'd always had. She still wore her bonnet – the black short veil and the starched white face brim. We always used to wonder if nuns had hair under there.

"Sister Catherine." I started nervously, waiting for her to respond.

She nodded, seeming sad. "Do you remember me? I'm the girl who –"

But she cut me off as if I was still a student who had spoken out of turn.

"Marsha Smart" she affirmed, staring at her knobby hands and whispering over her beads.

"Yes, Sister. Marsha Smart Watkins. This is my Mom Debbie and daughter Sue Laurice Watkins. We came to visit you."

Her steely grey eyes looked at my daughter. A sick little titter that blossomed into a weak hack erupted from her throat.

"Sue Laurice." Then – "And Mrs. Smart"

I'd heard that elder nuns had a lower percentage of dementia the more languages they spoke but the next comment was particularly jarring.

"I appreciate the visit ladies, but I know the real reason you are here."

"Well, I didn't –" I started to sputter but again found myself corrected.

"A sin to tell a lie, dear." She started but added. "I won't be here much longer. I need to stop telling lies too and Father Nolan wouldn't begin to understand." Her fist went to her lips and she coughed again. "Sit, you three. I won't be stood over."

There was a window seat which Mom and Sue took. I sat in the guest chair beside her wheelchair. She began:

"I was wild long ago. Flora was too. We were peas in a pod. We would steal things – cigarettes mostly and odd trinkets. Our families could not control us. So we were sent to the nuns to straighten us out. They could beat us in those days or make us scrub floors until our knuckles were bleeding – or shave our heads – or not feed us sometimes. This other Sue was a little "goody" little angel. She never did anything wrong and never got punished. So we messed with her."

I sat, shocked but in rapt attention at the story. She took a sip of water and continued.

"One night we got her out of bed and chased her outside but then a car came and hit her. Poor thing went straight to Heaven I think." Sister crossed herself and went on "Worse though, it was Mother Superior driving the car but she wasn't wearing her habit – just regular women's clothes and she smelled like whiskey."

Holy double life. My eyes bugged as I listened.

"She blamed us for the poor child running into the street after hours and brought down the Divine wrath on us if we ever spoke of it to anyone. Then she picked up the poor girl and wrapped her in her dark habit cloak and told us to go to our rooms. We thought she buried her somewhere."

"Sister –" I interjected, not sure what I was feeling. My Mom's face reflected horror and my Sue, bless her wanna-be Goth heart had an "Oh cool" expression. "She had a mother, I thought." then I corrected myself because I had been talking about what a ghost had told me.

"Her father was killed in the war. Her mother, poor thing, turned to drink in despair. It's how she was at the home. Sister Evangeline told everyone the girl had run away. There were a few weeks of phony attempts to find her. We were told to say that too. I think her spirit hung over the three of us. Mother Superior for making us lie and us for obeying. I knew you could see her spirit, girl – well Marsha. I saw it sometimes at first and so did Flora. I just didn't want it to be real. I wanted it to be over."

Go away, go away, don't you come back no more!
Go away, go away, and please don't slam the door... (slam!)

"Sister Evangeline told us the only way we would be ever forgiven and to make that demon go away was to devote our lives to the Lord and to teach other children. So we did. We were in the novitiate when we heard Sister Evangeline went into the cloister and the school closed. I think every so often a student with a bright, clear mind could see her, but we always talked them out of it. When they found the child's bones two months ago poor Flora died of a stroke. We never knew she had been put in the shaft. We never smelled anything more than maybe a dead animal in the attic and it was always locked. If we had known—"

Sister bowed her head then looked up at me. "Sue came to me too and I said I was sorry, but she wants to be put to rest and I'm too old now."

"Man, that sucks." My Sue said. "All those lies and messed up lives. And you were just kids to be made to do that. That's abuse."

The elder nun nodded, sad but seemingly relieved.

We sat with her the rest of the afternoon and then said our goodbyes. She gave us blessings that somehow seemed more sincere that the kind religious folks give you.

We claimed the bones – said we were friends of her family. My Sue wanted to take them to Oahu but the idea of shipping them in a small crate and then finding a spot in a local cemetery was too much. We opted to have her placed in the diocese cemetery and paid for the headstone which read:

"Susan Lorrenz of the Holy Sepulchre Belfry
At rest but not forgotten"

We took plenty of photos but when we went to the home to show them, we found Sister Catherine, once the "mean girl" Katie Marie had died the night before in her sleep.

But when I looked around the hall
I couldn't see her there at all!
Go away, go away, don't you come back no more!
Go away, go away, and please don't slam the door... (slam!)

Omens from the Shore

Kevin Chapman

A Strandvarsler Tale

"Natalie! Nat! Nat!" Duncan was yelling, interrupting me again.

"Nat! Lee! I lost my sandal. Give me the shovel."

I knew there had to be something here under the sand, couldn't risk taking my eyes off the screen. I yanked the shovel out from where I had stuck it in the sand.

"Christ, Nat!" My shoulder felt a twist as he jerked the shovel from my hand. "You almost whacked me in the face with that thing."

I didn't bother looking back at him, instead continuing to follow the grid pattern I'd laid out in my head. Two steps to the left. 'Nothing! Dammit.'

"Are you listening to me?"

"No." Even if he couldn't see me do it, I rolled my eyes at him. "I. Am. Busy."

I also didn't need to see him to know that the 'huff' sound I heard was him pouting.

"I'm going to kill Mel for telling you about that damn bracelet." Duncan whined followed by something banging on wood.

Surprised at how close he was, sitting on a driftwood log when I spun around, "She didn't just tell me about it. You saw everyone fawning over it. Saying how smart she was."

Duncan opened his mouth to say, "-I cut him off, "She literally held it over my fucking head and gloated."

The detector beeped. My eyes cut to it immediately. It was my boot. The sensor was on my foot. I could scream.

"Honey." Cocking his head sideways. "We've been at this for three hours. Three hours and we haven't seen one other person. There's nothing here."

"You don't think I know that?" I said, scanning the sand and moving further into my grid.

I got a quick beep. The screen showed something small was close to the surface. My heart skipped a beat, only to be broken when I uncovered an old pop tab, two nails and smashed Bic lighter.

"UGGGGH!" I stamped my feet, threw the detector down, kicking it away. "I just want to find something with my brain. Not sit down and have it poke me in the cooch like she does with everything else in life."

Kicking at the bits of lighter, I missed, the wet sand giving way under me. Stumbling until I fell backwards over the log Duncan sat on. 'Of course.' Here I lie. My boyfriend staring down at me in the muck, a failure.

"Come on Babe, get up," he said. "We're going home."

He kicked his leg over the log to kneel down next to me and before I knew it his strong arms pulled me up to sit.

I shot him a glance. "Thanks." I said with a weird guilty feeling. Why I felt guilty when I hadn't done anything, I don't know.

Duncan's expression was fixed with a flat smile. "It's no big deal." He said.

It is a BIG deal to me." I said, clenching my jaw so hard I felt it click.

"FUCK! FUCK! FUCK!" I kicked the log with each word.

It had an effect. The smell of lake air was pushed out by the smell of death carried by flies as the log to rolled away. Crab scrambling back from the stench as the wind blew a sickeningly sweet smell right at me. Bile to rise in my throat. "Oh gross."

Duncan yelled, "Oh God!", turned heaving. He managed to choke out, "What is that?" before falling to his knees.

I didn't answer, my stomach was squeezing in on itself. Words weren't possible.

As the breeze began to take most of the heavy stench away, I was able to stop yakking.

Duncan hacked up a thick line of spit, "Oh God, it's a body."

I'd never seen someone go pale before. Duncan's ruddy cheeks were white. He clapped both hands to his face

"I think-" Duncan said as he threw up again, this time into his hands. "I think it's a woman."

Relief flooded through me. "Oh, Thank God. I thought it was a dog."

"What the fuck?"

"What are you staring at me for?" I asked. I couldn't place how Duncan was looking at me, his mouth open with something I couldn't place.

"Thank God?" He spit, scaring a fly that was about to land on his lips. "Natalie, this is a person." He looked down, "Someone has to be wondering where she is."

I couldn't see the body from where I sat. Only a cloud of yellowjackets and other buzzing things.

Once on my knees, I duckwalked over to where I could see into the little depression where she was.

'She?' All I saw was ripped clothes, mangled greenish flesh, and wet blond hair. What wasn't crawling with some sort of bug, was eaten away. The bottom of the shirt was ripped open to reveal that not only were the guts gone, but that I could see into the hollow space of the rib cage.

The smell of moldy cheese made my mouth water in disgust. "How do you know that's a woman?" I had to spit. So close to puking again.

Duncan broke it down in steps, "Face is too bloated to tell either way." Cocking his head, "and the clothes are pretty generic. But look at the shoulder."

Pointing at a rip in the shirt, "I think that's a bra strap." Moving down, he added, "I can see a hint of blue fringe on the underwear inside the pants."

My eyes rolled, "I really do not want to know how you know to look for this stuff." I got a little closer. "Anything else?"

"There is a name on her safety vest," He nodded to the left side that was partially buried. "But I'm not getting close enough to read it."

Pinned above the name was a crushed plastic rod. "Wonder what happened to them." I said as a light popped on in my head.

Excitement began to simmer as I leaned in over the body. "Hey, you know what this means right?"

Rubbing his right eye with a finger, Duncan took a step back "I'm afraid to ask. What?"

I grinned up at him. "I win. I, I mean WE, we found a body. I win."

That look was back on Duncan's face, he took a deep breath before saying "Jesus, your parents fucked you guys up. Really? That's all you can think about. Winning against your sister?"

"Dude, we'll be on TV for this." I did my best to pretend to stand straight and look into a news camera. "Yes, we found that poor woman's body over there." I sniffled. "It's so sad."

The stink eye I was getting from Duncan smelled worse than the body.

"Dunc. Come on man. You know what I go through." I poked the body in the chest. "Ugh." My hand felt unclean and made me shiver. Wiping my finger off in the sand gave me tingles up my arm.

"You'll help me right, Baby." I said slowly looking up at him.

"Unreal...just." Duncan said. His voice trailing off as he shook his head.

'He'll see.' I thought as looked over the thing laying there. 'I just need to prove it to-'

"OH FUCKING HELL YES!" Pumping my arms up in triumph. It was everything I could do to not grab it right there. "YES! YES! YES!"

"What?" Duncan was immediately back down in the sand with me. "What is it?" Grabbing my shoulder, "What's going on?"

My heart swelled. I could kiss him.

"Look!" I said staring at what used to be a hipbone. Next to it half buried in the sand, poking out was the tip of a wrench.

'Mine. Mine, mine, mine.' I ached to have it.

"NO!" He reached out to stop me before I even moved my hand. "You cannot steal from a body."

His hands cupped mine in my lap. "Come one, let's go to the car, we'll call the cops." He tried to cajole me with, "I'll even get you custard on the way home."

Duncan knew me, knew how to calm me down. After looking me in the eyes, he also knew what I was going to do anyway.

I don't remember touching the wrench. I remember the voice in my soul.

'What did you do?'

"Okay what was that?" I asked looking around confused.

"Natalie Storstrand."

"Huh?"

"Nat. natalie. natty baby. can you hear me?" Duncan's voice sounded washed out.

A strange woman's voice cut clear through to my soul. *'You will not listen for him now Defiler of the Shore. You are MINE.'* The words took up a place in me, I didn't know existed. "I was CONTENT."

"Who are," My voice cracked, "you?"

'You steal from my body. You shatter my peace with your selfish greed and to top it off you don't even bother to learn my name.'

I tried to turn to Duncan to see if he heard it too, but I couldn't. My body didn't respond.

"LOOK AT ME." The voice demanded.

Duncan was waving his hand in front of my face. My body moved by itself so I could stare at the corpse.

Visions flowed into my mind.

Lush coastlines from all over the world with the smell of salt air.

I felt awe at the sight of Gibraltar.

The calm of watching the open ocean late at night.

The irony of my dead body floating past a lone willow tree before a storm caused my lifeless body to drift ashore.

'Wait. My body?'

The strange voice was back. *'I've sailed around the whole world. The water was my home.'*

The rotting face turned to face me. "I wanted to be here forever."

"What the hell?" I screamed and jumped up.

The jawbone moved up and down in the sand. An arm pulled itself up and pointed at me with a maggot covered finger. *'You took everything from me.'*

"Well take it the hell back." I said tossing the wrench down

I looked to Duncan. His mouth was moving with no sound. There were police lights in the distance.

'It's too late to go to him.'

My heart was beating overtime. I needed to run but my feet wouldn't move. Against my will, I slowly sank back down to my knees.

The voice returned to drive through me, *'The storm buried me in the sand. All that was left was rest.'*

A heavy burden clawed its way onto my back. My throat closed as a frozen hand closed around it and a knot of emptiness began to squeeze my chest.

'Do you feel that?' She asked. *"That's the hunger when you are torn from your ever after."*

I began to beg. "Please. I'm sorry."

'All I know is that YOU cut this place from me, and I can never return. Who's more sorry than me?'

My own body was consumed as a veil of her seething rage fell over me. Clenching my jaw tight. My hands trembled as they slid through the sand and under this rotting thing.

Cradled close like a sleeping child, again I wanted to heave as bugs began to crawl on me. A black clump fell from the rib cage and dangled by an even blacker vein.

The emptiness she forced on me grew as what I could see shrank. I could only focus on directly in front of me. My skin began to itch.

'Do you feel it?' The voice asked. *'There is another safe harbor for me.'*

An unseen damnation forced me forward. I had no choice but to go. One step. Then another.

Directly in front of me I saw a crowd. People holding up their phones. Cops holding up their guns.

The cops were saying something.

"Keep walking."

A bright flash. I felt the impact of a bullet on the wrench. My wrist bent backwards but I didn't let go.

My wrist felt broken. I screamed.

Another flash. Air ruffled as a bullet went over my head.

A ghostly arm reached out to span the thirty feet between us and raked across the officer's face. Three more shots hit the sand in front of me as he collapsed.

Compelled to move, pain lanced through me. Each step was a stomp as I fought for my life. It was hard to see where I was going through the tears. Onward I marched.

"I need to stop." I pleaded, with all my will I resisted. It meant nothing.

'Move! A holy ground is ahead.' The voice became clearer, more hateful, *'Refuse, stop, do not take me there and I will weigh down on you. I will remind you of all wrongs you have done in the book of Life. All the regrets you have left in your heart. Your will die in sorrow, and you will never know peace. We will wander forever.'*

The weight on my heart became heavier. Her call to rest became my burden with demand to be brought to a new place.

"To the right." I heard and up the hill we went.

Each step forward a problem.

Cars on the highway slammed on their brakes narrowly missing us.

The pull of rest taking us directly to buildings.

The spirit pushed down on me when I had to go around locked doors.

Bees and flies lingered about. Landing on my face where the bullet cut my cheek.

Catching glimpse of myself in the glass. Eyes sunken in. Hair stringy with sweat. Hand swollen and red. A horrid reflection of the body in my arms and the same on my back.

I would see it. Each time I would take a heavy breath and move on.

Squad cars would try to block the path, but as soon as I approached, they would drive off. The head would roll back and forth with each step.

Duncan kept pace with me the entire time. Several times he tried to catch my eye. This curse wouldn't let me respond to him. My arms were cramping wanting to drop the weight and not being able to.

"Where are we going?" I asked as we got to downtown. "How much longer?" Exhaustion stabbing into my ribs.

"The holy ground is ahead." Was the only answer.

On and on I went until...

I ran into a man.

A tall black man in a double-breasted suit wearing a huge bright yellow mask.

He wasted no time.

Looking me dead in the eyes, "You stole from the body, didn't you?"

I could hear him, see him. I opened my mouth to speak but was cut off by the ghost.

'*Leave-*' The spectral hand reached back to strike.

"Quiet!" He said in a deep voice as he looked above my head. "What's your name?" Calmly he stuck his hand in and pulled up the vest the body was wearing. Rubbing his thumb over the name, "Amy. Amy Tanck? That's your name?"

'*It was. Not anymore.*' She growled. I felt her surprise jolt through me at being known.

"It's still your name." The man said. "Always will be. I'm going to need you to slow down though." He said nodding his head at the Police behind him. "They're upset about you killing that one at the beach."

'*The Holy ground. I need my-*'the ghost, Amy, was cut off again.

The Man grabbed hold of my shoulders.

The pain stopped. Everything stopped. The burden was still there but less.

Amy stood there, looking like a real person, a normal person.

"What is...?" She glanced around with a confused look on her face. I probably had one too. The three of us stood there in a misty nothing.

"Where are we?" I asked.

"That's not important alright." The man introduced himself. "What is, is that I am Wyatt. Times like this though, people call me The Yellow." He pointed to the big mask he wore.

"My friends and I are people the city calls when stuff goes off the rails and they want it cleaned up." Jerking a thumb to the side. "You can't see my partners right now. But believe it or not, they are doing the lion's share of the work here." He held his hands out to mimic something big.

Looking at me, he tapped his ear, "Mostly keeping you from being shot in the head." I could see his eyebrows raise behind the mask as he shook his head. "That's their plan if this doesn't work out."

"So we're on the clock. Moving on, here's the short version." He pointed at Amy. "You died at sea." He pointed at my hand, "Natalie here, took the wrench off your body after you washed on shore."

"Not going super into the weeds with it, the basics are," He pointed at me again, "You interrupted fate."

"Sailors, have a connection with open water." Taking hold of Amy's shoulder, "People die all the time. You though, washed up on shore. Just a guess but, I'm betting you were destined to become a Woman in White."

Amy looked down and her work clothes.

"Don't get hung up on it. It's just the name for souls that warn people." Wyatt said and then continued, "More than likely you hadn't accepted it and settled in yet."

"Accepted it?" Amy asked.

"Not everyone takes well to being a haunting spirit."

A young woman's face flashed into the mist next to Wyatt. "We're ready. The roads are cleared."

"Okay, be there in a minute." Wyatt replied.

Amy had pulled her long blond hair over her shoulder and was running her fingers through it with a worried look on her face. "What now? Am I in trouble?"

Laughing, Wyatt answered, "Trouble? You're dead. What they gonna do? Take your birthday away?"

Amy chuckled at that. For the first time, she sounded nice.

"Here is what is going to happen." He explained. "You set out on a walking journey to your new rest." He shrugged, "That means, I can't drive you. Sucks but that's what we have."

Wyatt added, "The two of you have to work together on this."

We both shouted, "Together?"

Even with the mask I know he was giving us both a look. "Yes." Stepping between, he steered us both to a direction. Through the mist I could see a break in a police line.

"My best guess is where you are being pulled to is Erie Street Cemetery. It's the closest real Holy Ground in the area considering. It's ten blocks away. Go straight down here and take a right at Ninth street. Fifteen minutes more. Simple."

Wyatt pulled us closer. "This is also where it gets tricky. As you get closer, Amy, you might start feeling like you are dying again. Might. I don't know. The important thing is" He clapped me on the shoulder, "Don't panic."

Amy pulled away from him, "Don't panic?" Her voice cracked, her arms wrapped around herself, "I drowned. It was horrible."

Taking her hands in hers, Wyatt's deep voice softened. "I'm sure it was traumatic." He glanced off to the side, "But each person's afterlife journey is their own."

My team and I are going to do our best to back you up." He took a deep breath, "Both of you have to be brave and push yourselves. I will see you there."

My heart skipped a beat, "See us there." It was my turn to panic. I felt like fainting.

"What? Where are you going?"

Turning back to me, he smiled and replied with, "Have to pick up the Pastor. He doesn't drive."

Bringing us to stand next to each other. "Again remember, work together, be strong together and get to that cemetery. It's not going to be easy, but I believe in you."

"I have to go." With that, Wyatt stepped away and pain came rushing back.

Amy began shouting in my mind. *'It burns. The drawing it burns.'*

I bent over double as the crushing weight of Amy's despair washed back over me. My arms trembling with strain of holding her corpse. I fell on my ass. The body in my lap. My vision blurred out and narrowed back down to blinders I had before. Through that I saw the girl who stepped into the mist to talk to Wyatt. Behind her was my Duncan. My sweet Duncan. The man who two hours ago sat me up when I fell down. He was here now, waiting for me. I had my focus.

"Amy. Amy!" I shouted. "We have to move." I forced myself to my feet. My fingers clawing into the brickwork of the wall next to me without letting go of the body.

Through it all, I kept staring at Duncan, my red-headed goal. Before something else was dragging me along. Not anymore.

"Come on." I took several deep breaths. "We have to go."

In response, all I got was a wailing cry. A pitiful wail that reminded me of heartbreak.

I couldn't move. There was a crushing squeeze in my chest holding me back.

"Amy." I yelled. "Amy!"

Nothing. Only the sound of her sobbing.

Now it was my turn to be angry. "Bitch, do you want to go to sleep or not?"

'I can't. I can't. I can't.' Amy cried over and over. How does a ghost hyperventilate even?

I took a cue from Wyatt. "Slow down." I said to her and myself. As repulsive as it was, I hugged the body closer. "You can't what?"

Amy's voice was a jumble between barely audible and shouting, *'I can't go through that again.'* Her voice drifted off into a mumble before roaring back with another vision. *'I remember it all.'*

Without warning I was seeing through her eyes. Securing cargo on the deck of a ship in a violent storm. *'We were hauling ore. Those containers, they were sliding...we weren't equipped.'* Through a haze, something moved. Pain, then confusion before hitting the water. A mouthful of water for every breath. Lungs burning. Blackness. *'After the storm. I felt a calm. My uncle died at sea. On a trawler. Thought this would be the end.'* I felt a pause from her, like she was thinking, then irritation. *'Then you came along.'*

With everything in my heart, I tried to impress upon her, "I'm sorry. I really am. But how could I know this would happen?"

The woman who was talking to Wyatt was pointing at the police and down the road.

Duncan was across the road. He was holding the hoodie I kept in the car. I tried moving again. I was able to move one step.

"I saw what happened to you." I gambled.

'What? Are you going to say you know what I'm going through?' Amy sniped back.

"No."

I hope this works, I thought. *'Duncan. I love you.'*

"I know about loss," I told her. Deep breath. "You lost your life." Another breath. "I'm losing my family. I don't want to lose him too." Looking across the street.

'The rod?' She said. I knew who she meant though.

"Yes." I took one more step, my legs wanted to crumble. "He'll blame himself if we don't make it."

The way Amy replied, *'Good man.'* I felt she would have been nodding her head.

Wyatt's partner was back. This time with another guy. They were both shouting at me and motioning me forward. I could barely hear them.

I did my best to nod and take another step.

"We have to move." I huffed, out of breath. One more step. Then another.

Control of my body released greatly, *'I guess we do.'* Amy said with an emptiness.

Walking became easier. I took a few more steps, then a few more. Now it was like walking up a steep hill, not a field of fire.

I kept moving forward. "What's the matter?" I asked as we passed another police blockade.

'I am terrified.' Amy whispered. *'Where will I go?'*

"I don't know." Was the most honest answer I could give. "Where did you go last time?"

'I don't know either.' She said.

My turned side to side, as if she was looking around through my eyes. It felt like a nervous thing to do. The body in my arms seemed more sad than scary now.

'It was dark, I was drowning. The waves took every breath the fall didn't knock out of me.'

The was a cold spot forming in me.

Amy kept talking as I walked on. *'The last thing I saw was the lights of the ship through the storm leaving me behind. Then it went black. It was peace. Tranquil.'* I felt hot as a dust devil swirled about me. *'Then, you two showed up.'*

I looked straight into her rotting eyes. "I said, I'm sorry."

'I can still be pissed.'

"Fair." I answered. Clenching my jaw to remain calm. My wrist was starting to throb even more now. I wasn't sure what was heavier, the wrench I couldn't put down or her. We reached East Ninth street. Wyatt had said to turn right. I did so and immediately I was filled with mixed emotions. This had to be what he had meant.I felt the fear. Disgust. A thousand eyes watching from office buildings. One woman was pointing and laughing.

"Bastards."

A sense of cold, then hot, then the windows next to us all shattered with cracks.

"Hold! Hold! Don't shoot her!" Came a man's voice behind me.

The sound of running was muted, but I could actually feel the aura of someone closing in on me. Before I could even think to turn to face him, he was in front of me. Goddamn he was fast.

"If you can, keep calm. The police are nervous." said the new guy. "We have to keep moving."

'Wyatt said they can't hurt me.' Amy said as the weight on my soul returned.

"But they can hurt me though." looking up the hill at the police. I saw several shotguns pointed at me. "What happens if I die?"

'Just move then. Let's get this over with.' Amy ordered without much conviction to it.

I started moving again. The shotgun stayed pointed at me but let me through. In the distance there were more police lights. My lungs began to burn from the stress.

'I can see the waves.' Amy said in panic.

It got harder to move forward.

"It will be ok. We can do this. Come on."

As I passed a pizza parlor full of faces stuck to the glass window, I decided enough was enough. Amy's tragedy can't be how I die. Mel would just love it if I failed. Mom would agree with whatever the news said. Duncan....I fucked up. He got dragged into this because of me. I have to get out of here for him. I refuse to let him down.

"No. Not again. No."

Amy's fear became my mantra. *'No. I refuse to be lesser because of others. Not again damn it, I want to go home. No more.'*

I pushed, and I pushed, and I pushed until, suddenly I was there. The cemetery. A big stone arch and gates directly across from the stadium.

Wyatt walked up to me. "I knew you two could do it."

I shook my head. "She is freaking out up there."

This close to Wyatt I was able to shuffle the body. "I don't know what to do."

"I think I do." Wyatt said putting an arm around me. "Let me introduce you to some people." Guiding me to the gates, "This is Pastor Dan. He's going to help us today."

I think my mouth fell open at the sight of the short bald man in a basketball shorts and T-shirt for a tattoo parlor.

"Him?"

"Him." Wyatt smiled.

"Him." Shaking my head. "This day. I'm telling you."

"Not done yet. Follow me." Wyatt said escorting me through the gates.

"Like I have a choice."

Amy was still lost in her own kind of hell and the compulsion was still pushing to go somewhere, but didn't know where yet.

Wyatt stopped. "Dan come here please." Wrapping his arm around Dan, he added, "Okay, I have to introduce the two of you to Stephen."

The mists where I first met Wyatt swirled back around and most of the pain went away. Behind a tombstone stood another ghost. *'Hi! I'm Steve.'*

I had no clue what to say. My mind was blank. *What the ever loving Fu-'*

For being dressed in whatever I guess was the latest goofy style for a long time ago, Steve was on the ball though. Passing right through a tombstone, he rushed over to Amy who was talking to herself as she stood there in a daze.

Wyatt patted me on the shoulder and released the Pastor, who faded out of the mists. "While the Pastor gets everything ready and they talk, let's take care of this."

My arms fell to my sides in agony as Wyatt took Amy's body from me and sat it down gently against the cemetery walls. Looking all the world like the best Halloween decoration you'll ever see, until it slumped to the side and fell to the grass. The head popped off and rolled away.

The murky mist of the spirit realm blew away and the real world came back to life. The woman I saw earlier walked up, Wyatt nodded at me and said, "Take a look at her will you." Taking my hand in his, he pulled the wrench out of my grip. When contact with it was broken my hand finally unclenched, I hissed with new pain.

Pulling a large sling out of a cargo pocket of her pants, "Needs an Xray to be sure, go to the ER." She said softly as she slipped it on me and took a close look at my face. "The cut on your cheek isn't deep, probably won't scar. Clean it daily with soap and water. Drink a lot of fluids for the next few days and rest. I highly recommend a tetanus shot."

"Thanks Noh." Wyatt said to her. Turning to me, he added, "She's in medical school."

"Was. Was in medical school." She corrected with an annoyed tone.

"You'll get there. Follow your dreams." Wyatt said.

Noh rolled eyes, "just so you know, we all think he's a giant Dork."

"Love you too girl." Wyatt turned back to me, "Natalie, there's a lot to cover and not a lot of time to do it in."

"Still on the clock?" I asked.

"Still on the clock." He said with a smile. "First thing don't talk to the cops without a lawyer. Just don't." He handed me a card. "This guy is good and affordable. Not an endorsement though. Second, get therapy. This is going to be with you for a while. Third, grow up."

"What?" I took a step back.

Leaning in, Wyatt pointed my attention to Duncan who was standing off to the side. "He told me what led up to this." Motioning Duncan over, "Natalie, you need to grow up. You dug deep and did a lot of that today." Licking his lips, "You wouldn't have survived, if you didn't have it in you. But stop focusing on negatives. Learn to be the best person you can be and do that FOR yourself. Not anyone else. Believe it or not, there are a lot of spirits out there that exist only to wallow in sadness and regret. Don't do that."

I didn't know what to make of all that. "Uh."

Duncan gave me a huge hug from out of nowhere. "Thank you! Thank you! I promise-"

"No." Wyatt cut him off. He poked me in the shoulder, "You." His eyes flitted between us. "Duncan's a good guy, he means well because he loves you. But you need to do the work."

"Um. I'll do my best." I blushed. I meant it, but I didn't know what else to say.

"Honest answer. I like it." He said with a grim smile "The paramedics want to look you over and the police want to talk with you. I have to get the burial started. Remember what I said though." With that he shook Duncan's hand and walked away.

Duncan gave me another hug. While I was getting the wind crushed out of me, Pastor Dan walked up. "I hate to interrupt but she'd like to say goodbye to you."

"Who?" I looked at him for the longest time before it dawned on me. "Oh shit. Her! Amy!"

I followed him over to a spot under a tree where Amy was waiting with Stephen.

Her ghost looked different from him. Less formed, more like a hologram.

"What happens now?" Duncan blurted.

I elbowed him in the side. "Dude." I didn't know what to say, so after a pause I asked, "What happens now?"

With a voice that sounded of rumbling gravel, Stephen picked up the conversation slack. *'She's going to take over for me.'* He made a motion with his hands of passing something to her. *'Literally.'*

When Amy spoke, a cold shiver went down my spine. Her soft voice had changed from how she sounded in Wyatt's mists to the rustle of a gentle breeze on a calm night. Peaceful. Calm. Exactly what you hear before something grabs you from behind.

'Natalie, Duncan.'

'Oh God. I gonna throw up.' My skin wanted to crawl off me.

Amy smiled. *'I've been told I'm the overseer of this place.'* Behind her a big black stagecoach rolled up. A skeleton sat in the driver's seat.

"Oh. My. God." *'I might pee too.'*

"Every old graveyard has someone to gather the souls and guide them to the afterlife. Judge the trespassers." Stephen explained. *"My time is up. Amy is in charge now."*

'I guess Fate's not done with me yet.' Amy whispered. *'Wyatt said he'll stop by from time to time.'*

'Good Pip that one.' Stephen said to her. *'You'll like him.'*

'Will I ever see you again?' I asked Amy.

'Only when you stop by.' Amy's form wavering in and out. *'Take care of my wrench for me.'*

"Oh, no. NO! NO! NO!" Shaking my head, "I've had enough. You can keep that thing."

'Too late.' Stephen said.

A solid weight materialized at my side. Amy grinned and leaned in close, *'I've decided I want you to have it.'* With a small shrug of her shoulder, she added, *'To remember me by.'* The heaviness tugged at my capris. *'It's yours now. Someday, you'll go to your grave with it too. I've already picked out a spot for you.'*

Spectral Stories

Lily Luchesi

A Paige Papillon Short Story

Paige Papillon watched Vera King light the candles on her altar. So many of them. It was All Hallow's Eve, and Vera lit candles for those she loved who departed. Paige knew two of them belonged to Vera's parents, whom she said died when she was twenty.

When there were four candles left — yes, there were *that* many — Vera's husband Jon took her hand and they lit those together.

The dancing flames reflected in the Kings' eyes, turning their brown hues to Hellfire. Paige gave an involuntary shiver. If she didn't know they were human and that vampires were extinct, she'd guess they were both the Undead.

Paige's boyfriend, Zeke, tightened his arms around her waist and she leaned into him. Being a paranormal detective took a lot out of her, and while she worried she might be missing an important case, it was nice to have a night off.

Vera treated Halloween like Christmas and held a small dinner party; they were just waiting for the final guests: Paige's best friend Shayla and Shayla's mate Maura, and Vera's cousin from England and his husband, whom Paige never met but heard a great deal about.

"A drink," Vera announced, "that's what we need now while we wait for the others."

Jon went into the house and came out with three glasses of highballs and one soda for Paige, who didn't like the taste of alcohol.

Vera wore a long red dress, and Jon a three-piece gray tuxedo; Mina and Prince Vlad from *Bram Stoker's Dracula*. According to Vera, they always dressed up in matching costumes, and the first set they did was Sherlock and Watson.

Paige and Zeke opted for Frankenstein's monster and the Bride. Except Paige kept the iconic wig black and pink, her favorite colors.

"I feel like we should be telling scary stories," Zeke commented.

"Our lives *are* a scary story," Paige commented. "You're a werewolf. I hunt monsters. My best friend is a witch mated to a cat shifter, and these two..."

"Are perfectly normal," Vera cut in, making her husband make a sound between a laugh and a scoff.

While Paige didn't know their whole story, just that they used to work for the government taking down paranormal criminals, she knew the horror novelist and the police sergeant were anything but normal.

"I could tell a scary story, though," Vera said thoughtfully. "We did things that never got put into my novels."

Jon gave her a wary look. Paige didn't understand the full implications, but apparently if the couple got too far involved in the paranormal world again, something terrible would happen.

Vera ignored her husband's look as she asked, "Do you remember that Hellish apartment building off of Cumberland and Foster? When we were arguing?"

Jon's eyes lit up. "How did the witches even cleanse that place?" He gave a shudder.

Vera leaned forward, a gleam in her eyes. "Wanna hear?"

Paige nodded vigorously, making Zeke chuckle. "That would be a yes."

Vera took a sip of her drink and said, "Then let's begin."

Some unknown time ago
Cumberland Apartments
Chicago, IL

Vera stood outside the six-story, 120-unit apartment complex, checking the time on her phone. She was supposed to wait here for the Chicago Police liaison, who wasn't a police officer but would ensure the civilians stayed safe while she investigated the strange happenings.

Whoever they sent was two minutes late. And she couldn't get into the building alone. And it was warm out; she was grateful for the building's overhang that provided shade.

A familiar-looking, restored, white Cadillac Coupe DeVille pulled up and Vera wondered if she would get too hurt to work if she chose that moment to go play in traffic.

Why him?

Former detective Jonathan King got out of the car and locked it before he crossed the street.

When he reached the roundabout driveway in front of the apartment complex and saw Vera standing there, his whole body went still.

Crossing her arms, Vera arched an eyebrow in challenge.

"You were already two minutes late, can we not delay any longer?" she called.

He sighed and walked up to her, and she cursed herself for not wearing heels. Now he was three inches taller than her. But she had to look normal, well, as normal as a Goth girl could get. And that meant no stilettos or stomper boots.

"Okay, if you're here, those two disappearances aren't the work of a normal human, are they?" Jon asked, rubbing his hand over his reddish-brown beard.

"Sherlock got the first clue," Vera drawled. "And that's why you got hired privately. We can't have the CPD looking into ghost cases."

He looked up at the building. "Yeah. The ghosts are ... there's a lot of them."

"You can feel them, huh?"

He nodded. "And ... something else. Something *wrong.*"

"Wrong?"

"I'd say evil, but I'm not even sure it's evil. It's just *wrong*," Jon said. "I wish I had better vocabulary but I don't. Not for this."

Vera ignored the chill down her spine. She and the local Paranormal Investigative Division director Frederic Dominic both suspected there was something more than a spirit or two causing the weird disturbances in this complex. But no one had been more than mildly injured, so the PID couldn't get funding to investigate it. Until two people vanished, and one more turned up mysteriously dead.

Jon didn't know about the dead guy. Yet.

Jon giving confirmation about the sheer number of ghosts plus something else didn't make her feel at ease. She wished her hunch had been wrong, but she never was. Much to her director's chagrin. And anyone else who had to work with her.

"Here, put this on." She handed him a closed jewelry case.

He took it to reveal a silver and iron cross with something inside. A capsule.

"Holy water and the Lord's Prayer. Ghost possession is as real as demonic, but the difference is, unlike demons, ghosts can't remove that necklace," Vera explained.

Jon nodded and put the necklace on, pocketing the case. He headed to the front doors, gait slow and deliberate, as if he forced each footstep.

Holding the door for Vera, he said, "Ladies first."

"Why didn't you enter then?" she quipped, stalking past him, head held high.

"Excuse me for that. I should have said 'liars first'."

Vera's hackles rose as if she were a cat and, while anger was her primary response, so was despondency. She would never have needed to lie if he wasn't ... who he was. Choosing to be professional, she walked to the elevator and pressed level 1.

"Elevator is safe?" Jon asked.

"A ghost could lock us in the stairwell as easily as they could the elevator," Vera replied. "In fact, easier. Hence taking the elevator."

This building was in disrepair; the elevator was old, the lobby carpet threadbare and stained. The laundry room down the hall sounded like the dryers were going to take off at any minute. The scent of dust made her wrinkle her sensitive nose.

The elevator clanked its way down and they got on, going one floor up. The buttons were faded, and some paneling was loose.

"What's the plan here?" Jon asked.

Vera smiled, glad he knew who was in charge.

"We get a full brief from a traveling agent who lives here, and interview some residents. After sundown, we actively smoke out the spirits."

"Okay, I have a legitimate question: why do we wait for night? Aren't ghosts stronger then?"

Vera pondered how to respond. "Not quite. Three in the morning *is* when the veil is thinnest and ghosts and other entities are more active and stronger, but the main reason we do things at night is because it's less likely for innocent humans to witness it or be injured."

He nodded in understanding as they exited the elevator into a hallway just as dingy as the lobby, but Vera smelled something else. She couldn't put her finger on it — she was exhausted and hadn't had enough to eat that day — but it smelled like death.

They walked to apartment 101 and she knocked on the door, while Jon turned and waved to a cute little old lady with oval-shaped glasses and a cardigan around her shoulders.

And then she walked right into and through the wall.

"She was dead." Jon's voice was low and even, as if he didn't want to freak out.

"*Is* dead. It's a mostly permanent state, Jonathan," Vera commented. "I don't think she's here causing problems though. Probably just chilling out until she decides to cross over."

The door opened, revealing a tall man with long blond hair, clad in jeans and a Metallica t-shirt.

"Just in time; my ride to the airport is here in half an hour." He shook Vera's hand but his smile was friendlier than just business acquaintances. "And you are?"

Jon introduced himself and declined the handshake.

"I'm Han Svenson, I work cases sometimes with the PID in Europe, but I've been here lately, working with the band Lycancore," he introduced.

"Not familiar," Jon replied. "If it was released after 1990, chances are I don't listen."

Han smirked and Vera rolled her eyes. "Lycancore is incredible. You just have horrible taste." She gave Han a look. "Are you going to invite me in?"

"Oh, sorry. Of course, come in. Both of you. Let me brief you guys before I fly out to start the tour." Han moved aside as Vera and Jon walked into the well-maintained but small apartment. If it was four hundred square feet, Vera would eat her favorite pair of boots. The whole building was depressing.

Han led them to a sofa and he declined to sit; instead he leaned against a huge suitcase after handing Vera a manila file.

"I recorded everything that's happened here the past three months specifically, beyond your typical haunting stuff. It's odd, though, that so many ghosts stay here."

Vera looked up at him, but Jon beat her to the punch.

"You think something is keeping the ghosts here?"

She forced herself not to smile; she loved Jon's cleverness, always had.

Han nodded. "They're elderly. Nothing to hold them here. Most pass peacefully in their sleep. But here's what makes me really think something is keeping them here: one person died in a hospital. Yet their ghost is *here*."

"Something stronger than the average ghost then," she murmured. Jon was right. Something *wrong* was in this building.

"Finally, the dead guy's ghost — *it* is gone. As if something allowed it to leave," Han finished, and Vera winced.

"Dead guy?" Jon asked.

"I was going to tell you about that ... it's not just missing people," Vera admitted. "But we didn't find out until after you got selected for the missing persons cases."

Jon gave her a look that made her blood run colder than it already did. "Withholding information until you have no choice is a bad habit, you know. Doesn't make people necessarily want to trust you."

Han glanced between them and must have decided it was time to hightail it out of there before he wound up in the middle of a lovers' quarrel. "Well, then, I'll be off. Everything else you need is in that file there. Good luck."

The door shut behind him in a rush, leaving the two in tense silence.

"For your information, it was decided I'd tell you what happened after you arrived today. The Director's idea, not mine," Vera snapped, her eyes fiery.

Jon didn't answer; instead he went back to the file. "I think I know who we can interview first." He showed her a section of the file the PID pulled from the security tapes. A young girl, maybe twelve, saw something in the windows. The shocked look on her face was unmistakable: she saw a spirit.

"PID lip reading experts translated what she said."

Vera leaned closer, smelling Jon's cologne stronger now, and read it.

"Why is that man watching us? ... Him. That tall guy in the foyer. To our left! ... But Mom! He was just there! He was really creepy!"

Vera hated that kids could usually see things but adults waved them off. That's how good psychics lost their powers. "There's another reason we need to go see this kid. And it came from your precinct, different division." Vera sighed. "They made a complaint against the dead guy for harassment."

Jon took a breath and stood up. "Let's go then. We can use that as our cover."

The apartment where the girl lived with her family was above and one apartment over from the one they were going to use as a base.

Jon knocked on the door, which was already decorated for Halloween with a bat and skull wreath, and a pretty middle aged woman opened the door, murder in her eyes.

"Excuse me, Officer, but my child will not be answering any more questions!"

Jon blinked at her aggression and Vera figured it was her turn to step up already.

"Ma'am, we just need to confirm something on security footage," she said. "This wasn't discussed before, and no one is looking at your daughter or anyone in your family for the death." *If they are, they won't be by tomorrow,* she thought. *Director Dominic can change the police files.*

The woman huffed, then turned and called, "Ash!"

The girl rushed to the door, eyes too big for her face and drowning in a band hoodie. "Am I in trouble again?"

"No, baby, you're not," her mom assured her.

Vera smiled down at the girl, who now looked at her with awe. "Hey, Ash, I'm sorry to bother you this afternoon, but I just want to ask you one question and my partner and I will leave you guys alone. Is that okay?"

Ash nodded, and Jon took out his phone to show the footage to her.

"You seemed to see someone watching you as you were standing outside," he explained. "Was it the man who lived in 103?"

Her face went even paler than it already was. "N-No. This guy, he was super creepy. All in shadow, and really tall, with a big fedora." She mimed his height and hat with her hands. "And he just stood still and stared. Like a statue. He didn't even look like he had a face."

"And you didn't see this man, ma'am?" Vera asked the mother.

She shook her head with a sigh. "No. I wish I had. He really spooked her. She didn't sleep that night at all."

Jon glanced at Vera, who gave a slight nod.

"All right, that's all we need, and I promise, no more police will be by," Jon told them. "The Chicago Police are closing the case."

"Thank you, Officer," the mom said.

The kid nodded, still staring at Vera as if she saw an angel.

As the duo walked away, Jon smiled. "That kid looked like she was seeing her future looking at you."

Vera couldn't help her smile as well. "I'm the last person she should want to be, but I hope maybe by seeing me, she can know she can grow up to be whatever she wants and not change herself to conform to society."

"Well... Did we get anything useful on the guy, or was that all for nothing?" Jon asked after she was silent and they got back to the apartment.

"We aren't dealing with a normal ghost, as we suspected," Vera commented. "It's a Shadow Person."

Jon cocked his head. "A what now?"

"They're spirits born from severe hatred and violence, and they usually haunt depressed people or depressing places ... like this building. But this one is strong if he can keep spirits locked in here. He's likely slowly feeding on their souls. Which means we have to hurry and get rid of him before he drains their souls to the point of nonexistence."

Jon blinked, taking it all in, then flopped back on the couch cushions. "For crying out loud, how does every case I work with you get stranger? Vampire on the run, crazy witch trying to kill me, werewolves losing control in the city..."

"Oh, Jonathan, you haven't even touched the tip of the strange iceberg," Vera replied.

"Okay. What about the dead guy? You do realize that kid's mother killed him, right?"

Vera nodded. "I could sense a revenge killer a mile away. Evil souls won't sustain a Shadow Person. I assume the dead guy went to Hell, as he was supposed to. But that does make this worse: the Shadow Person got stronger because of the violence."

"Perfect," Jon muttered. "All right. Let's go kill a ghost."

"First thing is to find out where its spirit stays. It can't cross into the astral plane, it can't cross into any of the afterlives," Vera explained. "That means it stays here somewhere."

"Apartment 103," Jon said. "Where the violence lingers for it to feed on."

That was twice today Jon was quicker than her on something. Normally, this would annoy Vera. But the only thing annoying her was how attractive she found his mind. Too bad the rest of his personality was abhorrent.

"If we can get inside, we can ward it now, in the daytime. Now, contrary to most monster lore, Shadow People can move about in the day, but the way that granny's ghost was so calm, it seems like he's nocturnal only," Vera said. "Typical warding. Holy water, salt, blessings."

"What will warding it from the inside do?" Jon asked.

"Keep it stuck in there when it comes back." Vera grinned. "One huge ghost trap. Then we can banish it."

They searched the apartment for a stash of monster-hunting gear, finding it in the partially empty bedroom closet. Silver bullet-loaded rifles, silver and iron blades, carafes of holy water, containers of salt, crucifixes, even vials of dead man's blood, which made Vera wrinkle her nose in distaste.

"I should probably do the warding, you make sure it doesn't pop up anywhere outside," Jon suggested after he got everything needed.

"Plus…" He trailed off, not wanting to talk about the *thing* that came between them.

Vera bit her lower lip so hard, she tasted blood and licked it away before he could see, soothing the wound. "Yeah. Sure."

He stared at her for a few seconds too long, and she was ready to shoo him out the door herself when he finally started walking to the exit. She followed, to keep an eye out. Both were already armed, because you never know.

Vera grimaced as he reached the door to apartment 103 and called him back. "Jonathan? Be careful."

"I'm always careful. You're the one who shoots first and asks questions never," Jon reminded her.

"Careful? *You?* Did you forget I read your dossier?"

"What of it?"

Vera smirked. "I have two words for you: rabid raccoon."

He gave her a level look before replying, "I guess I have a kink for things that bite."

Her smirk widened. "Touche."

He opened the door and visibly shuddered before cursing. "The vibe in this room is making me want to run away and never come back. How evil is this thing?"

"It feeds on pure souls and gets stronger around pain and suffering. How evil do you *think* it is?" Vera tossed back at him.

Now it was his turn to say, "Touche."

He went inside, keeping the door open, and she could hear him chanting in Latin. Meanwhile, she did some digging on the building's history. Director Dominic of the PID found files not yet digitized and got someone in their library to send over some interesting murder and "unexplained" death articles.

Could one of them have been the Shadow Person when he was alive? The man found dead in a locked room, perhaps? The guy who was found hanging in the closet after losing everything in a gambling debt? The man who—

There. That smell. It smelled like death, rotting and wet and cloying. Did Jon not smell that? Why did it just pop up so strong? Was there something that died in the walls, a large rat or raccoon? Vera wished she brought perfume with. Then it hit her.

If something was dead in the walls, the smell would be stationary. Whatever caused it could move.

"Jonathan!" she cried, her worry for him taking over. "It's coming; it's here!"

"What?" His voice was muffled, but then he cursed and Vera rushed to the doorway.

"Jon, I—" She cut herself off, cursing her limitations. Cursing her parents. Cursing just about everything.

"I feel it," Jon said. "Get in here; jump over the threshold. Don't disturb the salt."

She breathed a sigh of relief and did as he said, and the moment she was inside, the door swung shut behind her like in an old, bad horror movie.

The blinds on the windows were rattling; so were cabinets in the nearby kitchen. The place where the poisoned corpse of the man who lived here was still stained with blood that had leaked out of him. It hadn't been cleaned out yet, as if the dead man would be returning any moment. Everything felt wrong, and now they had an incomplete ghost trap and an angry Shadow Person to contend with.

Jon groaned, stumbling a bit. "The Dark energy on this guy is vicious."

"Imagine a demon," Vera replied.

"I'd rather not!"

The air in the apartment was oppressive. Vera was breathing, yet it felt like her lungs couldn't get enough air. It made the blood rush to her head, and that wasn't good. She needed that blood elsewhere, like in her limbs to fight off the Shadow Person.

As darkness began to take shape before them, she readied the cannister of salt to toss it at the creature, but before she could, it sent Jon flying into the nearest wall.

He cursed as he got up, bruised but seemingly okay.

"Get out of the way."

The voice that spoke didn't speak, and it wasn't a voice. It was like a slither inside Vera's mind, and it seemed like Jon heard it as well. This Shadow Person didn't seem capable of speech, and it was no wonder: it really didn't have a face. Just a blank black canvas of nothingness.

"What am I in the way of?" Jon wondered. It moved towards him, and Vera took that as her time to strike, wielding an iron blade at her side. She sliced downwards, but the creature vanished, only to pop up behind her.

It was cold, radiating malevolence. Vera had faced down some of the most vicious paranormal criminals, and never did she feel such dread before.

But ... it wasn't her dread. It was his. The Shadow Person's. His hate, his rage, his fear, his darkness. It was overwhelming. Were she a lesser creature, she'd have crawled into a ball and sobbed.

That wasn't the case, however.

She was Vera King. And she didn't cry. Nor did she give up.

Whirling faster than most could follow, she sliced into the Shadow Person, and its scream that came inside her and Jon's minds was so agonizing, she nearly dropped her weapon.

Is this what psychics and mind magicians feel? How have they all not gone mad?

The Shadow Person flickered and when it came back into focus, there was a gash through which Vera could see the apartment behind it.

"I hope you don't have high blood pressure," Jon commented as he threw rock salt at it as if he were playing in the Chicago Cubs.

This time the sound in her head was a hiss of pain, but more manageable.

Jon doubled over, as if punched. The Shadow Person faced Vera and she knew she could take one blow.

Yet ... the blow didn't come.

She grinned, remembering. "You're a Dark creature, and you can't hurt me. How does it feel to be powerless ... Christopher?"

It was a shot in the dark, guessing the name he used when he was human. But the way he kept beating Jon down to get to her sounded like one of the murder cases she read, of a man who killed his ex and her new husband in this building.

The rage she felt intensified, confirming her theory. And he didn't like that she knew his former name. His human name.

Jon, who recovered from the last attack, raised his gun with iron rounds, but hesitated to fire. That would get attention, and Vera knew he knew the last thing they wanted was attention from the human police.

His moment of vacillation allowed the Shadow Person's darkness to stretch, bringing a silver knife from the kitchen and launching it at Jon.

It barely missed him, and he lost his equilibrium, falling to the floor.

The Shadow Person, Christopher, advanced.

Shadow People, despite once being alive, cannot be killed by destroying their remains. Or else Vera would have done that alone. No, they need something to chase away their darkness. Holy water and prayer is one way, but it seemed Jon used all the holy water.

Vera had to get more, but first she had to get them out of this apartment and leave Christopher trapped there.

But first, she had to save Jon.

What seemed like a lifetime flashed before her eyes as the Shadow Person loomed over the man she loved, whether she wanted to love him or not.

No. I lost him once. I will not lose him again!

"Don't you dare touch him!" she cried, doing what had to be the absolute dumbest thing: she sliced its throat, or where a throat should be, with the holy water-soaked iron blade.

She felt the coldness from it run up her arm, to her chest, and she faltered, almost as if her heart stopped. And then warmth began to seep back in as her blood took over, banishing the darkness trying to invade her body.

The Shadow Person flickered once, twice, three times.

Then he began to change, revealing fair skin, brown hair, and a head with a bullet wound.

Christopher.

He turned to face Vera.

"How?" This time, it was his voice that spoke, not in her head. "How did you turn me back into this weak thing?"

Vera had no idea.

Jon did, however.

"Because, in case you missed the memo in kindergarten, buddy, light always triumphs over the Dark."

Christopher turned on Jon, but this time Vera wasn't worried. There was a telltale scent of sulfur in the air, and she knew what that meant.

As the ghost began to disintegrate into flame — flame that couldn't touch the living — she smiled at him.

"Hell doesn't like it when people cheat them out of souls."

With a roar of the flame, Christopher was gone, leaving nothing behind except the faint hint of coldness that was already beginning to abate.

Vera walked over to Jon and held her hand out to help him up.

He looked up at her, hesitant, and then took her hand and she easily got him to his feet.

"You saved me."

She shrugged. "Part of the job."

"You wanted me saved so bad, your good intentions made that ghost stop being an evil entity." Jon didn't seem to be able to let it go. He looked flabbergasted.

"Don't get it twisted, I'm no hero," Vera commented. "I'm just as evil as you think I am."

His warm brown eyes softened for a moment, and it almost made her forget what a jerk he'd been to her, over something she couldn't change.

"You certainly looked like one just now," he pointed out.

She smiled. "I can play dress-up if I want. After all, it's almost Halloween."

Vera finished the story, while Jon looked on a bit sheepishly.

Paige wanted to ask why they fought, but she bit her tongue, literally, to keep the words back. It would be rude.

Instead, she said, "It's silly you argued. Clearly you were meant to be."

Jon kissed Vera's hand. "A perfectly creepy couple, in our own way."

Zeke in turn gave Paige a soft kiss on her cheek. "I think this is way too romantic for Halloween."

She shook her head. "Not at all! Regular people have Valentine's Day. People like us? This is what Halloween is all about. Celebrating our creepiness together."

"Well, enjoy it while you can," Vera said. "You have cases to work tomorrow, Paige. In this city, Halloween means paranormal crime goes through the roof."

Paige smiled, perking up at the thought of a new horrific mystery to solve. "You can count on the Paige Papillon Paranormal Detective Agency!"

The End

Another Step

Cathy-Lee Chopping

*The ends of her long white hair billowed out behind her
Whipped by the breeze as she made her way across the grey sand,
Chill of the overcast twilight creeping through her long regal garments.*

*The first whispers of winter hung in the air
Damp, curling the evenings mist into beckoning fingers of malevolent
desire,
Calling for souls to follow them into the murky depths of the ocean.*

*She turned to the water, dark eyes forever searching
The rippling face for hands breaking the surface,
Though she knows she will never see them come.
He was gone beneath the grey, lost at sea many moons ago.*

*The mist crept higher around her legs, caressing and slowly fluttering
her skirts
She took another step towards the water.
Hand unconsciously breaking the growing tendrils of winters grip,
sending swirls of cloud before her.*

*'It looks so cold,' she whispers, bare feet sinking into the wet sand
She took another step, shivering as her damp garments suddenly felt
heavy around her.*

*An incoming storm flickered in the distance, stopping her at water's
edge.*

*Her fingers traced her lips, remembering his touch
As her other hand removed a heavy golden crown from atop intricate
braids,
heart aching for her lost Lover, her fisherman who vanished at sea.*

*A solitary tear traced its way down her dewy face
As she took another step into the icy clutches of the sea,
Skirts now soaking the water up greedily, pulling her further into the
water
She took yet another step.*

*One more and she would struggle to get free, skirts heavy
Again her eyes scanned the ocean as her feet became numb to the cold
The mist again beckoned to her, "Come to me,"
Cold fingers curling around her waist as she stands transfixed.*

*She watched the whisps as they reached up to her face
In a lovers embrace, her lovers embrace.
He had come for her.
She smiled and knew she would be with her Love soon.
He reached out and took her hand, she took another step.*

Now You See Me

Parker Stevens

The fist flew before she knew what was happening. Sarah's head snapped to the side and hit the window hard. Blood poured from her nose as she grappled with the pain. The tears flowed automatically as if her body was conditioned by too many times of repeating the situation.

"Shut the hell up." Jon said with a snarl as he grabbed her by the hair and pulled her face back to his. "All you ever do is whine." His free hand slapped her hard and her eye socket exploded with pain.
"Stop" she pleaded as she gripped his fingers, "Please stop."
"Shut up Bitch." He screamed as her fingers dug into his hand and clawed hard. She drew blood and he screamed turning toward her releasing her hair, seeming to forget he was driving. His hand clenched on the wheel turning it hard toward her as he reared back to hit her again. The insanity in his eyes chilled her to the bone and she knew in that instant he was going to kill her unless she did something. With her breath sobbing raggedly she grabbed the wheel and tried to gain control. He roared and jerked it back wildly. The car swerved wildly and before she knew it they were barreling head on into the guard rail.

The car screamed down the embankment and time seemed to still as it rolled. Sarah screamed but the sound was snatched away in the crash as the car hit and the world began to fade away. Sarah's last thought before it all went black was that at least he would never hit her again.

Sarah sat up in bed, the unnatural stillness wrapped around everything. She felt a chill roll down her spine and shivered. Her heart beat faster and the breath hissing out of her lips was so cold she could almost see it. The usual hum of electronics had faded and the night seemed to be sealed in a vacuum so quiet she could hear her heart beat thrumming in her ears. It had been six months since the accident that had nearly killed her and had taken Jon's life and every day was a struggle. Strange sounds when there shouldn't be, changes in air temperature, things going missing, not to mention the glimpses of shadow figures she'd often seen out of the corner of her eye. She wasn't sad he was gone, she was afraid he might come back. If she was honest, she was damn scared because she was terrified she was living with a ghost and she knew exactly who the ghost belonged to.

"Is anyone there?" she asked hesitantly, hating the tentative note in her voice. She pulled out the gun in the nightstand drawer flipping the safety off and held it level, not taking any chances. If Jon had taught her anything it was to always be ready for the unexpected. She slid out of bed and moved on bare feet toward the bedroom door, knowing she needed to check on the sound she'd heard, but at the same time dreading each slow step.

"He's dead" she whispered to herself as she flipped on the hallway light and stepped out into the hallway. She knew she was still trying to convince herself, but she knew better. She had grown up in New Orleans, and she knew if anything odd was going to happen it was going to happen here.

The light ended in a gaping pool of darkness that seemed to move on its own. A thousand spiders seemed to dance up her spine at the inky blackness where her living room should be. The darkness seemed to move and gather into a solid shape and Sarah brought the gun up again.

"I'll shoot." she called out as she stepped back, her feet moving almost of their own volition. "I know how to use this and I will if you don't get out of my house." She wanted to say she sounded brave but knew that was a lie. She knew the weapon in her hand was probably useless against the thing in the darkness but old habits died hard. The shadow moved again and Sarah pulled the trigger. Two shots burst through the darkness, splitting the quiet. Through the smoky haze Sarah saw the shape begin to solidify as a low laugh filled the space. Her breath caught in her throat as the shadow formed a familiar shape she'd hoped never to see again, her boyfriend Jon.

He moved so fast her eyes couldn't track him. One moment he was leaning lazily against the wall, the next he was in her face his fist locked around her throat. "Are you going to make me?" he asked with a smile laced with pure evil. He squeezed and her eyes bulged. "What are you going to do little girl?"

His face loomed close and she saw the gray pallor of his skin. His brown eyes were blood shot and sunken in, his face which had once been handsome was now gaunt. His teeth, that he'd once been so proud of now stank with rot. "What's wrong sweetheart," He asked silkily as he pulled her closer and took a long sniff of her skin, "aren't you happy to see me?"

"Get off me." She gagged as he pulled her closer and squeezed tighter. Her vision began to blur and she tried to pull his hands free. Her mind was rolling between horror at the wraith squeezing the life out of her and the realization her mother was right, ghosts did exist. Her hand sank through the forearm holding her and her brain begged for release.

"Aww cat got your tongue." he said with a laugh as he slammed her against the wall squeezing tighter trying to crush her airway. The blood vessels in her eyes began to pop and he laughed in joy. "you should've known you'd never get away from me that easily." Sarah knew he was going to kill her this time. Sarah struggled against his grip, her brain screaming that he shouldn't be able to hurt her, yet the proof of his ability was slowly chocking the life out of her.

Her mind spun in a thousand different directions and she found herself praying for help. Her vision began to blur at the edges but she knew what she had to do. She wiggled harder in the spirits grip making his hands slide. His hands gripped the necklace she wore and pulled.

Sarah struggled harder, her vision almost black, until she felt the snap at her neck as the pendant she wore broke.

Salt slid down the things hands and began to sizzle. The salt sparkled in the hallway light, its pink crystals burning holes in the ghosts skin. Jon's sunken eyes filled with panic as his arm began to burn and dissolve.

"You bitch!" he screamed as he opened his rotten mouth wide, his mangled tongue lolling out. "I will kill you."

"Not if I can help it you bastard." Sarah gasped as she grabbed the sage and lighter off the hallway table with fumbling hands. Her fingers trembled but she lit it quickly knowing she would only have one chance. She shoved the burning bundle into his mouth and watched as the horror in his eyes intensified as he began to burn.

His skin peeled off in layers as Sarah watched, gasping against the wall. He began to scream as he began to break apart. He stumbled toward her, reaching for her with his grisly hands. "You will always belong to me." He hissed as he crumbled.

Sarah pushed off the wall and walked over to him staring into his melting face, she was really sick of him. "I belong to myself and no one else." she said forcefully, remembering all the years of misery and abuse he put her through. She felt the anger well up inside her as she took the remaining salt and sage and pushed them into his chest. "And I'm done with your shit, get out of my house."

Jon stared in wide eyed disbelief and dissipated with a wet pop of inky blackness that faded away into shadow. The air snapped back into place and the sounds of the night and the hum of her air conditioner filled the quiet. The unearthly time freeze faded and Sarah knew he was finally gone. The house seemed to breathe a sigh of relief and Sarah did too as she slid down the wall and put her head back against it. She felt the tears sliding down her cheeks and she knew it wasn't because he was gone, it was because now she was finally free.

The End

You Forgot Something

Thomas Woldering

It was dark and wet in the back streets of Paris. I leaned against the cold building. I remember the rage, agony, and astonishment I felt as that woman stood over me. I could barely recognize her, but I knew she was more than she seemed from her strength; she had just broken my arm.

"You're that woman staying with the Viscount Leclerc, aren't you? God, you broke my arm. What are you?" I asked her. It was such a bad break my arm was almost flopping about when I moved it. I recall strangely thinking in the midst of all this what a pity it was my expensive suit was now ruined.

"You're despicable, Lamond Deschanel – a man of the worst sort. You abused Mariella and you shot my father. Thankfully, all of it is within our power to fix," she told me.

"Shot? That man - the interloper - is your father?" I said next in shock, but quickly shook it off and snapped angrily. "What business is it of yours anyway, woman? Mariella hasn't been behaving like a lady or honoring me as she should, and now I find there is another man involved? I have to keep her in line. What would you have me do? I..." My voice stopped as she lifted me up the wall by my neck with one hand. I couldn't believe her strength.

"As someone who understands humanity and compassion more than you, even though some would consider me evil. Did you really think you could be so cruel to the one you are supposed to love and never pay for

it? You make me sick." she dropped me into a puddle and then looked over her shoulder. "Rupert,"
From the darkness beside her, a small cloaked creature shuffled forward. I couldn't see his face at all, but I remembered the red glow of his eyes from under the hood.

"Yes, my lady?" the half-height, shrouded goblin said.

"By the authority of my father, administer his punishment."

"Me? You honor me, my lady. Ooh, this'll be fun."

"Punish me? What are you going to do?" I demanded.

"Shhh, I need to think," the creature responded in a high, creaky voice filled with the joy of expectation as he scuttled up to me. His wrinkly, blue hands glowed with an unnatural energy and he grabbed my shoulders. "Severatus".

"Deschanel! Stop daydreaming and seal those papers!" I jolted back to my desk at the voice of my supervisor, Mr. Howe.

There was an elderly woman with purple-dyed hair sitting in front of me, staring in confusion. I looked down at my notary book and seal, aligned her paper, and pressed the seal into it.

"There you are, Ma'am, have a great afternoon." I smiled as my foggy confusion at where I was started to clear. I was at work. I couldn't recall how long I must have been staring at the woman, but it must have been a while from how she stared back at me.

Mr. Howe walked over and perched himself on the chair the woman had just vacated. He was the youngest of the associates at the firm, and always wanted to assert himself to boost how Mr. Boyd thought of him. He reminded me of a bird eager to peck even at the smallest seed.

"I know you've been at this company longer than anyone can remember, but if you can't rein in these episodes, I'll have to report this to Mr. Boyd. It makes us look bad."

"Always seems to get this way in the fall. Won't happen again for another year after Halloween," I shrugged. Time had been the proof there. I had reached the age where I really stopped counting years, and I only ever had those thoughts of France in the early fall.

"Halloween isn't an excuse. We can't have you in here staring and drooling. Now, it's time to close up shop. Go home and rest so you're not like this tomorrow."

I was the last out of the office, like always. There just never seemed to be a reason to rush out of there. The world was always there, and it wouldn't cease to be there if I took my time. I pushed down on my fedora and headed for the train station. Nearby there was an advertisement for Coke Zero flashing by on a bright LED screen, and I stopped for a moment. How long had it been since Tab was new, or since everyone walking around me had been reading newspapers and not phone screens? I recall phones used to be a real luxury, and not the hand-held ones, the corded ones. Everything was bright, noisy, and engaging these days. I didn't care for it.

"Oh well," I shrugged and walked past a crowd of young boys watching another one dance wildly on a cardboard box as they called out *'that's so sigma!'* "Another new word meaning?" I murmured, "what will they come up with next?"

I went down into the subway next for the dependably half-hour ride to uptown where I had lived for as long as I could remember. The station smelled of marijuana again today, much more common recently. Something was different today, though, and it made me look up from my place in the crowd.

"Sir!" the voice of a younger man caught my attention as the train pulled into the station. He rushed through the crowd in my direction.

All I could think was that I didn't want to be involved. I turned back towards the train and waded towards the door as the man continued to push aside and upset people.

"Sir, could you please stop for a moment?" He called out again, raising the attention of a few in the crowd.

Was he coming for me? No, he couldn't be, I assessed as I stepped aboard, though he did look like he was really coming straight in my direction.

"Sir, there's something you've forg..." he trailed off as the doors shut between me and him.

It was me he was trying to reach. Why? I glanced at him and couldn't help but think I had seen his face somewhere before. I would have said it was a dream, but aside from the waking visions I had around this time of year, I never dreamed. He stared back at me through the train window, but I turned away and found a rail to hold.

A young woman nearby stood up and motioned for me to take her seat.

"Oh, I couldn't, Miss." I passed

"My stop's up next," she insisted, grabbing one of the top rail straps as the train shook.

I ambled to the seat and took it between the bumps and jostles. "Thank you kindly," I took off my hat, placed it in my lap, then took a newspaper from my briefcase and unfolded it.

"I haven't seen that in years," the young woman cheerfully commented.

Lowering my paper, I glanced up for a moment. "All these screens can hurt the eyes," I returned to the day's articles.

"I didn't even know they made those anymore," she continued to make small talk to me.

Talking didn't interest me, but it would have been rude to ignore her. "One must know where to find them, but they are made."

As I was about to return to my reading, she spoke up again. "So, did you know that man?"

I heard the question, but my memory was already foggy. "Which one?" I asked, truly not recalling for a moment. Her next statement surprised me into lowering my paper.

"The one outside the train," the young woman described more, looking confused now.

Just then, I recalled him. It wasn't like me to forget someone I had just seen moments before I loosely folded my paper and focused more on this girl. She had long, loosely curled brown hair, and wore an orange leather jacket and jeans which were threadbare up the legs. "No, Miss."

"Did you drop your phone? Your cane? He was saying you forgot something," she continued.

I studied her for a moment as the bumpy ride continued. She looked like a bit of an urchin from her jeans, but that wasn't much of a tell these days when half of the new clothes in the stores came pre-torn. She didn't seem like those teens on the street l had seen though. Why was she so interested in me? I decided to keep chatting.

"I don't have either miss, and I know I locked the office. So, it's nothing important."

"You sure are unshakable. I would be looking everywhere around me," she chuckled slightly. "I'm Rita. What's your name?" she asked and offered a handshake.

"Mr. Deschanel," I shook her hand. She was wearing an interesting silver, dragon-shaped ring which covered her whole first finger like a piece of armor. It seemed familiar somehow, but I didn't think it was appropriate to ask about it.

"So formal; charming. No on introduces by last name anymore," she commented, then seemed to study me for a moment. "You've seen so much, haven't you? Your eyes speak of more experience than many would ever see, but there's something else."

I wasn't sure what she was trying to say, but I smiled and nodded. "I have worked at my job for a long time, but I don't know what you mean. I don't see myself particularly wise. I am a man like any other, with a job that I need to do. I play my part."

She looked over me again with a smile, seeming captivated by me, but the train slowing drew her attention to the door. "You mean more and have learned more than you know, Mr. Deschanel. Have a good night," she waved and departed, but stopped just outside the train. I had turned back to my paper, but I thought I heard her say something in shock just as the doors closed. "You? Of course..."

At the next stop, I folded and packed my newspaper, quickly exited, and ascended the rickety brass escalator to the sidewalk across from my rowhouse. It was dark already, but my neighborhood was quieter and safer than other parts of the city; I prized that.

I stopped outside my door tonight and gently lowered myself down on the steps. I usually went straight in, but it had been a strange evening. Windows were decorated and porches were lit. I noticed a small group of children going by in costume.

"Halloween is today?" I mused aloud, shocked I'd lost track of the day.

"You didn't notice, Mr. Deschanel?" a young, dark-skinned boy in a dinosaur costume frowned from the next stoop over. "Where am I gonna get full-sized Baby Ruth bars now?"

Next to him, his grandmother fixed a stare on him that could have turned him into a pillar of salt if she'd had the power.

"Jesus, Emmet," she leaned forward and cradled her bowl of candy like an attentive goalie. "You take that back and apologize to Mr. Deschanel. People are worth more'n what they can give you.

"Sorry, Mr. Deschanel," he looked down, ashamed.

"Oh, I forgive you. It's me who failed the neighborhood here." I leaned over closer. "But I'll tell you a secret: your grandmother really loved those when she was your age.

"Really, Grammy?" Emmet wondered at his Elder.

Emmet's grandmother sat back demurely. "Well, you can't beat a Baby Ruth. Go on and catch up with your daddy and sister."

After I watched him leave, I turned to his grandmother again. Her name was Gloria. "How old is he now?"

"Twelve, almost too old to be doing this. Definitely too young to be hearing about me seventy years ago..." she criticized.

"You have so many great stories to tell." I stood up to head inside and smiled again. "Even if you don't think they're appropriate, he could learn a lot."

"Little boys don't hardly listen to their grammys anyway," she frowned for a moment. "Thank Jesus, Desmond is a good Pa for him."

"You're to thank for that, so your lessons are worth it. Even if you think you're too old to give them, I still see the same young girl, Gloria."

She blushed, but then took on a more serious look. "And I still see the same old man – Exactly the same old man. I ain't never told a soul, but you've gotta tell me the secret to that someday."

Unlocking my door, I shrugged, "I haven't a clue what you mean, my dear. Goodnight.

I took a light dinner of beef stew, and I could almost hear the disappointment outside at my light being off. I couldn't believe I had lost track of the date. It wasn't like me. I had been dependable handing candy out as long as I could remember.

"The day dreams really are worse this year." I admitted aloud.

I cleaned the dishes next and bathed, then went into my study. I spent all of my time away from work and errands in here. It was quiet and there were no distractions. I already had no TV, radio, or other electronics to distract me, but even the hum of the refrigerator could not reach my weak ears in the study.

I had a simple table, chairs, and a bookshelf, but it was empty except for books related to work. I had no interest in fictions – they were almost as distracting as television. I often found myself wondering why I had no interest in distractions. Other old men had no issue finding fun activities to take their time like fishing, bowling, playing chess in the park, but I just sat blankly. I had seen my share of the world, but it had never piqued my interest; I was a constant spectator.

In the stillness tonight, Gloria's words returned to me. She was right. I was old when she was young. So old I'd seen Mr. Boyd's father retire, and his father before him. I had watched Gloria grow as an orphan on the street, and when Mrs. Bixby died next door with no heirs and left her house to me, I had given it to Gloria. Now her son, Desmond, and his family were growing there. The world just kept passing by around me, and unlike other old men I felt no inclination to stop working. I was like an old machine from before they were built cheaply – no frills, but never stops running. I did feel tired frequently though, and not a tired which could be solved by sleeping somehow. It was more like the sole of a shoe worn down to its lowest layers, but evenly and without any holes. Still, I did not sicken or die like the successive generations around me – I just existed.

I calmed myself and tried to think back for a moment on when I had come to this old rowhouse or even this city – a meditation. However, I could only see fog in the depths of my mind. One other image came back to me – that ring. I put my hand to my throat for a moment, because in the daydream which has haunted me, I was quite sure the woman was wearing a similar ring. "What could be going on there?" I mused at the thought.

Just then, there was a ring at the door. I snapped out of my reverie. "What time is it? It must be past ten o'clock. That can't be a misguided trick-or-treater." I rose to look out of the peep-hole.

When I reached it and I peeked out, I stepped back in shock. It was the man from the subway station at my door. I didn't speak or open it.

He rang again. Who was he? How did he find my home? What did he want?

He rang a third time.

"Go away. I'm not interested. Please leave me in peace." I called from across the closed door.

There was silence for a moment. I thought he might be gone, but then I heard the mail slot lift. What was he trying to do?

"Excuse me, sir. Excuse me. I'm sorry to bother you at this hour. I need to talk to you. This may be the only chance I have."

I couldn't believe he was doing this. "You're talking now," I responded.

"I need to come in. There's something you've forgotten, and I only have this chance to tell you about it."

"Out of the question," I responded.

I had never felt unsafe in my memory. Even when I had walked down a bad alley, no one seemed to notice me. I had fought in a war or two, I recalled, and not a scratch on me. Right now, though, I felt terror grip me. I felt that if I opened that door, something would come to an end.

"Please, sir. After all this time I've finally found you. You're kind, generous, and loyal – all the things I never was. Don't you see this means we can leave together now?"

"I don't know what you mean," I said as I felt a pang of guilt. "Goodbye."

Whatever this man was speaking of, I couldn't face it. I sighed and went upstairs. The man had remained down there, I saw from my window. He stared up intensely, but did not try to enter. I returned his gaze, and something felt familiar about him. It wasn't enough for me to open my door, but it was there. I shook it off and turned in for the night, taking out my hearing aids so I couldn't hear anything further from him. For once, they were a blessing.

The next morning inexplicably started late. Neither the sun or the bells on my clock woke me – for both to fail at the same time was unlikely. The man had been gone when I awoke, and no one followed me on the subway. Mr. Howe smiled at my late arrival as he focused in and started circling like the buzzard he was.

Suddenly, he struck from behind, approaching from where I had to jerk my neck around to see him. "Must be nice to be able to stroll in to work an hour and a half late."

"Good morning, Mr. Howe." I put a hand on my neck at the spasm he had caused. "I assure you it won't happen again. This was a very unusual morning." I tried to keep cheery.

"No, I think I'm going to report this to Mr. Boyd. Daydreaming yesterday, late Today, This Firm has to maintain some professional standards."

I winced. "Are you quite sure you want to do that?" I knew Mr. Howe had only been at the firm for two years, and even though he was my supervisor he knew little about me or my long history with the firm.

"I'll decide for myself what I think is appropriate. I don't need advice from a fossil." Mr. Howe marched to the ornate oak door into Mr. Boyd's office.

I waited, starting up a newton's cradle set on my desk which had been idle for a while. Soon, a rumbling of voices from the office rose into an irate dressing-down, then ended in a bellow heard across the office as a chastened Mr. Howe scurried from the door - much more a mouse than a hawk or buzzard now.

The rest of the morning went quickly with a few documents to notarize. It was Just before lunch when Mr. Howe Finally crept back over to my desk.

"Did you know that would happen?" the young supervisor asked.

"I warned you it might," I sat back and folded my hands.

"Really? Asking if I'm sure isn't the way to tell me Mr. Boyd is about to rip off my head. You wanted that to happen, didn't you?" he accused.

"No, but it's better you learn now that jockeying for power only results in pain," I observed. "I knew after that night in Paris..." I recalled, but then realized I was thinking of my daydream.

Mr. Howe scoffed, "Paris? You never take a day off to go anywhere. It says you have thousands of hours of vacation, like you've never taken any vacation in eighty years and someone just let it keep accruing."

"I guess it's grandfathered," I commented.

"Is that a pun? I'm still watching you, ya know. Someday –"

"Dammit, Daniel, leave the old man alone." Another bellow issued from the now-open office door. "Did you forget about those papers Mr. Dewey needs in court?"

Mr. Howe bolted away as Mr. Boyd came out of his office with a grin the young man would never see. "Should have hired the other young one instead of him. What was her name – Ms. Reilly?" He chuckled, then focused on me. "You okay, Lamond? Ghoulies got you again this year?"

"A bit worse than usual, actually." I replied, trying to keep a cheery tone.

"Well don't worry about it. Your place here is always assured," he said as he grabbed his coat. "Can you mind things while I head out to lunch?"

"Of course, Mr. Boyd." I smiled at him, remembering when he had taken over from his father years ago. He was set to retire next year.

The door jingled as he left, and I took out my own lunch and newspaper. I was just starting to settle in when the door opened once more with a jingle. A man and woman entered. I focused in on them, and an icy fear gripped me.

"It's Ok, Lamond," she smiled as she and the man sat across from me. It was the girl from the train and the man from outside my door. The man was dressed oddly in a suit that looked to be out of the 1800's, and the girl was in a formal-but-simple black dress that made her look older than she had last night. She looked like she was in mourning. Both were quite different from the last time I saw them.

While I was terrified, what I knew was my job, so I decided to do just that. "May I notarize something for you?"

The girl, I remembered Rita was her name, set several papers on the desk before me. "Yes, actually."

I glanced at the papers and froze for a moment. What could be the meaning of these? Swallowing hard, I asked her. "This is a last will and testament for Lamond Deschanel." I read on "Naming Mr. Boyd as executor and Gloria Sullivan as beneficiary under condition..."

"That she pays forward your possessions to someone who can be trusted to care for them and make them grow, just as you did with Mrs. Bixby's." Rita continued.

"I don't understand. How did you know about either of them and who..." I just decided to come out and say it. "...is that terrifying man next to you?"

Glancing at him for a moment again, I noticed he seemed a lot less active and wasn't trying to engage me like he had yesterday. I slid back in my chair as next I noticed he was slightly see-through – a ghost!

"What is the meaning of this!?" I jumped and hid behind my chair as agilely as my aged body could accomplish.

"There's something you forgot. You forgot to die!" the ghost's expressionless face let out a haunting echo.

At that I bolted for the door, but felt myself stop in mid step. "Sorry to do this, but you have to sit and listen," Rita declared.

I felt my body pull in reverse through the exact moves I had made until I was back in my chair at the desk. Now I was terrified and helpless. I saw Rita was directing my moves with the finger on which she wore the long dragon ring. The ring glowed with an eerie indigo hue.

"Who are you? Why are you angry with me?" I asked, finding she hadn't frozen my voice, just my arms and legs.

"I am Ifrita Mazan, but my name probably means little to you. I am an enchantress, but your kind often just lump us together with witches. I'm not angry either, but I do mean to fix a mistake that was made by a sister of my order."

"Ghosts and now witches? Isn't Halloween over?" I sighed. I was completely defeated by her, just like the Frenchman in my daydream.

"All Hallows Eve," Ifrita corrected. "It's funny you should say that, because if you'd listened to this man on *'Halloween'* you'd have never known he was a ghost and you'd be lots less terrified. You see, he can only manifest more than a whisper of that howl he made on the eve of All Saints' Day. I've used my power to strengthen him, until the end of today, but it doesn't allow him to move or talk like he could yesterday."

"You watched him come to my door?" I felt more like I was being toyed with by an unseen puppet master.

"I don't usually follow people, but I felt something unique about you. It's why you caught my interest on the train. I had to be sure of the situation. I needed to see what he said to you and how you reacted. I had to look into your memories too, so I prayed the goddess make you sleep in a bit longer this morning so I could."

"Why do any of this?' I sputtered out, trying to not return the piercing stare of the ghost beside me. "Am I supposed to learn from this? Isn't everyone who lives forgetting to die?"

"You have learned. You've become loyal, generous, kind, hardworking, and everything you weren't when you lived in France in 1886 like him." Ifrita explained, indicating the ghost beside her.

"My daydream?" I looked at the ghost again and saw he was cradling a mangled-looking arm. While I had aged, I had to admit an uncanny resemblance. "I'm not under a spell, though. I've never felt I had to do something I didn't want to," I denied and struggled again. "Not until you forced me back into this chair."

Ifrita waved her hand in a smooth fluid gesture and I felt my arms and legs come free. I tried to rise, but found my chair was fixed to the floor and my rear to the chair.

"I hope that's more comfortable. Now. You've not been under a spell, you're the result of one – a Ruperted spell."

"I know that name," I shuddered, recalling red beady eyes. "But that's from the..."

"The recurring *'daydream'* you have just around the time when your friend over here manifests. It's a memory," she paused and then smiled. "I still can't believe it's really you," Ifrita suddenly took on a look that I could only describe as giddy with excitement. "You know you're the reason we even have that saying – *'Ruperting a spell.'* It means devising a spell, handing it off to someone not skilled enough to cast it, then suffering the consequences when they inevitably screw it up. It originally came from an elder sister in my order, the daughter of old Methuselah himself, who did exactly that. You, my friend, are a legend – a legend and a mistake."

"Hold on now. I'm not a zoo exhibit, and it's not right to call someone a mistake." I objected again. It hurt to be talked about like that.

"I can't help what you are, but I can fix my sister's mistake. You see, she meant Rupert to rend your soul from your body and cast it your body into the void. In that case, your body would have died and your soul would have dissipated eventually – entering neither heaven, hell, or any kind of afterlife." She shook her head sadly. "Not a fair punishment for what you did, but you personally pissed Merona off."

"Merona?" I shuddered again as the image of a young woman with fiery red curls tore through my mind. I recognized her, and I knew this was real.

"Merona Zmiychyka. She's still out there somewhere I hear, but probably hasn't given you a second thought. She was always too dismissive and pushed tasks onto others - like your punishment. Instead of banishing you to the void personally, she passed her spell to her familiar, who ripped your soul from your body and accidentally banished your body to Hoboken, New Jersey." She grinned with a bit of mirth and shook her head. "I don't know if anyone will ever figure out why you ended up there. So, your body found a job as a clerk at a law firm – a humble servant and the opposite of the arrogant, demeaning young viscount who you were. You aged to a point, but once you reached the age you would have died at, everything just stopped for you."

The revelation stunned me, and even though my memory and knowledge of these names told me it was real, I still hesitated to accept it. "If this is true, what does it mean for me?"

"It will mean peace and rest…" Ifrita leaned in toward me. "…but it will also be the end."

I nodded, sitting back and sighing. "I've seen this happen to so many others, I never even thought of what it would be like for me. Why now? Why this year?" The question occurred to me.

"France is a long way from here, and he only had one day a year to travel to you." The woman explained further. "I'm sure he's seen a lot on the way too – traveling over mountains and across the bottom of the ocean. He's had as much time to think on his own misdeeds."

"He had to walk the bottom of the ocean? Unbelievable!" I commented, almost guffawing at the absurdity, but stopped myself. "Not so strange as everything else today though, I suppose."

Ifrita noticed and politely laughed a little. "You're right. The real world seems absurd to people who've lived their whole lives in common society," she paused. "So, then what will you do? I saw your feelings, and I know the fatigue you feel from this ordeal. Do you not desire this?"

"I do," I thought of how worn I was and how empty my days were. It all made sense. "But then why am I afraid of him?" I pointed to my ghost.

"He represents all you were, and that was not a good man. You feel fear because you know you could go to your hell if you joined with him. I am not a judge, but I think you've both done your time." She reassured me. "This has been a living purgatory for you, and through it you will redeem yourself as a whole being."

I looked at the other me with new eyes then. This poor bastard of a man who took so many missteps, but never had a chance to redeem himself on his own. I could give him a chance at that, just like I did for Gloria. I no longer felt fear, but deep pity instead. I took the will, signed it, and sealed it.

I swallowed hard and felt heat and tears flooding into me after doing such a final thing. "There is no greater love than to lay down your life to save another, so if I can save him – save us, then I will let this go."

Ifrita smiled and waved her ringed finger to release her holding spell. "And that is why I am confident you will be redeemed. Now, all you must do is take his hand and nature will guide you into the beyond. Good journey to you, Lamond Deschanel."

I leaned forward and took the ghost's good hand. A look of peace spread across his face as he stood and melted into me. Then, that warmth, peace, and restfulness spread to me. In a thousand years, I couldn't describe how relieving it felt. Ifrita rose and crossed the desk to close my eyes as my soul and I left my body resting back in my office chair and passed into unknown eternity.

The End

House of Nightmares

Cassandra Jones

Chapter One

I flipped the windshield wipers on. Did we really need a thunderstorm on Halloween night? It was a good thing none of us were wearing face paint. It would be completely messed up before we made it inside the house.

We'd been invited to a party at a house on the edge of town. Everyone knew the stories about this place. They'd never stopped teenagers from trying to sneak into the place, which is what they'd have to do for this party. If the police showed up it would be shut down before we could blink.

My best friend was sitting next to me in the passenger seat. He'd been the one invited to the party. Then he was told to bring his friends along. Fisher always got invited to these parties.

My gaze moved to the rearview mirror. Fisher's girlfriend was with us, along with her best friend, my little sister. Sloane normally didn't do things like this. She preferred to stay home and study.

"Is this really a good idea?" Harlyn asked suddenly. "What if the police come?"

"Relax." Fisher looked back at her. "Everything will be fine babe."

"I hate it when you call me that." She shook her head.

"You never know if they'll show up or not." Larisa chimed in. "Is there even electricity in the house?"

"Why can't you two be more like Sloane?" Fisher grumbled. "She's not being paranoid."

"Actually." Sloane looked at me. "If it's too creepy I'm not going inside. I'll wait on the porch or in the car."

"Why did you come?" I laughed.

"Because you wouldn't stop bugging me about it." She pulled up the hood on her costume. "You said it'll be fun."

"He's right." Fisher winked at them.

The girls had decided to wear witch costumes. I knew Sloane's was from a couple of years ago. She hadn't planned to go out on Halloween this year.

Harlyn and Larisa's were new though. They were also more revealing than Sloane's. Hers came to her feet while theirs were a lot shorter.

Of course, they were eighteen. My sister was only sixteen. Our parents had planned to have a houseful of kids, but only had the two of us. They were happy with me and Sloane.

I took another look at her in the mirror. She was right about me bugging her. I just didn't want her to be home alone tonight. Mom and dad were going to a party at a friend's house.

I planned to be home before them. What was the point of staying out late with a storm like this?

"What was that?" Sloane looked behind us.

"What?" Larisa asked. "Did you see something?"

"I thought there was someone standing back there." Sloane shook her head. "I must've been seeing things."

"You had to be." Fisher smiled at her. "Why would anyone be standing out in this weather?"

"He has a point." I agreed. "We'll be there soon. Then we can get out of this storm for a bit."

"Do you think they cleaned the place up a little?" Harlyn scratched her cheek.

"Sure. The place is spotless." Fisher shook his head. "Why would they clean the place they had to sneak into?"

"It was just a question." She snapped. "You don't have to be so rude."

She was right about that. He'd been giving her attitude all evening. He was definitely going to be making up for it later.

My gaze moved to the mirror again. Sloane was still watching the sides of the road. What exactly had she seen? She was acting strange. I had never seen her so nervous.

I continued to drive down the road. We should have been there by now. I had to go slow because of the rain. It was taking twice as long to get there as it normally would.

A flash of lighting lit up the sky. I took a deep breath when my eyes landed on the dark figure. Why would someone be standing on the side of the road? Even better, how had they gotten this far ahead of us? That had to be the same figure Sloane had seen.

"There it is again." Sloane pointed to the shadow figure. "How did it get in front of us?"

"That's not possible." Larisa shook her head. "They can't walk faster than a car."

"It's the same person." Sloane chewed her lip. "At least, I think it is. It's too dark to really see."

"Maybe it's someone playing a joke on us?" Harlyn put her arm around Sloane's shoulders. "I'm sure that's all it is."

That might be true with those guys. If we didn't get her to calm down I wouldn't make her stay at the party. I could always take her back to the house.

The house finally came into view. It was about time. I was ready for this night to be over. I wasn't the biggest fan of Halloween to begin with. I never had been. I rarely even watched horror movies.

Stopping in front of the house, I turned the engine off. I wanted to make sure my sister was okay. If not we wouldn't be staying long.

"Why are we just sitting here?" Fisher opened his door.

"I want to make sure Sloane's all right." I looked at her. "I can take you home if you want."

"I'm okay." She forced a smile. "We drove all this way. I don't want to ruin everyone's fun."

"We can leave whenever you're ready." I grabbed her hand. "Let's go have some fun."

"Where is everyone?" Larisa stopped on the porch. "I hear music, but no one's here."

"They have to be here." Fisher pushed past her. "Open the door."

Larisa was right. The house was completely empty. There should be at least fifty people here by now. Where had everyone gone?

This was definitely strange. I knew the guys throwing this party wouldn't take off without a good reason. So, where were they now?

I looked around the room we were standing in. They had obviously wanted to make it creepier. Along with the dust and cobwebs, red paint had been thrown everywhere. It looked like a bloodbath in the place.

"Is that paint?" Harlyn grabbed Fisher's arm.

"What else would it be?" He pushed her away. "I'm going to check out the house."

"What if it's blood?" Larisa followed him down a hallway.

"Yeah right." Fisher laughed.

Sloane was still standing by the door. She hadn't moved an inch. I didn't think she would go any further inside. I couldn't leave her alone.

I leaned against the doorframe. We could wait here for them to come back. There was no reason for all of us to risk getting lost in this place.

Our friends disappeared further into the house. I didn't think they would find anyone else. Maybe the cops had already shown up. Of course, they would've taken the speakers with them. No way would they have left those behind.

"Why isn't anyone here?" Sloane hugged me. "I don't like this, River."

"Me either." I confessed. "It's too weird."

"I think we should leave." She looked up at me. "Please?"

"We have to wait for the others to come back." I smiled at her. "We might as well leave if no one else is here."

Harlyn and Larisa came back down the hallway. I didn't see Fisher anywhere. Harlyn probably got tired of his attitude. I didn't know why he was acting that way. Knowing my best friend he was probably showing off because of who had invited him. Of course, they both looked scared. Had he done something to scare them?

"Where's Fisher?" Harlyn asked.

"I thought he was with you two." I shook my head.

"We can't find him." Larisa said.

Chapter Two

"What do you mean you can't find him?" I raked a hand through my hair. "He went that way with you."

"We were looking around and he disappeared." Harlyn chewed on her lip. "We only looked away for a minute."

"He's probably hiding somewhere to scare you." Sloane was quiet for a moment. "Did you find anyone else?"

"Not a soul." Larisa sighed. "We should've stayed home. It would've been more fun."

"Fisher, stop playing games." I called out. "We're leaving in five minutes. You better be ready by then."

I listened for any noise he might make. The house was completely silent. When did the music stop? Had one of the girls turned it off?

They were all still standing here with me. It had to be Fisher. There was no one else it could be.

I took my phone out to check the time. I wasn't in the mood to play his games. None of us were.

"Come on, Fisher." Harlyn yelled. "Let's get out of here."

"Why don't we leave him?" Larisa scratched her cheek. "It would really teach him a lesson."

She started towards the door when it slammed shut. I tried to open it. What was going on here? Had someone locked us in? Was it Fisher? Had he gone out the backdoor?

I looked from one to the other. They all looked terrified. I had to get them out of this house. They never should've come here.

Maybe there was another way out? We had to find out. I didn't intend to stay here any longer.

"Did you see any other doors?" I asked Harlyn and Larisa.

"We didn't really pay attention." Harlyn admitted. "We were too busy looking for Fisher."

"Let's see if we can find one." I started down the hallway.

"River, wait." Sloane grabbed my arm. "This is a bad idea."

"I know you're scared." I smiled at her. "We have to find a way out."

"There's something wrong with this house." My sister looked around. "We can't go any further."

"We already did." Larisa sighed. "Nothing happened."

"I can't go in there." Sloane backed against the door.

What was wrong with her tonight? What was it about this place that had her so scared? We had to get out of here somehow. Didn't she see that?

I walked back to her, putting my arm around her. We couldn't leave her by herself. She was already starting to panic. Sloane worried me sometimes. She had been having panic attacks again.

She'd had them a lot when she was younger, but not in a few years. This was one of the worst I had seen. I had to calm her down.

Her breathing was my biggest concern. I had to remember what mom and dad did to help her through these things. I hoped it worked.

"Sloane?" I grabbed her hand. "I need you to look at me. You have to calm down. I'm right here with you."

"I'm scared." She looked into my eyes. "I want out of here."

"That's why we need to look for another way out." I kissed her forehead.

"I'm staying right here." Sloane sank down to the floor.

"Stay with her." Harlyn said suddenly. "We'll go take a look."

"Okay." I sat next to my sister.

Sloane was staring straight ahead. Was she expecting someone to show up out of nowhere? Why was she watching the stairs like that?

I slipped my arm around her shoulders. I had to make sure everything was okay with her. Besides, she was starting to freak me out staring like that.

We sat there for a few minutes waiting for our friends. I had no idea where Fisher had disappeared to. Most likely the same place everyone else had.

Sloane was right. There was something off with this house. Were the stories really true? Was this place haunted, or cursed?

"There's a door in the kitchen." Larisa came back in, followed by Harlyn. "It won't open either."

"There's more of that paint or whatever it is in there." Harlyn sat next to Sloane. "A whole puddle of it."

"This place is weird." Larisa sat in front of us. "There was no sign of Fisher in there, or anywhere else we looked."

"I told you." Sloane shook her head. "We never should've come here. Now we're trapped. It's too late."

"What are you talking about?" Larisa scratched her cheek. "It's just an empty house. Those stories aren't true."

"What if they are?" Harlyn twisted a strand of hair around her finger. "What happened to everyone? They just disappeared. What about Fisher?"

"Fisher is probably hiding to scare you." Larisa looked into the next room. "He's been rude to you all night. I don't know why you deal with him."

"He's not hiding." Sloane looked at me. "Fisher isn't coming back. The house already got him."

"What?" Harlyn frowned. "Sloane, how do you know that? Do you know something we don't?"

Did she? My sister was acting like a stranger. She had never talked like this before. Was she keeping something from us?

How would she know anything though? This was the first time she had ever been in this house, wasn't it? How else could she know anything?

"I've been doing research on the town for a school project." Sloane wiped her tears away. "Some of those stories are made up. There's another one that is supposed to be true."

"Are you going to tell us about it?" Larisa rested her arms on her legs. "Or should we guess?"

"A long time ago something bad happened here." She paused for a moment. "Something to do with witches or something. They summoned a demon according to the story. It took over the house."

"How?" I leaned back against the door.

"Like it became part of the house." Sloane pulled her hair up into a ponytail. "Supposedly, it makes the house do things. It makes it hurt people. Haven't you ever wondered why so many people go missing here?"

"You're not serious, are you?" Larisa laughed. "That can't be true."

"It is. "Sloane looked at me again. "Why do you think I didn't want to come here?"

"Because you read the story and got scared." Larisa told her. "Are we going to sit here all night, or find a way out?"

What was wrong with Larisa? Why was she getting so angry at Sloane? She was only telling us what she had heard. There was no reason to be so angry.

We were all trapped here. It meant we had to work together. We didn't need to be going in different directions and getting lost. Hadn't we already lost one person tonight.

Where exactly had Fisher gone? I know he loved to mess with Harlyn, but this was extreme for him. He didn't make her worry about him like this. Something had to have happened to him.

"What can we do?" Harlyn chewed her lip. "We don't even know what happened to Fisher. What if he's hurt?"

"You can't think like that." I told her. "He's somewhere playing a game. He just wants to mess with you because it's Halloween."

"Then, where did everyone else go?" Larisa snapped.

"Larisa, are you okay?" Harlyn frowned. "You're yelling at everyone for nothing. That's not like you."

"There's nothing wrong with me." She stood up. "I'm not going to sit here and look stupid. You three can do that."

"Larisa, wait." Harlyn watched her walk down the hallway.

"Is she okay?" Sloane chewed her lip. "She's acting weird."

"I know." Harlyn frowned. "I've never seen her act like that before."

Neither had I. Larisa was usually the happy-go-lucky type. Nothing ever got her down. She didn't snap at people. Was she just mad because we were stuck in this house?

We couldn't ask her until she came back. I had no idea where she'd gone. I assumed the kitchen was back that way, but hadn't been any further than the doorway.

Sloane still looked terrified. Was the story about the house true? It was pretty creepy to think about. I didn't want to think about demons and witches. I definitely didn't want to think about a house that could hurt people.

Could I be wrong? Was the story true? I didn't want to stick around to find out.

Chapter Three

I looked at my watch. It had been half an hour since Larisa had stomped off. Where could she have gone? None of us wanted to go anywhere by ourselves and Sloane hadn't moved.

Were Fisher and Larisa in this together? I wanted to believe they were messing with us. It was better than thinking of them being hurt. Could everyone be playing a trick on the three of us?

There was no noise in the house at all. It made this even creepier. It was also getting colder inside. I had no idea how to make things better for the two of them.

The storm raged on outside while we sat on the floor of an abandoned house. This was the worst Halloween ever. I doubted any of us ever celebrated this holiday again. That's if we got out of this place.

"Where could she have gone?" Harlyn sighed. "She's never acted this way. Do you think it could be the house?"

"I don't know." I looked from her to my sister.

She was the only one who seemed to know anything about this place. Maybe we should've done some research before coming here. None of us had believed the things we'd been told our entire lives.

Sloane hadn't mentioned anyone acting strangely after being here. It was possible no one knew that part of the story. If no one got out of the house they couldn't tell anything.

"You mean like the house making her change somehow?" Sloane scratched her cheek. "I guess it's possible. If the demon makes the house do things, maybe it controls people too."

"This sounds like a horror movie." I shook my head. "Can we leave now?"

"I wish." My sister looked at the stairs. "Larisa?"

My gaze followed hers. Larisa was standing at the top of the stairs. She was staring at us as if we were invisible. Her eyes were glazed over and her hands were covered in whatever that was on the floor. Could it really be blood?

Harlyn went to her best friend. She had been so worried. This was only going to make things worse for her. She led Larisa back to where we were sitting. Could she tell us what had happened to her?

"Larisa, are you okay?" Harlyn put her arm around her.

"They're dead." Larisa looked at her hands. "All of them."

"Who?" I took a deep breath.

"The kids from the party." Larisa swallowed hard. "I found them upstairs in a bedroom. I don't know how I got there."

"You don't remember storming off?" Sloane took her cape off, handing it to Larisa. "You can wipe your hands on that."

"Thanks." She forced a smile. "The last thing I remember is us looking for Fisher."

"Sloane was telling us what she learned about this place for a school project." Harlyn told her. "You got angry, yelled at us and left."

"I yelled at you?" Larisa looked at Sloane. "I'm sorry. Did anyone find Fisher?"

"No." I leaned back against the wall. "He wasn't up there?"

"I didn't see him." She stood up suddenly. "We need to get out of here."

"How?" Harlyn asked. "The door won't open. I don't want to leave Fisher if someone's hurting people."

"It's not someone." Sloane stood up as well. "It's the house. We came inside and it won't let us leave."

"Let's break a window." I shrugged my shoulders. "We can get out that way."

"What can we use to break it?" Sloane asked me. "There's a baseball bat over there."

She was right once again. I guess someone had used it for their costume. I would use it to get them to safety. It didn't matter if I got out as long as they did.

I hoped it actually broke the window and not the bat. I had no idea what it was made out of. It could be plastic for all we knew. Harlyn handed it to me. Definitely not plastic. It was a metal ball bat.

I made sure they covered their eyes before I swung the bat. Nothing happened the first time it hit the window. It might take a few tries.

"River, wait." Harlyn grabbed my arm.

"What's wrong?" I turned to face her and Larisa.

"Did you hear that noise?" Larisa wrapped her arms around her middle. "It sounded like someone was being hurt."

"I didn't hear anything." I said, staring at my sister. "Sloane, what is it?"

"Upstairs." She covered her mouth with her hands.

We all watched in horror as Fisher was thrown down the stairs. He landed at the bottom with a sickening thud. There was blood all over him.

Harlyn bent down to check on him. I knew it was too late to help him. The angle of his neck was a definite sign. My best friend was gone.

I had a feeling he was only the first of us to meet this fate. This was a house of nightmares. It wouldn't stop until we were gone.

"River, let go of my foot." Larisa said suddenly.

"I'm not touching you." I took a deep breath as she was pulled down the hallway.

"Larisa." Harlyn grabbed her hand. "River, help me."

"Hold on." I grabbed onto Harlyn. "Pull her back to the door."

We made it almost to where Sloane was sitting when something knocked us backwards. Larisa's screams filled the air as she disappeared. I sat up slowly looking around. What had hit us? Was it the house, or the demon?

Harlyn was sitting next to Fisher hugging her knees. What were we going to do now? The house had taken two of our friends. If we didn't try to escape it would take us next.

I picked the bat up again. It was time to stop playing games with this place. We were leaving as soon as I got this window broken.

"Cover your eyes." I swallowed hard. "It's time to get out of here."

"Be careful, River." Sloane turned her back to me.

I swung the bat as hard as I could, but nothing happened. There was no way these windows wouldn't break. I just needed to keep hitting it. It would be better if I had something bigger to use. Something with more force.

The window finally started to crack. It wasn't much, but at least it was breaking. I had to get enough of it out of the way for Sloane and Harlyn to get through.

A noise from upstairs caught my attention. Why did it sound like people were running up there? The footsteps were coming down the stairs towards us. How was that possible? There was nobody there.

We were in serious trouble. Was this the house playing tricks on us? Was it the ghosts of everyone the house had killed? I didn't want to know.

"River, what's that?" Harlyn pointed to the stairs.

I could see what looked like shadows standing up there. They were black masses with long, skinny fingers and red glowing eyes. Had they summoned more than one demon here? Or was this the work of that one demon?

One of them ran down the stairs towards us. I took a deep breath as it grabbed Harlyn by the throat.

Chapter Four

"River, do something." Sloane grabbed my arm. "We have to help her."

"I don't know what to do." I shook my head. "How do you stop a shadow?"

"Wait." Sloane took a flashlight out of her pocket.

I watched her shine it at the shadow figure. It let out a demonic yell before dropping Harlyn to the ground. I couldn't believe it worked.

Harlyn crawled over to us. I could see the welts on her neck from the thing's death grip. What had it planned to do to her? Were we even safe in this spot? I doubted it.

I looked around the room. Whatever that thing was, it was gone now. So were the ones at the top of the stairs.

"What was that?" Harlyn clutched at her throat. "Is that what hurt Fisher and Larisa?"

"It had to be, right?" I hugged her. "Are you okay?"

"I think so." She wiped her tears away. "Thanks to Sloane. How did you know that would work?"

"I didn't." She confessed. "I just figured it was made of shadows, maybe it doesn't like light."

"Is that the only flashlight you have?" I asked her.

"Yes, but it has a brand new battery in it." Sloane smiled at me. "I figured we might need it coming here."

"I'm glad you're always prepared." I kissed the top of her head. "What about your phone? We can use the flashlights on them too."

"Fully charged and turned off until I need it." My sister looked at me, then Harlyn.

"Mine's eighty percent." Harlyn stuffed the device back in her pocket. "I also have Larisa's She must've dropped it, but it's sixty-five."

"Good." I checked mine as well. "Mine is charged pretty good as well. Leave them off until we need them."

"We can't stand here all night." Harlyn shivered. "Those things might come back."

She had a point. We could try to wait it out until daylight, but that was hours away. We might need to find somewhere else to hide for a bit. I knew Sloane wanted to stay by the door. I didn't think it was a good idea any longer. Not after the shadow grabbed Harlyn.

It was pretty dark in the rest of the house. Most of the candles had gone out. Maybe we could go into the living room. If there was a fireplace we could build a fire. The light might keep those things away.

"Sloane, can I borrow your flashlight for a sec?" I took it from her. "I might have a plan."

"Where are you going?" She demanded. "I told you it isn't safe."

"It's not safe here either." I pulled her into a hug. "If there's a fireplace we can build a fire. We can stay by the light of it."

"I hope it works." Harlyn followed them into the next room. "I'll grab those flyers by the door. We can use them to start the fire."

"Sloane, can you hold the light?" I handed it back to her.

I tossed some of the flyers into the fireplace, along with pieces of wood from a broken chair. It would also warm the house up a little as long as we found more wood.

My gaze moved to the wall next to the fireplace. There were logs stacked up. They would come in handy. I grabbed a couple of them and put them on the fire.

Taking the flashlight I looked around the room. I was hoping they had left something to eat, or drink. I saw a few bottles of soda sitting on a table. That was a good thing. I put them next to our spot on the floor.

"What's that?" Harlyn pointed to another table. "Is it some kind of lamp?"

"It's a lantern." Sloane grabbed it running back to us. "It's battery operated."

She flipped it on. It lit up half of the room. It was even better than the firelight. We all sat down next to one another trying to get warm. If we stayed here we might be able to keep whatever those things were away.

We listened to the crackling of the fire. It was the only noise in the house. I was pretty sure things wouldn't be that way for long. What would this place try next? We had already lost so many people tonight. Why couldn't the place just let us leave?

We should have listened to Sloane. We could've stayed at our house and had fun. At least we would all be alive right now. If I hadn't agreed to drive everyone here this wouldn't have happened. I knew it was all my fault.

Harlyn and Sloane were hugging one another. I wished I could get them onto the porch. If they weren't inside they might be okay. Of course, we had no idea of knowing if it would even work. For all I knew the house would never let us go. Whatever those things were, they might follow us home.

My thoughts went to Fisher and Larisa again. How were we going to tell their parents what had happened to them? I knew Fisher's father would say it was my fault. He would be right about it though.

"Are you guys thirsty?" I opened a bottle of the soda. "It's not cold, but it's better than nothing."

"It could be worse." Harlyn took a drink. "We could be stuck with nothing at all. I mean, we have no food anyway."

"We'll be okay." Sloane smiled at her. "How long do you think we'll be able to stay here without anything happening?"

"I wish I knew." I sat the soda back where it was. "I think the light might be keeping them away. I just hope there's enough wood to keep the fire going all night. We could always break the table and use it."

"What if the firelight isn't bright enough?" Harlyn chewed on her lip. "This lantern won't last forever, and neither will our phones."

"We'll figure it out when it happens." I put my arm around her shoulders. "I promise, I'll protect the two of you."

"What if they hurt you?" Sloane leaned against me as well. "I don't want either of you to get hurt."

"The house is going to do that." Harlyn shook her head. "Look what it did to everyone else. Why are we any different?"

She was right once again. I had to try to make them feel better somehow. We couldn't think about what was going on around us. We needed something to keep us occupied for a bit.

We could play some kind of game. Maybe they would want to talk about stuff. There were several things we could do. Although, I needed to keep a watch on the doorway for those things to return.

The silence took over the room again. I wanted something to happen. It was better than waiting to be surprised. Who would the house try to get next? It had already come after Harlyn once. Would it stop before it got her? I had to make sure it did.

I refused to let it do anything to them. They were only here because me and Fisher wanted to come. It wasn't their fault. None of us had known about the curse this place carried. The stories had been told to scare us, nothing more.

I had a feeling there were some older people in town who knew the truth about this place. They had most likely lost someone here as well.

I wasn't sure how long we had been sitting in the same spot. I tossed more wood on the fire so it wouldn't go out. That seemed to be helping keep those things at bay for now.

My gaze moved to my sister. What was she looking at now? She gasped right before something grabbed her wrist.

"River, help me." Sloane screamed. "Make it stop.'

"Sloane." Harlyn grabbed her other wrist. "Don't let it take her."

"I've got you." I grabbed her under her arms. "Harlyn, help me pull her back."

We kept pulling as hard as we could. Whatever had a hold of her was stronger than all three of us. It seemed a whole lot stronger than the other one. We were all being pulled towards the living room door, and away from the light.

"River, please." Sloane cried out. "I don't want to go."

"Sloane, hold on." I put my foot against the doorframe to brace myself.

Harlyn did the same thing on the other side. As long as we didn't let go this thing couldn't take her. We had to hold her tighter.

Something hit the floor next to my foot. When had she put her flashlight back in her pocket? As fast as I could I grabbed it shining it at the doorway. The thing let go of her letting out an eerie scream.

"Get back to the fireplace." I yelled. "As close as you can."

"The light's not working." Harlyn hugged Sloane. "That thing got her right beside it. We have to do something else."

I sighed just as something grabbed my foot. The next thing I knew I was being dragged into the hallway.

Chapter Five

"River," Sloane ran after me. "Leave him alone."

"Sloane, grab him." Harlyn lunged for my hand. "River, use the flashlight."

I did what she told me, but it didn't work this time. That wasn't good. I thought the light hurt these things in some way. Had we been wrong? Or was this something completely different?

Whatever it was we were all being dragged to the stairs. Would it throw us like it had Fisher? Or would it do something else to us? I didn't want to find out.

"You have to let go." I looked at them both.

"We can't." Sloane started to cry. "We can't let it take you."

"You don't have a choice." I tried kicking at it. "If you don't let go it'll take you too.'

"Then it'll take us." Harlyn pulled harder. "I'm not letting it take you. We have to protect one another if we want to live."

I watched in horror as she was pulled backward. This couldn't be happening. There was no way Sloane could help us both. Especially not when she was in danger as well.

Sloane's eyes went wide with fear as a shadowy hand grabbed her around the throat. It slammed her into the front door. She wasn't moving. How bad was she hurt?

Harlyn was screaming from somewhere down the hall. I could only imagine what it was doing to her. I felt myself being pulled up the stairs before slamming into a wall.

My gaze moved around the hallway. Those shadows were everywhere. Their glowing red eyes stared at me. What would they do now?

Another sight caught my attention. There were bodies everywhere as well. Some were missing arms, legs, and even heads. Was that what was going to happen to me?

"River, where are you?" Sloane called out. "Please answer me."

"I'm upstairs." I called back.

"I'm coming to help you.' She started up the stairs.

"No, stay there." I yelled. "It's not safe up here. Stay by the door."

"Are you okay?" She asked.

Was I? I probably wouldn't be for long. I made my way back toward the stairs so I could see her. I had to keep her away from those things.

Sloane was standing against the door staring up at me. She looked okay. Why hadn't they tried hurting her? Was it because she knew the story of the house? Whatever it was I would use it to our advantage.

"Let my sister go." I stared at those shadowy figures. "She didn't want to come here. She's just a kid."

"She told you not to come here" One of the shadows said suddenly. "She was the only one who listened to the warnings."

"Does that mean she won't be hurt?' I demanded. "Let her leave.'

"We can't do that. No one can open the doors until daylight. You will both die here."

"River, run." Sloane threw something up the stairs.

I ran to my little sister. Did she have a plan? I hoped so.

Sloane hugged me as tight as she could. I realized we were against the door, but she was in front of me. What was she doing?

"River, Can you reach the doorknob?"

"Yes, why."

"Open the door.' She smiled at me.

I opened the door causing us to fall to the floor. We were on the porch. How?

"It's daylight." Sloane hugged me again.

We had made it until morning. I helped her up, dragging her with me to the car. We had to tell everyone the truth about this place. We had to make sure our friends were remembered. I would make sure no one ever came here again, even if it had to be torn down.

"Are you okay?" Sloane leaned against the car.

"Yeah, are you?" I kissed the top of her head.

"I am now." She wiped her tears away. "What's going on now?"

I took a deep breath as the house started to shake. The screams coming from inside were horrible. The house was caving in. We were still too close.

"Get in the car.' I opened her door. "We have to go.'

"Hurry." Sloane cried.

I drove away from the house. My gaze moved to the rearview mirror. There were lights flashing from the windows. A strong wind suddenly started taking the house apart, like it was in a tornado. Was it because we had escaped? Had we broken the curse?

I had no intention of ever coming back here. Sloane wouldn't either. This house had taken so many lives. We had gotten lucky. No way would we give it another chance to get us.

Our friends were gone. We couldn't bring them back, but we could tell the story. Make sure everyone in town knows what would happen if they went there. And we were never celebrating Halloween again.

"I'm sorry I brought you guys here." I took my phone out to call for help.

"It's not your fault, River." Sloane kissed my cheek. "Do you think anyone will believe us?"

I had no idea if they would. As long as she was safe I didn't care what they believed.

An hour later we were sitting in the living room with our parents. The police had gone to that house to check it out. They had told us there was no house there. It had simply vanished. Did it mean we were all safe now? I sure hoped so.

The End

Wear Wolf

Ashon Ruffins

The sirens blared and the bright white spotlights cut through the top of the tree line at the concrete monstrosity of a facility at the bottom of the hill. The echo of the high-pitched sound was offensive. I knew the facility would be trouble.

Fifteen years ago, I made the woods of the North Dakota home after burying my husband. Nobody will find him. Serves the drunk right for killing my dog. The smile on my face was the last thing he saw. I had this place now. It gave me everything I was looking for: peace, quiet, and the beauty of nature. It wasn't perfect. Michael still showed his ugly mug around here now and then. It's been more often these days. Even in death, he still stared at me with his damned silly grin. He always stood in the same corner of the living room, near the window and the front door, with dead white eyes and his throat still sliced open. Typical Michael, even in death he tried to steal my peace. Is it any wonder I needed to be free from him? Free from everyone? Fifteen years without a neighbor, surrounded only by trees and the native wildlife. Peace. I had much to work through, and I needed every minute of those fifteen years. They built the facility a few years ago. Since then, it had spewed out the constant noise pollution of diesel trucks and intercom announcements down there.

"What the hell is going on now?" I mumbled. I walked toward the front door, past Michael. He stood in the room's corner, his head turned as his dead eyes lingered on me.

Standing on the front porch of the cabin, warm breath visible when it touched the bitter cold air, I peered through the tight frame of the binoculars to see what the fuss was about. There was nothing to see. Nothing but a few flashing lights and tons of fallen snow. They clearly searched for something. Whatever it was, it's important. The facility was always surrounded by rumors.

Whenever I went into town for supplies, the low brow morons that lived there would gossip about it. Initially, it began with typical conspiracy theories associated with secret facilities. Ridiculous tales of refrigerated alien bodies, bio-weapons, and inter-dimensional travel were at the forefront of the rumors. The latest one I heard appeared to have stuck with me was that it was some sort of genetic engineering facility that focused on the crossbreeding of species. They conducted experiments on creating animal and human hybrids and kept them inside. Tales of twisted genetically altered freaks held in glass prisons for observation after being developed in a lab. The thought of it horrified me. I don't like animal cruelty, just ask Michael. The siren stopped and the spotlight ceased its search. Darkness once again owned the woods. A deafening silence followed.

"Finally!" I yelled, tossing my hands in the air.

With the closure of my eyes, I tilted my head back and inhaled the cold air, filling my lungs, as I took in the quiet. No blaring sirens. No bright search lights. Only the pleasurable memories of blood as it poured from Michael's throat. I smiled. The perfect Halloween night, costumed, candy, and quiet. Although the one-piece cat costume was not ideal to wear standing outside without any coverings for my legs.

The perfection of the night was short-lived as the high-pitched howl of a wolf echoed in the distance among the trees. A wolf's howl was unfamiliar here. Since I arrived, there had been few in the area. It was not what I'd hoped. Wolves had a special place in my heart and I spent some free time reading and watching videos about them. The sound of the howl was different. It was deeper, louder, as if it was from something much larger.

Back inside my cabin, eager to get back in front of the comforting warmth of the fireplace, I extended my hands and rubbed them together, hoping to eliminate the chill that assaulted me. I exhaled sharply; the white visibility of my breath caused me to shake my head in disbelief. The cold didn't follow me inside. The cold was here because of him. Anxiously, I attempted to catch a glimpse of the corner, aware of what awaited me. Michael still stood in the corner, same grin and same dead milky white soulless eyes. This time something was different about the way he looked at me. He lifted his hand and pointed at me with his index finger extended. His nails were black and covered with dirt.

"If I could, I'd slit your throat again and instead of burying you, I would burn your body and make sure nothing was left. Stop with the torture. Just kill me already."

Somehow my tone was calm but my hands trembled from the overbearing cold. Whatever he was warning me about, I didn't care. I sat in the chair and picked up a piece of chocolate from the candy bowl next to me. The orange tinted glass bowl with tiny hand painted bats on it was a favorite. Won in a costume contest at a friend's party. I miss Halloween in the city. The décor and the costumed kids brought a fun element that gave me joy. One of the few joyful things I shared with Michael. I sat in the recliner near the fireplace, the heat almost non-existent. Thoughts of the sirens and Michael's filthy pointed finger lingered.

A howl again echoed in the night's air. I rush to the window and peer outside, still unsure why the alarm went off. The alarm and the wolf howl were no coincidence.

"What the hell are those?" I whispered.

In the depths of the darkness of the wood line, two yellow round objects glowed and hovered. The silence of the night was shattered once more by a low rumble emanating from the same area as the glowing eyes. My chest pounded rapidly, filled with anticipation of what it could be. I knew what it was. Excited I would finally see one up close, I smiled.

After all these years, I will lay eyes on the perfect animal. I turned and rushed to the refrigerator, grabbed the fresh steak I planned to prepare for dinner, and ran back to the front door. Michael was still in the corner watching me with that shit-eating grin, no longer pointing.

I stepped out onto the porch. My skin bumped over due to the cold air. Illuminating the area, the orange hue of the jack-o'-lantern was the sole source of light. As the fur-covered beast emerged from the woods, my eyes widened with excitement. I've waited so long to see one. The wolf trekked toward the cabin. Even at a distance, I could see its brow curled. Its blood thirsty eyes and sharp canine's baring down on me as I unwrapped the sixteen-ounce porterhouse steak. The blood of the steak soaked through the plastic wrapping and covered my fingers.

"My word. Aren't you a fella? I could have fed my husband to you. Would have made clean up a lot easier," I whispered, loud enough for it to hear me.

Still, where did it come from? No wolves in this area for fifteen years and now one pops up after all that commotion on the other side of the hill. I tossed the meaty steak at its paws. Its head never wavered; hungry eyes never averted away from me. This wasn't what I imagined. The wolf's growl was apparent even from the distance between us. It started toward me. Its massive paws sank in the snow's thickness, one after another. Legs tingled, unsure if from cold or rising apprehension as the beast neared. I back away toward the door, mirroring its steps. This made little sense to me. There was no animal that I feared. I loved them all, especially wolves. This... thing was unique. It was mean, and it was hungry. It was as if I could feel its intentions toward me and they were not good. Its pace quickened. The stride covered the ground faster than I could get to the door. Sound of its teeth snapping became louder as I struggled to open the door.

I slammed the door behind me, its claws feverishly scratched at the door. I leaned against it and tried to slow my breathing. Inhaling deeply, I cut my eyes to the corner of the room. Michael turned his head toward me. His sinister grin was wider than before. His soulless eyes conveyed joy as he watched me run inside in terror. The scratching ceased as I crawled away from Michael in the cabin living room. With shallow breaths, I made my way under the nearest window and lifted my eyes above the windowsill. The darkness consumed the night and the light inside the cabin only allowed my reflection to stare back at me.

"Shit. It's too bright in here," I mumbled, still feeling Michael's eyes upon me. "What the hell are you looking at?"

No response. Only his goddamn stare.

A growl once again presented itself on the other side. This time closer to the window where I stood. Glowing amber eyes pierced the darkness and stared back through the window. My hands trembled at the sight of them. Leaning forward, I stepped closer, peering outside, only jerking back when shards of glass flew at me. The beast jumped through the window, its massive paws and canines lead its assault. Arms covering my face, I fell to the hard wooden floor. Blood poured from my hands as I crab walked backwards over the broken glass trying to put as much distance between me and the beast. It now towered over me in the living room. Breathing shallow, my chest rose and fell as I struggled to get on my feet. The stench of the mixture of blood and feces permeated off of its filthy fur assaulted my nostrils and turned my stomach. I've read nothing about a single wolf which behaved this aggressively. Its size and behavior were unusual, and the glow of its eyes was unnatural.

As I stood, the arm of Michael caught my eyes, as he again lifted it and pointed at the beast in my cabin. Focused on Michael's dead hand, something that sounded like a broken growl filled the room. The louder it became, the sooner I realized it wasn't broken... there was a rhythmic sound. It was laughter. A sinister laugh resonated in my bones and sent chills over me.

"W-What the fuck are you?" I yelled, with a curled brow and tears in my eyes.

A patch of furred flesh fell from the wolf onto the floor of the cabin. Another followed. More slid from its blood covered frame as its claws retracted and paws flattened and split. I watched as its canine frame buckled and reformed, its moist blood-soaked flesh slid about the floor. Its body jerked violently, and its laugh persisted. I watched as it made its way to its re-formed feet. The snout fell from its face, exposing its human shaped nasal cavity and jagged teeth. I stood in shock and watched at what I thought was impossible. The creature sprinted toward me and struck me in the head. Everything went black.

The enticing aroma that filled the air awakened me. Blurred vision, I could only tell I was facing the kitchen and there was a large red figure that stood inside. That thing must have knocked me unconscious and tied me to a chair. As I regained consciousness, the twine burned my bound wrist and my leg throbbed with unbearable pain. My eyes came into focus, and I screamed in agony at the sight of the sizable chuck of flesh missing from my leg.

"Looks like you're finally awake. I'm glad. I hoped I didn't hit you too hard," said the creature that stood in the kitchen. The voice was raspy, a blend of animal growl and human.

I screamed again after I lay my eyes on it. The creature stood in front of the stove, stirring the food of a pan. Its muscular structure, covered in a thick blood-colored mucus, was exposed. The eyes bulged from the skull and its teeth were jagged and sharp. The perfect tool of a carnivore. I watched as it stuck its finger into the pan, the meat was still red, much like a rare steak. Blood trickled down the side of its mouth as it chewed.

Somehow, without flesh for eyelids and brow, it conveyed a look of elation as it tilted its head back in enjoyment. "I knew you were worth it. You taste divine. I've watched for years as others prepared food in the lab. Sometimes they would share, but always raw. Always subpar. You, my dear, are not subpar."

"Why are you doing this? What the hell are you?" Tears fell from my eyes as the pain from my leg became unbearable.

"You know what I am. You saw me," its voice was still raspy as it chewed.

I watched in terror as it walked closer to me, a trail of bloody footprints left behind it. "I saw a wolf. A beautiful creature of nature. You are something from hell. What I saw was impossible."

"I only wear the wolf form to hunt. This is what I am. A devourer of flesh." It picked up a large kitchen knife off the table near it. The thick blood colored mucus dripped from it as it continued toward me.

Michael appeared in the kitchen's corner, his dead white eyes and sinister grin affixed. I glared at him as his face seemed to fill with satisfaction. Agony returned as the knife slid into my thigh again and sliced more flesh away. Warm blood poured down my calf. I screamed for help into the void of darkness toward the broken window. The room spun as it continued to slice pieces away from me. The aroma of sizzling flesh once again filled the air as my eyes became fixated on Michael and that fucking grin. It was the last thing I saw before my eyes closed.

Souls Waiting

Beth Bayley

The Souls stood in the darkness waiting for the light
Staring into the mists of time

The dim light brightened exploding on the bonfire
Shooting flames high into the night sky

The Souls shuffled back waiting for the veil to thin
Murmuring with excitement as the heard familiar voices

People laughed and sang old songs
Celebrating Samhain, dancing around the fire as the veil thinned

The Souls moved closer to the veil
Smiling and laughing at their descendants full of happiness

Everyone danced faster, blowing kisses to their Ancestors
Telling them they weren't forgotten

The fire died down. The veil closed. Celebrations over for another year
The longing would begin again in the mists of time.

Paralicyst

Michael P.A Harding

It was late in the evening when Sadie's eyes began to falter and slowly closed against her will. Lines of text and data danced and juddered in a disorderly fashion, refusing to conform, deftly eluding her vain attempts to focus. They were free now, revelling in sharp staccato movements beyond the constraints of their ordered world. Nothing more could be gleaned from them and no actions taken despite their rearrangement. This didn't stop her from triple checking once more that the work was securely saved. If only she was less efficient, she could take more time or delay the inevitable. Sadly, Sadie was far too proficient for that, one of the safeguards she needed was to appear professional.

Neuroticism was an understatement, much to the chagrin of her colleagues, in regards to her work ethic. They could never understand how many constraints she placed upon herself to appear as a functioning member of society. They awoke from poor sleep or sweet dreams, arriving at the office a touch bleary eyed at worst. Respite was a luxury she couldn't conceive of. Sleep was a hunting ground for nightmares, one Sadie survived, night after night, but only by observing her ritual.

Every action was performed slowly, as she spoke aloud the confirmation of each act. Ritual is a blend of performance and task, and this one was no different. Lessons imparted by the ceremony were for her and her alone, to re-affirm identity and to tether her to a bland reality. Sleep was akin to wading into dark waters; thick with swirling sediment and laden with the scent of rot. Each stage of her performance was intricately choreographed, as if she was a will-o-the-wisp lighting small candles on long stemmed lilies on the surface of a marsh. Sleep, as she referred to it, was far too treacherous and cunning to allow repetition. It would divine her intentions and use them against her. Memory was her most powerful guide in the dark, the memory of who she was, or at least the facade she'd constructed. There was no joy or purpose in her life's achievements; everything she did was simply another tether, another reason to survive the night. Sadie had outran the nightmare for so long that escape and denial were her only companions. It had become her purpose and her singular joy, to deny her last scream to the predator, until it starved in the dark or she could run no further.

The ritual began with the front door to her home. It symbolised her challenge to the nightmare on each night she returned to the house. Her survival until sunrise was proof she'd lived to see another day and for a few hours, Sadie gained a temporary end to her torment. She walked slowly to the front door, cold hands rubbing her neck and trying in vain to ease the tension she found there. When she reached the threshold to her home, she paused, placed her hands on her hips, and sighed once more. Every night without fail she had to fight down the desperation, the despair and the questions of, why her? It had become easier over the years to simply accept it as her lot, but she had never entirely snuffed out the restless anguish coiled within her. In silent resignation, Sadie allowed the burden of futility to set in until she repressed her meek yearning for escape, and got on with her business.

"I am Sadie Melinowe", she declared firmly, forcing her eyes to stay open as she turned purposefully from the closed door to the central hallway of her home.

"I am Sadie Melinowe, and this is my house, this is my life, and in the morning, I will see the sunrise", she said firmly, staring down the hallway, daring something to appear.

Satisfied the coward would remain unseen until she slept, Sadie turned to the right and flicked the old, heavy light switch to the entrance way. The house was built a century ago, with two wings either side of the main hallway, a study and games room on the left and a living room, kitchen and laundry on the other. Light switches for one room were positioned on the adjoining wall of the room that came before it. Her ritual had been shaped by this, the steps of the dance determined by how best she could enter and exit a space whilst remaining in the light. Holding onto truths was the only way to survive, and so whilst Sadie controlled the lights, she also held back the dark. Every step she took was measured and decisive, a strategy for survival honed by the truths of trauma she had collected throughout many sleepless nights.

Sadie entered each room in turn and ensured nothing was out of place. Standing in one room whilst it was filled with light, she forced herself to stare into the darkness of the next. Counting down with long, slow breaths, Sadie switched on the next light and stepped over the threshold. Lies swam in darkness and caroused the shadows into play, and she fought to banish the imagined threats with sheer will, before illuminating the space. Not until she had calmed the slight shake in her breathing, did she permit herself to stop staring into the dark. Continuing this pattern until she returned to the front door of the home, Sadie challenged the darkness once again. Now the aging bulbs of the home dimmed and cooled around her and only the hallway light remained. *'Everything is simply in stasis when the light goes out'* she assured herself, *'the house is just awaiting the dawn in quiet stillness'.* She would be the same, Sadie knew, simply still and quiet, until she could escape from sleep.

Embracing darkness was one challenge but willingly entering her bedroom was another entirely. Ritual and procedure promised numbing, perfunctory action, that would absolve her of conscious thought. Tiredness evaporated and exhaustion was forgotten, as Sadie embraced functionality. It made the acceptance of finality even more difficult when she found herself staring down the narrow corridor.

Every night she would stand here, weighed down by the burden of her torture, whilst considering the benefits of surrender. Surely there was some way her pursuer could not reach her, she reflected bitterly.

Stepping forwards slowly, head lowered and hands still on hips, Sadie entered the hallway. In front of her, the dim yellow glow of the hallway light did its best to counter the deep darkness behind. Running fingertips across the bare walls, she reflected idly, as she often did. For years she had lived in the house and yet never once had she bothered to make it a home. Why would she, though? People who had lives and purpose were given cause to reflect on the memories they hung from their walls. Sadie had nothing worth remembering, and the thought of seeing her ephemeral existence reflected back at her was more horrifying than what she was about to endure. Pausing beneath the hallway's pull cord light switch, Sadie's shoulders sank and her eyes closed. A long sigh escaped her and with a languid reach for the cord, the hallway too, was plunged into darkness.

Sadie stepped into her room and left the door slightly ajar, leaning against the cold wooden frame. Despondent and defeated, she waited for her eyes to adjust to the darkness, where the dull orange of her bedside lamp spilled into the hallway. It was enough for Sadie to see that the scratched wooden floors bore no new scars after the light had gone out. She contemplated walking out right there and then leaving no memory of her life behind, save for her work. Allowing herself a moment, Sadie began to wonder how long it would take someone to discover some trace of her.

Indulgent melancholy soon gave way to deeper exhaustion. The pulsing ache around her eyes and the stiffness in her bones left Sadie threadbare and worn. Shuffling over to her bed, she pulled back the thin covers of cold, colourless fabric and collapsed. Pushing herself beneath the covers and resting her head on the single pillow that lay nearest the lamp, Sadie made a meagre attempt to cover herself. Cold was an ally to her, it was harder to sleep when you caught a chill, and it had often provided escape. She hardly noticed it now though as her breathing slowed and for the briefest of moments, Sadie's eyes closed and her body was peaceful.

This sanguine state was broken when the small tufts of cloth, dispersed unevenly across her cloth sheets, pressed into her skin with an ever increasing insistence. They tended to be annoying, if she tried to cocoon herself in bed, but evidently tonight this had been done for her. Instinct woke her and she began pressing against her bonds. Not only were the covers wrapped tightly around her, but as she strained her eyes and looked down, it appeared as though they were moving. Where reality evaporated and illusion took hold, dreams were not far behind. Dreams at least offered a salubrious sanctum where the recesses of her mind could sort and order what provocations the subconscious could not discard. In the shadow of that order however, chaos reigned, nightmare stalked, and Sadie knew it was time to run.

Pain was not her cause for urgency in escape, rather it was the illusion of warmth that ran from unseen wounds. Blood was a vital tether to the reality she couldn't abandon. She wasn't really bleeding, of course, but the flow of crimson was like sand in the hourglass. Tufts of bound thread became cruelly sharp, twisted into barbed wire that lacerated her flesh. Every moment she bled, she was less and less likely to wake. In distant reality she was in the same position she'd collapsed in, eyes open and unblinking as paralysis held her. Before Sadie learned to escape her predator, she'd awoken in hospitals, surrounded by a new nightmare of breathing tubes, monitors and the echo of concerned voices. 'You cannot die of sleep paralysis', said all the specialists and experts assuredly. Perhaps not, she thought, but exsanguination of the soul through the exhaustion of the flesh was a real and ever present threat.

Reminders of reality were powerful here, able to alter the imagined world she was trapped in. Pulling hard on her tether, the slowly constricting wire loosened into loops of idle string, falling from the bed like languid snakes. She willed herself to rise slowly, but suddenly the room whirled and gravity gave way to madness. Sadie, the bed and the barbed wire twine all spun forwards and drifted slowly, like junk jettisoned into space. Her bedroom door was now beneath her, and the innate human dread of deep, dark water ran in rivulets from her mind. The borders of the door frame now became dark rocks in a raging sea which couldn't be held back.

This manipulation was a mistake on behalf of her predator, a distraction it had attempted many times and one she'd always narrowly avoided. Dark water induced panic, but the sense of creeping dread from somewhere beneath her, induced an even greater fear still. Climbing up and over the headboard, her torturer crawled slowly, like a stalking arachnid at the edge of her sight. The door ahead held no fears greater than what lay behind, and so she set her jaw and held her breath. Straining fingers reached for her scalp but clawed only air as Sadie let herself fall away from the bed and into the dark.

Long lines of wood grain turned to churning dark water as a fall of mere meters became miles. Sadie didn't scream, she didn't have the time for luxuries like becoming mindless in her terror. Her predator would be frustrated and furious now his quarry had escaped. Unreality in this realm of nightmare allowed her to perceive the trail she left behind. Blood flowed like crimson cloth and the further she fell, the more threads her hunter could grasp. The flowing strands pulled taut, almost imperceptibly, as hands of flensed and sickly wet flesh eagerly grabbed at the cloth. Sadie turned her head slightly to glimpse blood slick arms, made of too many joints and bones, catapulting towards her. The sight of him always lost her ground. Even as she turned back to the ocean trapped within the door, she knew he was close. Sadie needed to see him, she needed to understand how he was hunting her tonight. Desperation is all she observed, somewhat surprised. Her pursuer was many things, but he had all her nights to stalk her. Impatience was a common trait of his, but desperation was new.

Observing its behaviour engendered logic to madness and gave her a reprieve in the miasmic twilight of paralysis. Sadie's fall turned into a dive and she lanced towards the oncoming ocean like a comet. In a moment he was upon her; she heard bones snap as his arms contorted into a cage and felt his moist breath on the soles of her feet as seven tongues strained to taste her. She speared the dark in a perfect performance of will and defiance. Plunging into the dark she breathed deep, stealing precious moments of distance from her predator. She knew that somewhere in reality, her heart would palpitate and her paralysis would be disrupted. A soul bound between two prisons knew how to ration a pause in the monotony of incarceration. Such meals were rare but invaluable in sustaining her flight from her terror. Long moments had passed since she entered the water and she was completely alone. Perhaps her pursuer was intent to let her sit idle, hoping to lull her into a false sense of security. Sadie simply waited, falling slowly as she devised her next escape.

With a gentleness she didn't expect, she languidly came to rest upon something cold and hard. At first, everything was in darkness, so she reached out and felt for what she had fallen upon. A rough texture like stone met her fingers, but it was hard to tell precisely what it was, as all feeling in this realm of nightmare was like a numb echo in her mind. The echo gained form and shapes emerged, like static spirits in a polaroid, the longer she dared to look. Sadie noticed they were illuminated by a pale, wan light, far above, but how long it had been there she couldn't tell. To her surprise, it was not some trick, but the impression of moonlight, or perhaps a bedside lamp, reaching down towards her. Process was a crucial tether, and she always left the bedside light on in case she was lurched from nightmare into wakefulness during her paralysis. Growing confident her desperate predator had exhausted himself for a moment, she tried to make sense of the senseless realm.

Dead coral stretched out for eons all about her, threaded with dark claret red seaweed, like the stains of clotted blood on cloth. No life was in the reef, it was all dead or dying, but Sadie thought she could make out the impression of bones nearby. Sensing no looming terror on the edge of her sight, she risked a closer look nearer to where she lay. Now she understood why her hunter had not followed her down here. Sadie's chest constricted as suddenly as her consciousness altered from respite to restriction, and her mind beheld the reality of deep water as she began to drown. Convulsing as the depths filled her lungs, she could not scream at the horror all around her. Innumerable mounds of corpses; broken, twisted and strung with rotten flesh, were heaped on the ocean floor, creating valleys of the dead that fed the stagnant sea. Survival kicked in at last and even as she was trapped in the panic of drowning, Sadie raged against her fate and sought freedom. All her struggles only managed to turn the heavy soil of decomposing bodies into a cloying mud that dragged her further down into the corpse reef.

Paralysed in absolute terror, Sadie's immobile body was powerless and her wide, unblinking eyes failed to shut out the grotesque visions. This only served to worsen her predicament, as she sank deeper into the reef of bone which gave way to more rot-mud and bloated flesh. Corpses began to fall in and fill the hole her struggles created. The shimmering light of her lamp pierced the veil of her nightmare for mere moments before being swallowed up by the heaving mounds of death. There was only the terror of entrapment beneath the corpse pile and by the worst realisation of impending mortal peril. Sadie was poised on the very edge of inevitable death and the eternal void. She screamed but made no sound, joining the silent chorus of the corpses that suffocated her.

Thunderous heartbeats drowned out all other sound as paralysis broke and Sadie lurched from darkness into the weak light of morning. Her mind raced and even as her sleep filled eyes opened, she could still see an ocean of screaming corpses that bore her name. Paralysis was slow to wear off and she groaned as her lethargic limbs struggled to move. She wanted to sit up and to not lie in the same position she was in when the reef consumed her. The worst part of the nightmare was even as the details faded like a receding tide, the feeling of terror remained ever strong. The bed creaked as she doubled over, sitting on its edge and trying to breathe through the overwhelming furore of what she'd endured. An hour passed before the hammering of her heart quietened to a dull and distant boom in her chest. The light seeping through the thin blinds of her room became ever brighter but the pervading sense of dread did not ebb away. It was less of a shock now but more a constant tremor within her soul that persisted as she returned to what she knew would ease it; the methodical execution of her banal reality.

Moving from the bedroom to the bathroom and then to the shower and once more to the bedroom was a pattern Sadie knew well. She checked each light in each room was switched on before she entered. Every room was then observed to determine if there were any unseen terrors lurking in her peripheral vision. This continued as she prepared for the day and allowed herself time to mask the exhaustion pervading her daily life. Hardly anyone at her office would consider her as charismatic, but she needed to appear approachable on occasion. It wouldn't do to admonish her staff for their shortcomings without being able to offer an encouraging handshake or smile when discipline had been dispensed. It was all she had; interactions with the other drones and the ability to appear as though she was invested in her work. If anyone was to ask her what she really achieved at the end of each day, Sadie wouldn't know what to say. Her mask of an empowered professional was well and truly ready, but it faltered suddenly, when she reached her front door.

Looming before her, the dark oak door consumed her vision, as though she stood in the desert and beheld a great monolith that consumed the horizon. The door imposed itself upon her as a megalithic structure of impossible vastness. She blinked her tired eyes and sincerely hoped this was merely a false perception from exhaustion. Surely, she thought, the deep age lines of the wood, were not in motion. It was impossible for it to be a heaving, churning mass, where the medullary rays of ancient amber sap crashed together like foamy horses of the sea. Sadie breathed out and tried to control her frayed nerves and the illusion mercifully disappeared. Forcing herself to focus on the day ahead, she put her hand to the door and stopped sharply as she grasped the faded brass handle. Pain lanced up her arm and a terrible cold struck her, forcing her back, confused and scared.

Stumbling away from the door, Sadie's slight touch had been enough to release the lock and the door swung slowly inward. Her breath was cast from her lungs, her chest grew tight and the curtain of reality drew back. The shadow of the door passed across her, nightmare eclipsed reality and she was beneath the sea once more. Surely this was the most cunning and devious trick her tormentor had played yet. How cruel it had become, and all because she had shown the audacity to outpace it for mere moments. Collapsing against the corner of the entrance and hallway, she failed to gain her balance. Pain struck her sharply and her skin was caught on the edge of the old metal light switch. Blood ran in small rivulets down her neck and she knew this was not the faint echo of reality in the world of nightmare. This was warm, visceral and far too real a sensation for the realm of sleep.

A soft breeze passed across her as the door gently bumped against the stopper on the skirting board. Staring out into the achingly bright day outside, she heard muted bird song and the distant sound of a lawn mower whirring across spring grass. For a moment she saw how drab and bland her house had become. Once the warm wooden and copper furnishings had been such a stunning aesthetic for a neighbourhood where so much was new and ever changing. The outside world appeared to her as an impressionist painting. It was distant and preserved from a bygone era and its soft light shone in to illuminate her misery. Her house was devoid of light and life, suppressing all sound and being fit only to obstruct the vibrancy that existed outside of it. The door swung back on its hinges and obscured the vision of possibilities beyond her prison. Sadie felt a distinct sense of loss and sadness for being parted from such a pleasant and peaceful place.

A darkness now loomed within her. Sadie registered a disruption to the usual monotony of existence that fused together form and function in favour of emotion. How long had it been since she'd truly experienced the raw and unfiltered fury of an unbidden feeling that wasn't pure terror? Even within her dreams, the sense of bitter satisfaction she experienced from outpacing her predator was simply a performance on behalf of her waking consciousness. Grimacing from pain, Sadie rose slowly to sit upright and briefly yearned to touch the handle once again. She wished to dive into the waters as she did in her dream, for the fleeting chance that this time, she might emerge above the waves. Briefly she hoped maybe in the dark ocean world, there was a gentle current that flowed like the breeze beyond the door. Maybe it would carry her to rest in a coral of abundant life, and she would be lulled into a gentle sleep by the rhythmic heartbeat of an opal dream.

Even as Sadie felt the forgotten promise of emotion reaching through the ether, she knew it was foolishness to permit its existence. This happened from time to time; at least, that was the way she remembered it. On occasion Sadie played tricks on herself, like a child waiting on the step for a wish which would never arrive. She looked about her and forced the banal reality she saw there to set in. She had not felt anything, Sadie told herself, and she would not allow childish fantasies to form hopes, only to have them crushed when she was inevitably trapped in a sleepless nightmare once again. Such visions of mundane suburbia had appeared so wonderful but now were absent from her mind. Why torture herself when it was clear there was no reward to be gained. Stagnancy was no vile evil; it was simply the best existence life held for her. There was no value in challenging her torment only to risk it becoming worse.

Secured in the knowledge she was better off enduring this known horror rather than risk the ire of one she did not, Sadie forced herself to stand. Patting at her neck, she was surprised at how quickly her wound had clotted, and she dabbed at the emerging scab. She couldn't afford to show even the slightest hint of weakness in the office; she was at all times pursued by those below her, and forever held at arm's length by those who she might replace. Even the barest opportunity to undermine or diminish her place in the great machine, would be an invitation for someone, somewhere, to strike her down. Comfortable lethargy set in, and she stood firm on the easy ground of compromise between survival and servitude. Finally she was ready to leave but couldn't bring herself to open the door by the handle. Pulling it back, she disregarded the outside world, and made her way to the car.

Her day at the office was not remotely memorable, it never was. Repetitive meetings, reviews and the murmur of nearby colleagues was naught but ambient noise now. Whenever she would return home, all she would remember is how painfully bright everything was. Low hanging rows of lights, chained to the ceiling by black coated links of metal, always seemed to be far too intense. Computer screens, tablets and the burning sunlight which breached the concrete courtyard where she took her break, alongside other cogs and functionaries, was all too much. Nauseating banality lessened as the day passed and the sun dimmed, and she suffered through her journey home, surrounded by the staccato blare of horns and furious shouts. The benefit of returning to her house so she could now continue her work without the interruption of people bothering her with question after question. Here her screen was dim and the lights were low, only retaining enough brightness to make sure she could discern reality from dream.

Sadie had assigned her unusual morning to a part of her consciousness she rarely reached for, and didn't allow any distractions when she returned home. Just as she did every night, she moved from room to room, ensuring all the lights were turned on and everything was in its place. She could confidently discern reality from illusion when the lights were on, whenever she felt something was lurking just out of view. At some point, she was sure she would eat something and check for messages on the phone which never rang. Occasionally a sudden jolt of fear struck her as something unexpected invaded her vision. A blur of dark movement darted from just behind her shoulder and into the hallway. Sadie caught it in the reflection on the glass of her microwave door but dismissed it as a phantom. Water lapped back and forth, filling the sink as she cleaned her cutlery. The reflection of her yawning countenance in the frothy waves mirrored the pale corpses on the ocean floor. On each occasion she recoiled momentarily and then forced herself to be calm. She observed the room around her and saw 'the nothing' it held, the stagnancy and the grey. Long moments passed as she allowed the absence of her house to sink in and calm her infuriatingly frightful mind.

The night wore on as it always did and she worked until she was unable to see the numbers that danced like irascible children on a theatre stage. Resigned to her plight, she began to enact the ritual tethering her to reality and hoped it would lead to an easier flight from her predator. She turned off the lights, observed the quiet spaces and tried to reassure herself. Whatever happened was simply an anomaly and not worth concerning herself over. Mindlessly she ran her hand over the light switch where she'd cut herself and was forced to pause in confusion. Why she hadn't realised this when she suffered her injury, she couldn't tell, but the light switch was clean of blood. Of course it would be, the switches in the house were baroque certainly, but they were hardly sharp. Ritual obsession meant she knew every inch of these fixtures without question. Why on earth then, had she thought it possible to lacerate her skin and draw blood? Fingers smudged prints onto the brass easily so any stain would stand out like a sore thumb. The impossibilities Sadie beheld shook her confidence and a pit opened within her stomach as for the second time that day, the sacred boundary between nightmare and reality had blurred.

Sadie moved forward slowly, distracted now by the realisation she'd been wounded by something unseen. Her usual obsession with checking and triple checking her ritual acts subsided and new buds of fear bloomed in her soul with each attempt to logic away what she perceived. Entering her bedroom, she sat slowly and stared at its drab, stained walls for a long time, as she desperately tried to calm herself before going to sleep. Being panicked only served to make her inevitable paralysis far, far worse. Eventually she left reality and began her flight from her predator, though she couldn't remember when she'd fallen asleep. It was far less egregious a pursuit than she'd suffered the night before, though she couldn't shake the feeling her captor wanted to be seen. She awoke in her bed with her legs curled up to her chest and her arms extended out, as though her body was tensed to make a great leap.

Reality proceeded as it always did and the day dragged by, although Sadie was a little more sluggish in leaving the house than usual. Office life represented her escape from madness but it held no relief. Every expectation required monumental effort to fulfill, and she barely managed to adjust her clothes and ensure she looked prepared and professional before she left the house. Her mind shifted slowly into gear; remembering which day of the week it was, if any executives needed to be avoided and recalled the names of those subordinates requiring admonishment. Sadie was genuinely concerned she might fall asleep during the monotony of the day and awake screaming. However, no such embarrassment took place and she returned to her house soon enough. She was several hours into replicating pointless data, before she was struck by a horrific realisation. Sadie became painfully aware, as she submitted her packages for review, that it was in fact Friday. Two whole days of exhaustion lay ahead, which she would have to endure without the soothing balm of her inane work. Time always seemed to drip like molasses as Sadie rotted in her house over the two insufferable days of the weekend. Her tethers to reality were always frayed and unreliable during this time and she dreaded what cruel punishments lay ahead.

Preparation was key during the long monotony of the weekend and Sadie couldn't risk a bulb bursting. Such a disruption to her ritual would steal all control from her. Darkness was a blade her predator used to split the fabric of nightmares and spill into her reality. Rising from the desk, she turned to leave and gather what she needed to survive the coming ordeal but barely left the room before she stopped short. The entrance way and the kitchen beyond were pitch black. As a mental exercise, Sadie had learned to take note of the distinctive thud made whenever the antique light switches were flipped. Seven times she had heard the dull impact and reverberating hum of wound wire, as she turned all her lights on, one by one. So deep was her paranoia she went to great lengths to purchase light bulbs that made a sudden and shocking whip-crack sound whenever they burst. There was no possible way Sadie would miss the sudden cacophony of a light bursting or the sudden dimness in the light around her. Something was very wrong, the assurance of control fell rapidly away, even as she tried to grasp at it.

Old houses were prone to faults, she knew, and perhaps the mains protector had been triggered and needed to be reset. Moving with trepidation over to a thin window, she peered outside through the dirty glass to see if the streetlights were still on. Before she even reached the glass, the lights flickered and shone again, as though a sudden fault had now resolved itself. Relieved but a little confused, Sadie sighed, shook her head and walked back towards her computer. Her study didn't await her there when she turned around, but rather she was somehow standing at the entrance to her bedroom. It was not an unpleasant sight, the warm glow of her bedside lamp was cast over fresh sheets and it all looked surprisingly inviting. The invasion of her reality and the lawless rearrangement of nightmare robbed the room of its allure and she began to weep at the sight. The rules had been broken now and her tethers were on their last winding threads, moments from snapping and casting her into the abyss.

Walking backwards, slowly at first and then faster as fear took control, Sadie careened into the front door, just as she had slammed against the wall the day before. The hallway was far too long for her to have reached its end already and she cried out in confusion and fear. Hitting the oak hard, she flung her arms back, trying to slow her descent. Instead of wood grain, Sadie instead felt the ice cold impact of freezing water on her back and was suspended by roiling waves. Forced to exhale her breath from what felt like falling vertically, panic set in as she somehow felt the sensation of sinking. Soft echoes of tears flowed as she was steadily consumed by depths bound within the door. Her bedside lamp was so distant now, it shimmered and faded like the moon being obscured behind dark clouds. Everything was in darkness and she was at the mercy of the ocean. Just as she slipped beneath the freezing water and her lungs filled with terror, her tormentor appeared. Sadie sank back from her home whilst it stood, watching from inside her house, as she drifted away. For all her fear there was rage too, a brimming fury for this monster who couldn't be sated. It reached out towards Sadie and she tried to look away from the dark silhouette, turning her head and keeping her eyes tightly shut. Denying the sight of it had saved her before but all the rules of this realm were failing. The familiar cracking and snapping of the many-jointed arms were akin to a foul shrieking in her ear, and as twisted fingers reached towards her, she swiped at them in futile defiance. When she did, her arm was clasped in the warm, puss laden grip of the predator, who dragged Sadie back to her home and above what passed for the surface.

The ocean receded rapidly and she was hurled from the doorway, slamming into the hallway wall and collapsing against the floor. Looking back, Sadie lost all courage as her tormentor now revealed itself entirely Crouched down and forcing its way past the door frame, the entities sagging flesh and diseased bones were brutally compressed together, the sound of pulped meat gurgling from within its skeletal form. Sadie watched the ugly maw that served as its mouth part slowly. Stunted teeth like blood stained pearls were slathered in congealed saliva and the scarred skin split apart as it made a mockery of human speech.

"P - l - e - a - s - e," it managed, the word exhaled like a death rattle from a sick and dying man. W - a - k -e," it pleaded.

Sadie woke screaming at her computer desk and could not stop her collapse into hysteria as she fell from her chair. There was something truly terrible about what she had suffered. More than all the years of torment, hearing it speak was beyond her worst fears. Aspects of its visage she couldn't comprehend, were seized upon and made worse by her imagination. Drawn from a patchwork quilt of all the memories of torture she'd ever endured, Sadie screamed and begged for her vision to be taken from her. Hours later, as dawn broke and the new day began, she was still curled up on the floor, shaking from her ordeal. Eventually a single thought of purest clarity filled her mind, one she couldn't ignore.

'Why does it need me to wake up?' she thought, and then she reluctantly voiced the question she dreaded to answer, "what is it afraid of?"

All her tethers were now falling away from her, and the longer she dwelt on what had happened the further from certainty she drifted. Not once had she fallen asleep in front of the computer. The nauseating ache which reverberated throughout her brain as she stared at the screen wouldn't allow it. Between the paranoia at the risk of forgetting her ritual and the need to consume her mind with work, it had simply never happened.

Something had changed in the last few days; the stagnancy she wrapped herself in was now broken. Years of the same monotonous repetition and tedious survival for the sake of bitterness had continued, unchanged and unchanging. Now her predator had shown itself to her and had sought only to beg and plead with her as a child might plead with its mother. Were she not treading on the precipice of madness, she might've been enraged by the audacity of the thing, to seek aid from her when so much of her life had been consumed by it.

Sunlight always lost its warmth as it passed through the grimy windows of the old house. When all her tears were spent and trauma gave way to survival once more, Sadie was unsure how long she'd lain on the floor. It could be late afternoon or maybe even heading towards sunset, she thought, which meant the evening was soon approaching and the lights must all be turned on.

"Why..." she said quietly, mostly to herself, "why should I bother?"

Sadie continued to ponder on this point even as she wiped the back of her cold hand against her cheek and pushed the last remnants of tearful anguish away. All the exhaustion from years of terrified flight seemingly consumed her in an instant, and Sadie forced herself to painstakingly enact her ritual. There was no point and she shouldn't bother, but there was nothing else to be done. Passing between rooms with the resignation of an automaton, her numb soles pressed against the dusty floors. There was a comfort to be had in distancing herself from concern. Eventually she simply allowed herself to be propelled around by the innate memory of repetitive action. It wasn't that she wanted to be parted from the world, she just had nothing left to fight with.

Sadie sometimes fantasied she had someone, anyone, who would know her name and care enough to ask her what it was like to have been running for so long. The answer was as indulgent as it was true. She'd said it many times to expensive, slightly condescending professionals who feigned interest.

"Imagine that you're a child in the back of a car," she would say, "on a long road home from some distant journey. You've left the fresh country air and now the familiar tainted smog of the city passes through the crack in the window above you. Despite the unnatural scent, you're told you're going home. Boredom is victorious and you begin to lose the battle against sleep but can't drift off completely. A soundless beat plays somewhere. Yellow light spills across your eyes as street lights flash again, and again. Though you're traveling, there isn't a journey here, there is just the dull light and cloying darkness. You sense the longer you've been traveling, the less reason you have to make it home".

No street lights illuminated her house, she noted, but at least the honeycombed glow of the bulbs affirmed they were active; although it was hard to tell how long they'd been on for. The pattern of ritual had led her to the hallway once again and she stood still, trying to coax her muscles to keep moving. Tethers were her safety and her survival, but they'd been cast aside without an inkling of their whearabouts. Outside a storm was rising, she noted with dull interest. The barest hint of a breeze passed in the small crack in the oak, and even in her fugue state she could discern the gentle bumping of the door moving on its hinge.

'No point looking there,' she thought, it was getting late, and the edges of her vision were growing dark.

She felt breathless and weary beyond words, as though her lungs were burdened with every breath she took. It was painful to recognise how far she'd deteriorated in so short a time. Best to look left, as she did every night, and walk towards the study. Once there, she would reach the entrance to the room and raise her hand languidly to the right, where she would flick the first of the seven switches. 'Let the numbness continue and accept that whatever will be, will be' she thought without concern.

Sadie scowled as her fugue state was disturbed and she turned back to her front door as a realisation dawned on her. The heavy trance she'd fallen into couldn't stop the fear from now unfurling within her as she looked at the door. There had been no crack in the oak and no split in the wood where the breeze could come in. She knew she would've noticed a hole in her front door, it would be impossible to miss. Wind continued to howl through the crack. She smelt the brine of the sea and heard the crescendo of waves as they fell upon each other. Doubling over, Sadie lurched from numbness into sudden feeling, recalling the flood of the ocean, the fall backwards into the waves, the arms and fingers with too many bones, snapping and popping as they closed around her. A cage of fear descended down and bound her, as the sickening assuredness of waking from the nightmare, instantly vanished.

Slowly moving forwards, against all her instincts and even as tears ran down her face, she placed one foot in front of the other. Every step banished the numbness and brought agonizing clarity back to her mind, as though the blood in her body had begun to flow again. Sadie hissed with a dry, stifled scream as her need for understanding overpowered her terror. Placing both hands against the door, Sadie slid down the lifeless oak until she was level with the anomalous damage. Leaning heavily against the door, she forced herself, inch by inch, closer to the wound in the wood. The deep brown umber swallowed up the light and she had to draw herself down and to peer through the crack, where she hoped to simply see a quiet suburban street. Where she expected street lights and driveways, jagged obsidian rocks and impossible waves of dark water surged upwards to a distant sky.

Even as she registered the revelation, Sadie forced herself back instinctively, skidding across the floor, trying desperately to catch her breath. The door swelled in her vision but even as she raced backwards, she couldn't get far enough. Her nails cawed into the hard wooden floor and found grooves there, carved by hands that weren't her own. A sound like a gargantuan wave crashing nearby froze her in place, and she turned at the sound, expecting to be swept away. Instead she saw the kitchen, which was pitch black, save for the soft orange embers that swung to and fro. The ocean roared but all Sadie saw was the bulb cooling rapidly after something had snuffed it out. Unconsciously holding her breath, she continued to stare at the ghost of the glow in disbelief and denial that somehow, her ritual was failing.

More sparks and bursts of sound exploded about her as she looked this time to her study, the lights there had gone out too. Fresh waves of panic grappled with survival instinct and Sadie inched her hands backwards, clawing away from the looming door which continued swelling in its vastness. Another blast followed by a further sharp crackle of energy came from behind her. Her scream was drowned out by the roaring fury of a steadily encroaching sea. Panicked beyond thought and barely able to breathe, Sadie looked behind her and was unable to tear her eyes away from the bedroom lamp at the hallway's end. The bathroom light had indeed gone out and the hallway light above danced erratically, like a ship's sail caught in the maelstrom of a dreadful storm. All of this was terrible to endure but what awaited her in her bedroom was far worse still.

Sat on the floor, collapsing and folding its immense form into itself, was her predator. Gangly limbs, made of moist bone and matted hair, were folded out and across themselves, as it sat cross legged before her. Its right hand was gouged into the floorboards of her bedroom, as though it had, like her, dragged itself back and away from the oak door, or perhaps towards it. Though she begged any power that would listen to gouge her eyes to remove this vision, she could not turn from it or force herself to run. Exhaustion was absolute and her heartbeat became a sonorous drone. The thing looked exhausted as well, its torn flesh draped over driftwood and ivory bones. In a mockery of the human form but one that was haggard and spent. Slowly, very slowly, Sadie followed the trail of unwound skin and brine slick furs, to where the creature's left hand rested.

"Don't, please..." Sadie began, and was reviled by the look of disappointment and frustration the thing returned in answer. Yellowed orbs like faded yolks, swam within thin membranes of translucent flesh. Something of her weariness was reflected there, as though it endured hardship in its relentless pursuit of her. Their gaze was locked, the predator and the prey observing each other and knowing each other with terrible clarity. She saw again the pleading there, as though it waited for her to do something, but Sadie was now far beyond thought. At last it let out a long, rattling sigh, and as Sadie screamed, it turned off the light.

Sadie could still sense those rueful orbs upon her as the light from her bedside lamp was shut out. The last light she had left was the one above her, the low hanging hallway light that swung back and forth. A raging sea seemed so close now as though at any moment a torrent of water would burst through the house and drown her in an instant. Marooned upon jagged rocks amid the storm, there was nothing she could do to survive. The wind howled through the wound in the door, and the light played over her face. The bulb swung up and forwards, and she saw the darkness unfurl in front of her. It swung backwards and behind her view, and the darkness lurched. Spiraling flesh strands and limbs of snapping bone flung up and over her, swallowing the space in the hallway and suspending the shadow that lived in the dark. The light swung back once again but stopped suddenly as a single finger of entwined teeth and too many knuckles, threaded through the circle wire at the end of the hanging cord. The oceans roared and Sadie's scream was one and the same as reality and nightmare became one. The warden of her nightmares moved the gaping wound in its face to speak, the words delayed and confused by the breath it stole to utter them.

"I-f y-o-u d-o-n-t w-a-k-e," it wheezed, speaking with its many tongues but exhaling with her breath, "w-e, d-r-o-w-n."

It pulled the cord, the bulb burst, light flashed out, and now at last, everything was swallowed by the darkness.

Eons, seconds, nevers and nowheres passed by and were forgotten, before Sadie returned to something resembling consciousness. Light was an unknown concept here, but there was awareness and a perception only the soul understood. She'd been carried off by an ancient ocean, long ago, from a place she didn't care to remember. Like a child slowly stumbling towards familiar sounds, Sadie felt the impression of scratching, scraping and buzzing against her mind. Drifting from nowhere to somewhere, she was carried by currents to a place of still reflection, but she wasn't alone.

Hunched over on the edge of an obsidian outcrop that heralded the plunge towards a cavernous maw, was her tormentor. Below her, she knew, were the numerous corpses she'd once feared, their mouths forced open by rigor mortis. Aged claws picked and scraped at one such limp and lifeless vessel, as her predator turned the body back and forth, seeking any morsel it could draw from the spent corpse. As if sensing her, the creature glowered up, able to hold her gaze in this place where she'd gone beyond fear and abandoned all resistance. It knew what she felt, what the last vestige of her soul was capable of transmitting across the void, like the faint crackle of radiation that registered the last words of a distant star.

"Starve" she pulsed out into the nothing, and she knew it understood her meaning and the bitter satisfaction with which she spoke the words.

Once again the creature seemed to be exasperated by her inability to understand and accept something, as though it too had reached the limits of exhaustion and simply embraced the futility of its pursuit. Slowly it gazed upwards, its shoulders sagged and a palpable wave of desperation rippled out from its impossible mind. Sinking its many elbows back into the corpse laden sand of the outcrop, it ignored Sadie and merely continued to gaze up. An odd choice, she thought, in a realm where there were no directions, simply here's and there's. Sadie did conceive however that there was an above and a below. When this truth dawned on her, she then sensed a weight sinking behind her. Another weight, and then another and another sank slowly to join the corpse valley below, and Sadie reluctantly perceived the ocean around her. Descending like the remnants of a dandelion adrift on the breeze, came broken, starved and withered corpses. Her corpses, she noted, and where once existence had swaddled her in nothingness, now a deep sorrow bloomed and then filled all that was left of Sadie Melinowe. There were so many broken parts of her, all torn and wounded in some way, all of them desiccated husks, worn and wasted.

Turning back to her tormentor, she no longer beheld it with fear, but rather sought an understanding. She wanted to determine some reason as to why all this had to take place. It recognised the look and stared back, and she thought for a moment that it shared her sorrow or at least was caged by some similar version of it. Corpses impacted against the ocean floor and kicked up dark muddy plumes of silt and suffering. Long moments passed as the prisoner and the jailor beheld each other honestly, without the assumed roles of predator and prey. Understanding passed between them and Sadie knew then, though it had often rattled at the cage bars, it was no more than a fellow cellmate, begging for release.

Rituals and reticence had done nothing more than grind down the will Sadie once had, until she was nothing more than a shell, like the ones that sank about her. Real or imagined, tears flowed and she wept softly, unsure of how long she had really been pursued by her captor. Was it years or days? Months or decades? It had been a long time, she was sure of it, but understanding flooded into the space where delusion once dwelt. A great force pulsed out into the drifting corpses, as her weeping turned into a scream. Too long had her screams and insurmountable emotion been bound up. She'd forgotten where it ended and she began.

All the reasons Sadie had ever found to recede from existence and trap herself within procession and procedure fell apart. For all the primal terror her captor exuded, it was in reality nothing more than a moth to the flame. He had been blinded by the allure of her suffering and was too greedy to flee from her whilst he could still escape. The desperation she had sensed was very real. Her tormentor had eaten every scrap of Sadie's will that it could sustain itself upon, and now wanted to escape her mind before it joined the corpses down below

Sensing the form of her hands, face and limbs, Sadie beheld the being who had ruined so much of her life. It attempted to plead one final time but confusion now contorted its features. It could not give voice to the words as it discovered it was unable to steal her breath. Passing beyond the precipice of total fear, she'd embraced the void, and it held no more threat for her. With acceptance came a sense of calm, and for the first time in her memory, her soul was sanguine.

"Wake," she said, with a firmness she didn't expect and a voice she could barely remember, "I am Sadie Melinowe, and I will see the sunrise."

Light spilled in then, a dazzling strike of brilliance the depths of the ocean couldn't subsume. It burned with an intensity unfamiliar to Sadie, but she welcomed it and whatever else came next. The currents of other oceans were roused then and bore her from the dark obsidian shelf, where her tormentor was now trapped in the panic of drowning. Sadie paid him no mind, she was bound for other places where she could burst from the ocean and into the air, where the darkness couldn't hold her. Sadie's vision blurred and the dark sea churned as she was carried toward an opal dream. She could've sworn, as she was lulled from consciousness, she heard bird song from somewhere above.

The breeze was cool and gentle against her face, lapping at the tears falling across her cheeks, like a faithful hound concerned for its master. Warmth prickled her skin and she couldn't discern if she found it painful or not. Dappled light danced on the soft grass and the swaying leaves of the old tree above went someway to tenderly easing her emergence into the sunlight. Between her fingers, tall blades of grass tickled at the dry skin and it felt good as she let her fingers slip into the soil. Breathing deep in the fresh air, Sadie let the tears flow, but she smiled and felt the unfamiliar sense of relief take hold. Rolling onto her back and basking in the sun, Sadie was tired and exhausted, but for the first time in years, she felt genuine relief, and an absolute yearning for sleep.

The door to her house had been left ajar after she'd burst outside and collapsed. The oak swung too and fro, disturbing the heavy dust upon the floors and allowing light to spill in. Methodically and precisely, something with uncomfortably long limbs and bones which slipped and shuddered into place, slithered towards escape. Each time the door swung wide, it would risk one movement, then another until at last it crawled out, low and spider-like. The outside of the house was in disarray, having been untouched for years. The discarded scrap and detritus provided all the shelter the thing needed to retreat swiftly from its captor. Reaching the unkempt bushes lining the properties boundary, the creature stopped and risked one last glance at the thing which had held it hostage for so long.

Decades had passed since it had been lured into the trap so masterfully set for it. Trauma and tragedy had oozed from Sadie, her fledgling soul was so easy to terrorise then. Drawn to her weakness, the creature had slipped into the moments between dream and waking, gorging itself until its belly burst, reknit and then burst again. The font of endless feasting was wonderful for a time but never seemed to end. Years of crippling torture in her daily life had broken Sadie long before she reached adulthood and suffered the predelictions that awaited her. Sorrow turned to silence and the dreams that once fed it, began to turn to ash in its mouth.

The future was irrelevant when it only held more pain, and Sadie had given in. As her walls lowered and her house became a prison, the creature raced to escape, but it was too late. By the time she had developed her accursed ritual, there was no way out. Every horror it could devise only served to strengthen her reliance on her repetition of the sacred steps, until it had almost starved. Now at last it could flee her unknowing grip and seek out a new victim. It cursed its pursuers, those who had used their child as bait, for humiliating it so thoroughly. Vengeance could wait, however, for now it needed to feed and there would be some lovely families nearby, the creature surmised

It began to slink off into the shadow of a nearby brush but suddenly stopped short. Swollen yellow yokes swam wildly, seeking the cause of its entrapment. Sadie Mellinowe's bloodshot eyes caught the things gaze and the predator became the prey. Where before Sadie smiled with the joy of freedom, now she glowered with embittered vindication. It could not steal her breath to imitate identity or soul and its rotten lungs wheezed uselessly in a failed attempt to scream. Flesh sloughed from its brittle bones and maddening terror enveloped it as Sadie stalked forwards, ignoring its muted pleas and glaring down without mercy. Every night for years on end, it had clawed at her sanity and savaged her mind. Long years of cruel attention were now to be returned tenfold.

"I almost forgot, you know," Sadie said quietly, as the sunlight spilled over her and into the dark where her quarry lay, "but you couldn't run forever."

Sadie watched the sun's rays unmake her nightmare as it was annihilated by the inviolate laws of reality. Warm tears spilled over aged skin Sadie didn't recognise and her joints creaked in disgruntled protest at her every movement. Important words had been spoken to her on the night she'd entered the house. Familiar voices had burdened her with a task she was too young to understand. Though desperate to recall who'd spoken, she only discerned the distant echo of stern looks and stifled weeping. So many stories had been spun and reached their end while she'd remained trapped and Sadie would never know why she'd been left to such a fate.

Birdsong rose as the joyful chaos of life unfolded, just as it always did. Sadie watched the last shadows of the night burn away with the day. She laid down on the unkempt grass again and closed her eyes, listening to the ambient song of life unfolding around her. Sadie's work was done, her toil was at an end and finally, she could sleep.

"I did it," she said, her voice drifting listlessly with the wind, "can I sleep now?"

The Old House

Carole Weave-Lane

The windows in the oddly shaped house, opened and shut
Listening to the chiming of the bell in the tower

A troll wearing mourning suit,
Answered all the bed and breakfast enquiries.
Deep within the cellar a dragon roared for its second breakfast.

Such a house was built on the Cliff tops
Where the ocean waves swept upon it

To its right of the door
an old cemetery was home for pesky ghosts

According to the local Minister,
It was but the resting home of ancestors,
For when he visited all was as it should be

But we know better, do we not
For at Halloween, it opens its doors to all us magickal lot.

Author Biographies

Kevin Chapman

Kevin Chapman is a Writer, US Navy Vet and survivor of a recent brain tumor experience. He's run the Cleveland Eastside Writer's Group for over ten years.

Kevin lives in Mentor, Ohio with his wife of thirty one years, Teresa. He has two of the barkiest dogs in the world, one cat that thinks he's Kevin's doctor and one cat that may be trying to kill him. He rounds that out with two sons, Jacob and Nicholas.

Adria Northman

Adria Northman is a new author from Canada who loves her own company and her three cats. If you could find her, it would be in a hammock in the trees at the bottom of the garden, reading books.

Adria loves her small home overlooking a small town where she also enjoys watching and listening to thunderstorms. Maybe you'll find her counting between the thunder to the lightning.

Adria also loves her herbs, spices and grows many of her own to make salves for herself and a few friends. A bit witchy? Maybe Adria will tell us one day.

Mary Woldering

Mary R. Woldering is an author, artisan, art historian, madwoman, visionary and devoted wife to Dr. Jackie F. Woldering, mother of Ruth and Thom and grandmother of five. She lives in Mentor, Ohio.

Thomas Woldering

Thomas Woldering is an Engineer, Quality professional, and aspiring science fiction and fantasy writer. He lives in Stockton, California with his wife and two children.

Donna Clancy

Donna Clancy lives on Cape Cod, Massachusetts in the U.S.A. She is a single mom of three grown children and happily divorced.

Her favorite genre is cozy mysteries and she has several series on Amazon at the present time; The Jelly Shop Mysteries, The Shipwreck Café Mysteries are self published. The Braddock Mysteries are released by Level Best Books. Trash to Treasure Cozy Mysteries and Paint and Sip Cozy Mysteries are published by Summer Prescott Books.

Several standalone books in the thriller/suspense genre and Christmas romances are also available.

You can visit her social media pages on Facebook

Have a great day!

Ashon Ruffins

A native New Orleanian and an Army Veteran. He loves the art of storytelling in all genres and believes the best lessons in life can be told through fiction. Ashon is the author of the Uncovered Darkness Mental Health Horror three book series and is also a mental health advocate. Ashon's debut novel Descent of a Broken Man was a Finalist for both the Best Book Award in 2022 (American Book Fest) and The American Writing Awards in 2023 in the Horror category. He enjoys spending time with his family.

Danny Buenaflor

Born in California at the tail end of the 20th century and currently resides in Arizona. With a love for the vintage and the futuristic, the romantic and the intellectual, the terrifying and the weird, he has entered the writing world by way of poetry and a couple of short stories released online, including his novella, The Incident at Blackgrove. He has also dabbled in screenwriting since he acquired his Associate of Science Degree in Film from The Los Angeles Film School. This is his first published work (and hopefully first of many). You can find him at his blog where he discusses everything that pops into his mind (when he remembers that his blog exists): darylonabarrel.blogspot.com

Lily Luchesi

USA Today bestselling and award-winning author of the Paranormal Detectives Series.

Her young adult Coven Series has successfully topped Amazon's Hot New Releases list consecutively.

She is also the founder of Partners in Crime Book Services, where she offers a myriad of services, including editing.

They were born in Chicago, Illinois, where many of their stories are set. Ever since she was a toddler, her mother noticed her tendency for being interested in all things "dark". At two they became infatuated with vampires and ghosts, and that infatuation turned into a lifestyle. She is also an out member of the LGBT+ community.

When not writing, she's going to rock concerts, getting tattooed, watching the CW, or reading comics and manga. And drinking copious amounts of coffee.

Lily also writes contemporary books for adults as Samantha Calcott, and dark/taboo romance as S.L. Sinclair.

Cathy-Lee Chopping

An author and mother of two from Perth, Western Australia. Her hobbies include reading and discovering new and upcoming authors, writing short stories when she is not procrastinating about her novel, listening to music and enjoying downtime watching reality tv about cooking and renovating.

Cathy-Lee started writing when she was 12 years old, but she started taking her writing seriously when she turned 21, and in the last 20 years she has amassed a huge folder of stories that have not yet seen the light of a publishers screen.

Cathy-Lee now has enough material for her own anthology of short stories, to which she is close to having published. She is also working on a fantasy novel, and she is really looking forward to publishing.

Cathy-Lee started publishing her secret works when a friend of hers passed away in January 2018. Evlyn was 34, too young to have been through a heart and two lung transplants over the last decade, and she once told Cathy-Lee that she was crazy to not want to show her work to anyone; that life was too short. Just days after she passed away, Cathy-Lee submitted her first ever published piece of work, 'Buried Love' to Plaisted Publishing House for their Ghostly Romance Anthology 2018.

This same friend once told Cathy-Lee, "A story not written is a story not told," this has motivated her to start publishing her work more for the public to enjoy.

Michael Harding

Michael lives in Western Australia, where he attempts to avoid the sun as often as possible whilst spending time with family and friends. His love of writing is inspired by his Mum, who read 'The Hobbit' to him at a young age, and who has always passionately championed his imagination and creativity. Often he could be found telling stories to family, passers by and any ducks that were kind enough to listen.

Fantastical stories of dragons and high drama in the stars have always captured Michael's imagination, and feature heavily in his writing. Although he often terrified himself by sneaking from his bedroom to catch glimpses of the X-Files, he grew up to have a deep appreciation of the horror genre.

The combination of fantasy, history and horror usually form the backdrop of his stories, whether they are written or shared on the tabletop with his dear friends. Although a great deal of his writing is done alone, accompanied by a pot of English Breakfast tea and Mr Cheeky Puss, Michael has often used roleplaying games to challenge his plots and complications. Flawed story logic and obvious plot holes are a lot more fun to re-write and fix when it is workshopped by the hilariously infuriating and always creative solutions enacted by his players.

In addition to prose, Michael has often written poetry, using it as a valuable tool for both breaking out of writing habits and to relax the mind. No matter what he is writing, he is incredibly thankful to have his Mum's keen mind and educator's eye, ready to review the text and catch his all too common grammatical errors. When he isn't writing, Michael enjoys music, painting miniatures, and yelling instructions to his beloved Chelsea Football Club, who rarely seem to hear him.

Cassandra Jones

Born in Fairmont, WV and raised in the small town of Four States, WV. (Yes, that's a real place!) She has loved to read since she was very young. At the age of thirteen she decided she wanted to try writing her own story. After taking Creative Writing and Journalism in high school, she began to love writing even more. She has won first place in a poetry contest and third place in a writing contest. She attended her first writer's workshop in 2015 and another one October 21,2017. When she's not writing, she can usually be found with her nose in a book.

She enjoys working on the family history and learning new things. And has an obsession with making creepy dolls. She also loves to spend time with family and friends. She has the best time at her book group called The Lunchtime Book Discussion Group that meets at her local library once a month.

Cassandra has been a part of over thirty anthologies, mostly for charities. She writes in several genres, Crime Fiction, Horror, Romance, Children's, and Poetry.